THE TWILIGHT WARRIOR

From
THE DRENGR RØKKR SAGAS

By

James W. Truax

Cover art by:
© vlastas via canva.com
Cover design and chapter art by:
James W. Truax

ISBN-13:
Ebook: 979-8-9887814-0-0
Paperback: 979-8-9887814-1-7
Hardcover: 979-8-9887814-2-4

To my son, Carter, whose industriousness and wit continue to awe and inspire me, allowing me to think that I may have succeeded in some small way as a father.

CONTENTS

ACKNOWLEDGMENTS

I would like to thank everyone who offered advice and support during the creation and publication of this work, of which there are too many to mention. Special thanks, as always, I give to my wife, Jennifer, and my children, Clara and Carter, without whom I could never stay focused enough to finish. Thanks are due also to my brother Bobb, who eagerly awaited each new episode, gave me great positive feedback, and encouraged me to keep writing. I extend a special thank you to Brian Penney who was a wonder in helping me edit the manuscript. And finally, thanks to all my Wattpadders who were kind enough to read and comment on my work.

THE TWILIGHT WARRIOR

From
THE DRENGR RØKKR SAGAS

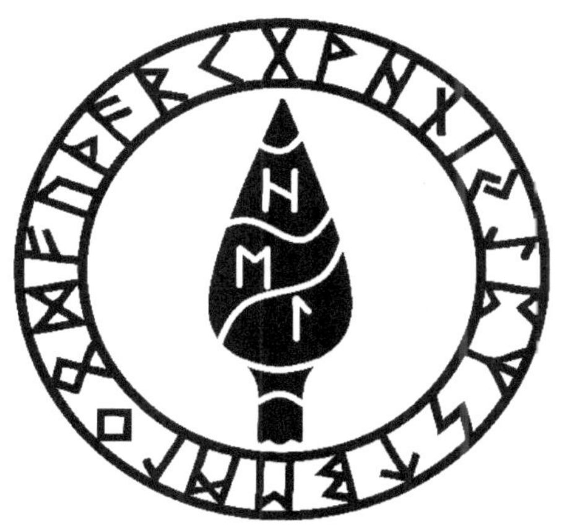

CHAPTER ONE

SPEAR OF GOD

A spiral suddenly rises from the undulating sea of black, swirling high into the air before floating gently down again and disappearing back into the pitch. Moments later, another spiral emerges, and then another, as flocks of carrion crows, alarmed by some unknown peril, take wing, whirl about, and light again upon the battlefield where two thousand men lay dead and dying. The earth, once abounding with wild grasses and bracken, is now a reddish-brown morass littered with broken steel and broken bodies.

I lie among them; my belly spilling my life's blood onto the ground to run and pool with the blood of my comrades and enemies alike. Above the din of squawking carrion, I hear the distinct cries of pain and fear, and the whimpers of resignation. There is a crow tearing at the flesh of a man beside me. I can see each feather so clearly that I could count them. I taste the sweetness of my blood and the sourness of my bile as I cough it out. At this, my dying moment, I expect my senses to be failing, and yet, they are at

1

their zenith, as if to drink in all they can before I pass. My last breath shall be choked with the stench of death.

There are men walking around me, putting the dying to the sword. "He's one of us. Give him an honorable death. There – his sword – give it to him," I hear one of them say before the sound of a dagger slashing a throat. By his language, I know he is a Norseman. Soon he will come to me, place my sword in my hand, and drive his dagger into my throat giving me an honorable death. And before he kills me, he will tell me that the gods are pleased with the great victory we have won, and he will lament that I will enter Valhalla before him.

"Victory or Valhalla!" I laugh aloud, throwing myself into a fit of coughing. Our battle cry rings empty now. The only victory is in survival, which I have not. So, it is Valhalla that awaits me, a glorious hall for the glorious dead. I shall sit at the great table with Odin, drink from his cup, and regale him with stories of my bravery on the battlefield and my cunning with women. Or perhaps it is just a lie, a dream of something better that exists to inspire men to give up their wretched mortal lives in the cause of conquest.

"Victory or Valhalla", I murmur. Yes, the gods will be pleased with our victory, but I will not be here to bask in the glory or enjoy the spoils. For me, this victory means nothing. I curse the gods that brought me to this end. "Odin and Frigg, I curse you! Freyja, I curse you. Tyr, Thor, and Loki, I curse you! I curse all the Aesir and Vanir, all the gods!" No sooner do I cry out those words, than a flash of light blinds me.

A woman approaches me from the light. "Are you one of the Valkyries come to take me to Valhalla?" I ask.

"No, Asger Agnarson, I am not," she answers. "I am Hel."

"So, I am bound for Helheim? My death wasn't glorious enough to warrant eternity in Valhalla?"

"No, your death would have been glorious enough for Valhalla, had you actually died." Her words take a physical form, bright wisps that flit and echo in hushed tones around my head.

"If I am not dead yet, then why are you here?"

"I am here because you called for me, Asger."

"I did not call for you, Goddess."

"Oh, but you did. When you cursed the gods, when you cursed my father, Loki, you called for me. A curse is a powerful thing, Asger, especially one uttered with a man's last breaths. Did you think you could lay such a curse upon us, and we would allow it?"

"I did not know, goddess. I … I am sorry," I stutter. I am transfixed by her beauty.

"Why do you look at me so, Asger?"

"You are not what I expected."

"I suppose not. You were expecting the Valkyries."

"No, that's not what I mean. It's just that you are so beautiful, more beautiful than any Valkyrie. I thought you would be a bit more …"

"HAGGISH!", she bellows and transforms into a hideously, aged woman, thin to the bone, nearly toothless, with long, straggly hair, and spindly fingers. Instantly, she is upon me, her face mere inches from mine. "Do you prefer me like this?"

"No, Goddess, no," I wince and turn away.

"Very well," she says calmly and returns to her former beauty. "Now,

Asger, as I was saying, we cannot allow your dead man's curse to stand."

"But I said I was sorry, Goddess."

"It does not matter that you regret it now. You see, it is a binding curse. Even the gods cannot overcome its power. We must answer it, and you, Asger, must answer for it."

"Goddess, surely, I am not the first man to curse the gods at his time of dying."

"No. But you are the first who truly meant it. And for that I condemn you."

"Condemn me? But I am already dying. How do you condemn me?"

"Oh, Asger, I am not condemning you to death. I am condemning you to life. You, Asger, will not die today, or any other day. You shall have eternal life, lest your curse take effect."

"I don't understand."

"You shall never die, Asger. You will live forever."

"I don't believe you. You haven't the power. In fact, I don't even believe you are real. You are just a phantom, an illusion born of my dying mind," I protest, convinced that my imminent death is causing me to see and hear things that aren't there. I blink my eyes, expecting her to disappear, but she does not.

"I assure you, I am no illusion," she says, taking up my sword. "Can an illusion do this?" She claps me across the face with the flat of the blade, snapping my head sideways and sending a sharp pain radiating through my jaw.

"AAHH!" I yell. I know now she is no aberration. This truly is Hel, the Two-Faced Terror, the Mistress of Helheim.

"Furthermore," Hel continues, "no one will remember who you are. Henceforth, anyone who once knew you will not recognize you, and anyone you meet will soon forget they met you. You will live in anonymity."

"What about my wife? My children?"

"They will not know you."

The truth of her words cuts deeper than my mortal wound, and I am filled with dread. "Goddess, please, you cannot do this."

"It's done. And what's done cannot be undone," Hel says with finality.

"Please. PLEASE. Do not do this. There must be some way for me to atone. There must be some way to end this curse you have laid on me."

"No, Asger, it was you who laid the curse. I have merely delayed its effect."

"What effect could my curse have, Goddess? I am only a lowly mortal."

"Yes, you are a lowly mortal, but still, your curse has the power to bring about Ragnarök, the end time. And so, you shall live on until Ragnarök, when all shall be destroyed and both gods and men are laid low. That shall be the end of your life as well. Until then, Asger, as your name means 'spear of god' that is what you will be – the Spear of God – my spear."

I feel tears running down my face. What is my sin that I have been so cursed, to live on and on and on, a stranger to everyone, even my beloved wife and children? The utterances of a dying man, spoken in fear and anger, should not be pretext for such a fate as mine. I sit up and cover my face with my hands.

"Do not weep, Asger. I am not without pity. I shall provide you with companionship for your journey. I have called on my brother, Fenrir. He will remain at your side."

With that, she vanishes. "Goddess! GODDESS! HEL! PLEASE!" I scream, but she is gone.

"Hey, look at this one. Not a scratch on him," I hear a man say from behind me.

"A coward who hides among the dead," another says as he comes around in front of me. "Cowards don't get to die honorable deaths. But they do get to die," he says as he shoves his sword into my chest.

Instantly, the man is gone, taken in a blur of blue, his sword wrenched from my body. I turn my head and see the man being ravaged by a great, blue wolf. A moment later, the wolf bounds over me and kills the man standing behind me.

I struggle to my feet. I feel for my wound, but it has already healed. I am, as Hel said – alive. I pick up the sword at my feet and thrust it deep into my belly. I feel it in my body, but there is no pain. I pull it out, but there is no blood. The wound seals itself and leaves no scar. Unbelieving, I thrust the sword into my belly again and again and again. There is no pain, no blood, and no mark. I stare at the sword. It is an instrument of death for everyone but me. I cannot die.

The wolf comes alongside and nudges me. He is twice the size of a normal wolf, with a thick coat, deep blue in color, like the fjords of my homeland. I look into the pitch of his eyes, and I know his thoughts. When he killed the two Norsemen, he was not protecting me. They could not have harmed me. He killed them out of sheer anger. I know that, though Hel bound him to me, he does not wish to be. His eyes burn with hatred, much of it for his sister, but more still for me.

"Come, Fenrir," I say and start walking. He leaps ahead, turns, and looks at me.

"Home," I answer his unspoken question. "I'm going home." I take a few more steps, but Fenrir again blocks my path.

"Yes, I can. And I will. You cannot keep me from my home and my family," I say firmly. "Hel said you were to be my companion. That means I am the leader. I say where we go, and you, as my companion, will follow." His eyes portend murder, but he knows he can do nothing. I start out again, and Fenrir follows.

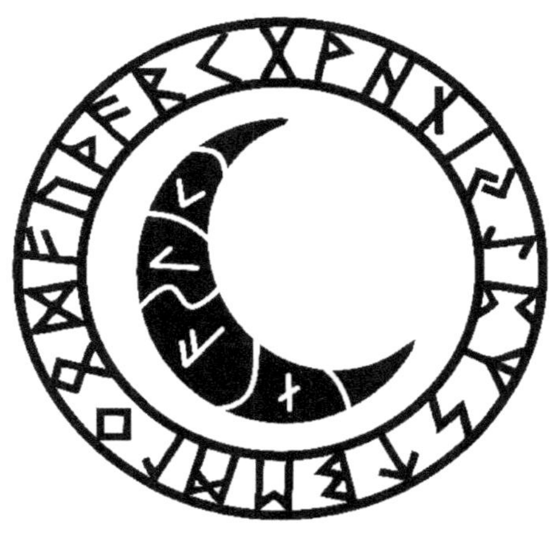

CHAPTER TWO

THE CLAN OF THE CRESCENT MOON

Shadowy figures emerge from the thick, early morning mists, appearing and disappearing in the swirling fog. A dozen, then a dozen more, then a hundred decrepit soldiers, slog their way through the bog, returning from a harrowing defeat. As we move among them, I see they are not soldiers, but the vestiges of felled giants, cleaved at the knees, their lower legs stuck in the mud and still upright. The fog lifts with the sunrise, and we climb a low dike, following it along the river Peene, leaving behind the dead pine forest in the flooded lowland.

It has been twelve days since we left the battlefield, but we have not encountered a living soul. A farmhouse we passed promised a hot meal and a warm bed, but we found the farmer and his teenage son slain and the house burned. His wife, daughters, and younger sons, had he any, would have been taken as slaves by the raiders. A set of muddy hoof prints suggested he'd had a draft horse as well, making him a wealthy man for this part of Pomerania. We followed the tracks until we came upon a mound of rocks, the last resting place of one of the raiders. The farmer had managed some vengeance for his family. I pulled the stones away hoping to find something of value, but his comrades had stripped him of everything, including his sword. Clearly, these thieves were not bound by honor, and this death warranted nothing more than a pile of stones.

We walk along the dike until we come to a village. A fifteen-foot palisade of beech surrounds the village, with two towers on opposing corners, allowing unobstructed fields of fire for the entire structure. An eight-foot moat, partially flooded, surrounds the wall and is fronted by an earthwork with long sharpened stakes embedded in it. The moat is bridged by a mound of stone and earth and covered by twelve-inch-thick timbers which are deeply grooved by carts passing in and out of the village. We walk through the open gates which are hewn of heavy oaken planks and banded with iron.

A woman shrieks at the sight of us and runs off. Three armed men approach, drawing their swords. "Is that a dog or a horse?" one of them asks as they spread out around us.

"A wolf," I answer casually, laying my hand on the hilt of my sword.

"You cannot bring your wolf into the village, skraeling," another says.

Calling me a skraeling, a weak, little heathen, tells me much about these men. First, though they know my language, they are not Norsemen. By their accent, I know they are slavic Wends, our so-called allies in the battle. Second, the insult is just an attempt to intimidate me, and a rather feeble one, since I can tell they are more afraid of me, a real soldier, than I am of them. Which brings me to the final thing I know; these men are blustering fools who've most likely never bloodied their swords.

"He's not my wolf. He comes and goes as he pleases. If you want him to leave, maybe you should tell him to leave," I say, edging my sword a few inches from its scabbard.

The third man circles around behind Fenrir. "We've had some of our livestock go missing. Perhaps your wolf had something to do with that," he says and lunges toward Fenrir with a killing blow. The wolf turns with blinding speed and bites the sword with such force that it shatters. The man falls with a shout, a shard of his blade embedded in his thigh.

Before he can react, my sword is at the throat of the man closest to me. As quickly, Fenrir pounces on the third, pinning him with his great paws. The man turns ghostly white as the great wolf gnashes its razor fangs mere inches from his face.

"You're lucky he ate that herd of goats before we arrived. Otherwise, he would make his supper of your head," I joke.

"C-C-Call him off, please," the man pleads, his voice shaking and barely audible.

I start to call Fenrir's name but stop myself. It will be difficult enough to explain a monstrous, blue wolf, but to tell these men, men I do not intend to kill, that this is Fenrir, the Hound of Helheim, the Bane of Odin, would be laughably ill-advised. They will forget me soon enough, but I doubt they will forget coming face to face with the Wolf-God.

"Blarulf! Release him!" I command.

Fenrir steps away, clearly displeased with my lack of cleverness, his disgruntled look saying, "Blarulf? Blue wolf? That is the best you can come up with? You are a moron."

"How did you come by such a monstrous beast?" the man says as he comes to his feet.

"We met fighting the Franks."

"You were at the Battle of the Sees? It was a great victory. That will teach the Franks not to cross the Elbe!" says the other.

"So, you fought in the battle, too?" I say, lowering my sword from his neck but keeping it at the ready.

"Well, no. We are billeted here. But if I were there, I would have killed Charlemagne myself. Is it true that he fell in the battle?"

"Charlemagne was not even there. But the Franks will come again, and perhaps Charlemagne will be leading them. You may yet get your chance," I laugh. "You should probably help your friend before he bleeds to death," I add, pointing my sword to the third man still lying on the ground clutching his thigh.

"But what of your wolf? Blarulf you call him?" the other asks. He is a bit too persistent for my liking.

"Like I said, we met in the battle. He comes from the east, I think. I understand there are vast packs of them, larger than him, roaming the steppe lands feeding on Rus. In fact, I think Blarulf may be a runt."

"What's he doing this far west?"

"Following the blood, I should imagine. A big battle means lots of dying men to feast on. And not just the flesh, he devours their souls as well."

The man's face turns white. Fenrir erupts in a chuckling growl.

"Now, if you could direct me to the nearest olstofa, I could use a drink."

The man points me to a long, timber hall across from a livery stable. "You never gave us your name," he says as I walk away.

I turn and say, "I am called Asger. Remember that name."

As I continue toward the tavern, I overhear the men discussing their encounter saying, "Did you see the size of that wolf? And the blue fur? … I heard those things live in the east. What was it doing here? … And what of that poor soul it was chasing. Probably a farmer … It must have killed his family … Good thing we ran it off. It could have slaughtered everyone in town … What farmer?"

Hel's curse is certainly effective. I held a sword to a man's throat, yet he forgot me in seconds. "A farmer," I laugh, shaking my head. Will Inger remember me? I must believe she will. My wife, my beautiful goddess, she will remember me. Love is stronger than any curse. And, if Inger remembers me, then perhaps the curse will be over.

I have Fenrir hide in the livery and tell him not to kill any horses. I enter the olstofa and order an ale from a buxom, young woman with ratty, blond hair and a scar across her cheek. I search the room and see a table of Norsemen, soldiers like me, clothes still stained with the blood of battle. I recognize one of them as Eric Halvorsen, the seventh son of Jarl Halvorsen. We've known each other since we were boys and have raided together on several occasions. Eric would know me if anyone would.

I sit on the bench across from Eric. He is regaling the others with a story of his bravery in the battle. Eric is always one for embellishment. He has a gift for storytelling, and all around him are enthralled by his tale, erupting in boisterous praise and laughter as he recounts in detail how he cut down twenty-two Franks. I always thought he would have made a good skald were he in any way versed in the history and traditions of our people.

"Last time I heard that story, it was only seventeen Franks," I say, making my presence known to the group, who burst out laughing.

"And next time it will be thirty-five," one of them laughs.

"I think forty-four," Eric says. "It is a much more lyrical number."

"And much less believable," another says, evoking another round of hearty laughter from us all.

"It's good to see you, my friend," Eric says to me. "I thought you were lost."

"You know me, Eric?" I ask, hopefully.

"Yes, I know you. Of us all, you were always the most cunning," Eric responds, having heard my question rather more as a statement. "When we were boys, the lot of us would get into so much trouble. Once we took a boat and sailed all the way to Skien. We broke into a store house and stole everything we could carry, candles, skins, tools, and gold, a ton of gold, gold coins, gold goblets, gold trinkets, like this one," Eric continues and pulls a gold crescent moon from under his shirt that hung on a chain around his neck.

"We each got one, see?", I say, holding up mine, finding it had been hooked into a crease on the breast of my leather armor, the chain broken and dangling. It is a precious charm of good luck. I am fortunate not to have lost it. "And don't forget, a barrel of fish," I add. Eric's eyes light up.

"Yes! And a barrel of fish!" Eric laughs.

"You see, Eric told his father, the jarl, that we were going fishing," I say. "It's a good thing Bjorn remembered to get the fish."

"It didn't matter much. Father found out soon enough. 'We don't steal from our own,' he said. Then he whipped me soundly and made us take everything back. Well, not everything." Eric twists his golden trophy in his fingers.

"We kept the fish, too," I laugh. "Our first raid. To the Clan of the

Crescent Moon!" I say hoisting my glass in a toast. Everyone joins in, laughing and drinking to our adolescent hijinks.

I feel truly alive again. Eric remembers me. The curse is not real, and soon I will be home with Inger, Gyda, and Brant. I know it has all been a dream. Hel, Fenrir, and the curse have all just been the machinations of an addled brain. I think, perhaps, that I suffered a blow to the head in battle. That would explain everything I have experienced all these days since. Tomorrow I shall board a boat, sail down the river, and then, home.

CHAPTER THREE

BLARULF!

A monstrous dragon head emerges from the morning mist, then vanishes. A second, even more hideous head, and a third, eyes gleaming with bloodlust, appear for a nightmarish moment before retreating into the hazy shroud. The great hydra glides in near silence, its many heads bobbing in and out of the fog searching for prey, its advancement marked only by the faint, rhythmic splashing of its hundred legs upon the river. I sit in the belly of the beast, pulling hard on my oar, as my drakkar longship and thirteen others make their way down the Peene, past Anklam toward the Szczecin Lagoon. From there, we will head north through the Peenestrom and enter the Baltic Sea at Peenemunde.

My friend, Eric, captains the rudder. To my despair, he does not remember drinking and laughing with me in the tavern. He knows me as a childhood friend only by the moon charm around my neck, but he doesn't know my name, even though I have told him a dozen times over the last several days. Likewise, the other men I am sailing with, some with whom I

15

stood shoulder to shoulder in the shield wall, do not recognize me and even question whether I am truly a Norseman. I was so sure I was free of Hel's curse, but I know now that even those I have known all my life, those I have drank with, raided with, bled with, have no memory of me. I can only hope against hope that Inger will know me, but I am beginning to fear that perhaps she won't.

Fenrir has taken a place in the bow, his enormous head resting on the gunwale, his mouth hanging open, his tongue flapping in the headwind. At least one of us is enjoying the journey. I recall as we were leaving, a Norseman complained that having Fenrir in the bow would cause the ship to ride too low at the head, making for difficult rowing and potentially foundering it. Fenrir removed his tongue with a lightning strike from his claw before biting the man's arm off. No one else said a word.

At Anklam, six more ships join our flotilla, laden with riches from Charlemagne's decimated army, booty raided from the local populace, and the recompense from Dragowit, the king of our Wendish allies. We have nearly two hundred slaves, many of which have been put to the oars. The women are passed around like skins of ale.

We are among the last of the victors of the Battle of the Sees to leave for home. A hundred of our number are remaining behind to build forts in the west along the Elbe. I know it is a fool's errand. Charlemagne has already established fortifications as far east as Lubeck in his continuing war against the Saxons. The battle we just won was against an advance guard of Franks who we vastly outnumbered. Still, two thirds of our army fell, most of them Wendish tribesmen. Should Charlemagne decide to move against the Wends again, he will surely conquer them.

At the Szczecin Lagoon, Eric decides to sail east across the lagoon and raid some trading skiffs. He loves raiding more than ale and women and never misses an opportunity to secure more riches, and more importantly, increase his reputation. He takes three ships, offloading much of the cargo onto those heading north. Fights break out among the men for whom should get to sail on this expedition, but I suspect much of it is for show. The men are weary from the battle, and none want to sail with Fenrir, for I have decided to go along as well, telling everyone I wish to release Blarulf, as he is known to my comrades, back into the Rusland to roam among his kind. In truth, I believe spending more time with Eric may jog his memory of me.

We take two trading skiffs within an hour, piled high with skins and silver, but the treacherously shallow lagoon is proving difficult to navigate, even for our shallow-draft longships. Our ship runs aground on a shoal, the bow driven deep into the muck. Perhaps the armless, tongueless Norseman was right – Fenrir's huge size is proving to be a detriment. Fenrir jumps from the ship and immediately sinks deep into the mud. He growls and snaps about angrily at his dilemma, biting off the dragon bowpiece as he struggles to free himself. The force of his blow shudders the ship loose and the oarsmen pull it clear of the shoal.

We are so focused on freeing our ship, we do not notice eight skiffs approaching, four of which are pulling two large, flat-bottomed barges full of soldiers. We sailed into an ambush. We pull hard on the starboard oars, while the rowers on the port side push forward on theirs. The other two ships do the same. Our longship turns like a grist wheel, but we are too slow. A skiff collides with our drakkar amidships, splitting the port side with its metal ram and killing an oarsman. Our ship lists heavily to starboard from the impact, and Eric is thrown overboard. Men from the skiff board our longship, swords and hammers flailing, as our ship rights and begins filling with water.

I draw my sword and enter the fray as another skiff pulls a barge alongside us. The soldiers jump onto our stern and attack my comrades from behind. I hack my way aft, but there is little room to maneuver on such a narrow ship, which is violently rocking in the pitch of battle. I duck a blow from one of our attackers and thrust my sword upward through his belly. A torrent of blood squirts from the wound as I pull my sword out, his heart discharging its contents with its last beat. I push him overboard as a sword comes down on my shoulder, cleaving deep into my chest. The blow knocks me backwards, and my blood sprays my enemy in the face. He stands over me, wiping his eyes clean so he can gloat over his kill. The surprised look on his face when I rise up, unhurt, will be a lasting memory. I separate his head from his body with a backhand stroke.

I glance momentarily at Fenrir. He is still stuck in the mud but is snapping and flailing at another of the skiffs, the soldiers of which are hacking at him with swords and shooting him with arrows. A net flies from the skiff and ensnares Fenrir. As he struggles to free himself, I see Eric swim to him and start cutting the net away with his knife. I chuckle silently as I think of what the immortal, blue wolf will do to those men once he gets loose.

I return to the battle, but it is clear we are losing. Most of the Norsemen are trapped between two groups of attackers, and they can't even form a shield defense since most of their shields are still hanging on the side of our ship. I see an opportunity to turn the tide, so I jump onto the skiff that rammed us, and then to the barge, bypassing the mass of battling men. My gambit works, and I cut down three soldiers on the barge before anyone realizes I am there. Another Norseman duplicates my feat, and together we move through the enemy like a scythe. I am wounded many times, but I keep pushing forward. My comrade dies gloriously doing battle with four men, but he is replaced by two more Norsemen with shields who managed to board the barge.

Though vastly outnumbered, we now have the advantage of putting our attackers in a vice. Many of them, believing there are more than just three of us on the barge to their rear, foolishly turn their backs on the remaining Norsemen in our longship. My comrades grab up their shields and begin pushing back against the horde, throwing many of them overboard. Within seconds, it becomes a rout, as the skiffs pulling the barge cut their ropes and start rowing away. The skiff that rammed us likewise tries to pull away, but we overtake it quickly. My remaining comrades and I board the skiff and we retreat, leaving our foundering drakkar and the barge piled with dead. Several enemy soldiers remain, but they are stranded.

We row our skiff toward the other two longships which are engaged in a heated battle. From a distance, it appears the others are barely holding their own against the horde, but our arrival will soon change their fortune. We ram our skiff into the other barge, causing many enemy soldiers to stumble and fall. We don't give them a chance to get back to their feet as we pour onto the barge and hack them to pieces. We form a small shield wall and push the few remaining on the barge into the water. Their barge being captured, our enemies have no choice but to retreat. They swarm onto their skiffs like roaches and row away.

A blue blur flashes above our heads as we celebrate our victory. Fenrir has extricated himself from the muck and is bounding, ship to ship, into the battle. He lands on a retreating enemy skiff and rampages through it. Twenty or more men are decapitated instantly, their heads popping into the air like a juggler's balls. The enemy dispatched, Fenrir leaps for another skiff. It is a magnificent jump, sixty yards at least, but he falls short, splashing into the water. He starts to swim after his prey, but our jubilant laughter at his failure stops him short. He turns and swims toward us, his eyes glaring. I have seen that look before; Fenrir is not amused by our mirth. I hope he returns to his normal state of disgruntlement before he reaches us. If he kills everyone, there won't be anyone left to row.

"Blarulf! Blarulf!" a spontaneous cheer goes up. "Blarulf!" The men, taking account of Fenrir's actions, have decided he's one of us. "Blarulf!"

As Fenrir approaches, I still see the sternness in his furrowed brow, but his eyes are softer, and he is trying very hard not to smile. I think maybe this is the first time anyone has ever paid him homage. "Blarulf!" I shout with the others, pumping my fist in the air.

Our victory comes at a cost. One ship is lost, and the other two are severely damaged; thankfully, they are both still seaworthy. We've lost almost a third of our number, mostly from my longship. We recover Eric, who was standing on what was left of the skiff that attacked Fenrir. From the condition of the enemies' bodies, it is clear Fenrir did not take kindly to being attacked and netted. We recover what valuables we can from the wrecked ships, enslave the surviving enemy soldiers, gather our slain brethren onto the enemy barges, and set them afire. They will be feasting in Odin's great hall this evening while we make our way to Peenemunde to rejoin the rest of the fleet.

CHAPTER FOUR

THE TRAVELER

A giant snake, a quarter *röst* in length, its ragged, gray scales hanging loosely on its rusted, iron spine, slithers up a muddy road toward the gates of the city. Its progress is slowed by fear and exhaustion as it struggles to climb the dike that marks the perimeter of the city's defenses. Each rib of its emaciated body holds a head hung in defeat, the visage of each etched with the miserable foreknowledge of a future of harsh servitude. The slaves, chained together by collars which cut bloody grooves into their necks, pass through the gates on their way to the auction block.

Peenemunde is our final stop before our journey home across the Baltic Sea. Eric says he wants to sail out in two days, but I suspect it may take a bit longer, our ships having been damaged and in need of repair. There are some thirty-seven drakkar longships and at least as many trading knarrs assembled here, most of which are already rigged and crewed, but have been held back while the jarls argue about the division of the spoils. Eric, though not a jarl, will be representing his father, Jarl Halvorsen at the

21

Thing. His older brother, Olin, was supposed to have been there, but had been mortally wounded in the battle and succumbed to his injuries the day before we arrived. Out of respect for Olin and Jarl Halvorsen, the other jarls and sons of jarls have waited for Eric's arrival.

Eric barely takes notice of his brother's death, requesting only that the body be wrapped for transport back to Lagarvik; he doesn't even wish to see it. I am not surprised by Eric's reaction. There has always been great competition between all of Jarl Halvorsen's sons, and Eric has been chasing Olin's legacy his entire life. Perhaps now Eric will find favor with his father, but I doubt it. Eric's reputation is damaged with his ill-advised foray into the Szczecin Lagoon, and the men don't trust him now.

Strangely, in his near defeat, Eric gained the admiration of one of us – Fenrir. It seems the Wolf-God is thankful for Eric's intervention when he was trapped in the net and now follows Eric around like a puppy. Occasionally, he looks at me from Eric's side, saying clearly that this is a man worthy of his company, whereas I am not. It does not matter; Fenrir is bound to me, and he knows it. He must go where I go, and his petty sideways glances only make me laugh.

Eric has been keeping his distance from me since the lagoon. I am still holding out hope that, given enough time, he will remember me. In truth, I am glad for his deliberate avoidance as it means he has taken some note of me. I follow him to a blacksmith's forge outside an olstofa where the Thing is to be held. As he hands the smith his sword for sharpening, I slap him on the shoulder and announce my presence.

"Eric," I say. "I see you have a new companion." I look at Fenrir who snarls at me.

Startled, Eric turns, quickly drawing his knife and holding it to my throat.

"Is that how you greet a boyhood friend, Eric?"

"Are you my boyhood friend?" he says, pressing the blade hard against my skin.

"Of course. Though you seem to have been avoiding me the past few days."

"I think you are not my friend. I think you are a demon sent by the gods to nettle me; you and this infernal dog of yours, though at least he has the good sense not to provoke me."

Fenrir's eyes flare at the insult, but he does nothing.

"I am Asger Agnarson, and I am your friend," I say as I gingerly slide the crescent moon charm around the knife and hold it up. "And, again, Blarulf doesn't belong to me, though he seems to have taken a liking to you."

"Crescent moon or not, I do not know you. I saw you die in the lagoon. I saw you cleaved in half. And I saw you rise again."

I understand now why Eric has been avoiding me. He may not know who I am, but he does know what I am. "How can that be, Eric. You were in the water. Perhaps you only think you saw me killed, or perhaps you hit your head and imagined the whole thing."

"I saw what I saw, demon. What do you want with me? What do the gods want with me?"

"I assure you, Eric, I am no demon. I am who I say I am."

"Is that so? Should I move my hand and open your neck? It's the only way I'll know for sure."

"I would rather you di…," My words are cut off, my throat slit to the spine. A short spray of blood erupts from the wound, and instantly, it closes.

Eric's face goes white, and he drops his knife. He stares at me, motionless. I notice the blacksmith, having witnessed my murder and miraculous recovery, throw down the sword and run away screaming. Fenrir pounces on him ripping his throat open with a razor claw.

The ruckus draws several others to the scene. Fenrir disappears in a flash, leaving Eric, me, and the dead blacksmith.

"What's happened here?" says a burly Norseman.

"That blacksmith is a Frankish spy," I say quickly. "Eric, here, recognized him, and when he confronted him, the smith attacked him with his own sword. Eric dispatched him with one stroke of his blade. It was a wonder to behold, the speed of it. That man was a fool to think he could best Eric."

I pick up Eric's knife and place it in his hand. He instinctively returns it to his belt but does not take his eyes off mine.

The men begin patting Eric on the shoulder and proclaiming his heroics.

"Frankish swine. He got what he deserved," says the burly Norseman. No one questions my account of the event.

I slip away and find Fenrir lying behind the stables.

"What do you think you're doing?" I ask. I can barely contain my anger. "You have ruined things for me with Eric. He'll never trust me now. He'll never come near me. He'll never remember me."

Fenrir looks at me, his eyes saying, "You are an idiot. He is never going to remember you. No one is ever going to remember you."

"You're wrong! Inger will remember me! My children will know their father!" I yell.

"Do you not understand? My sister has eclipsed your existence. There is nothing memorable about you." Fenrir's thoughts are as clear to me as if he were speaking them aloud.

"You're wrong. Eric knew me. He knew I could not die."

Fenrir shakes his head. "Knowing your secret and knowing you are not the same thing. With time, Eric may forget your secret, but until he does, he will keep his mouth shut about it. You really should be thanking me. The rest of these morons would wag their tongues. You may be the Spear of God, the Immortal Soldier, the Twilight Warrior, but now is not the time to foster that reputation. There is much we must do first."

"What do you mean? What must we do?"

"Give up your dream of home and family. They do not exist. You do not exist."

I can see he knows something he will not tell me, something he is not supposed to tell me, but almost had. He turns and runs off before I can press him further. It is pointless to follow him. As easy as it should be to track a large, blue wolf through the city, Fenrir is a god, and if he doesn't want to be found, he won't be.

Even so, as twilight fades into night, I find myself wandering aimlessly about the streets and alleys of Peenemunde searching for Fenrir. Perhaps it is because I have been stewing for hours on what Fenrir would not tell me. More likely, it is because I am drunk on ale, or whatever it is that they ferment here, having spent much of the afternoon outside the olstofa waiting for the Thing to end. Normally all Norsemen would be welcome, but this particular Thing was strictly for the jarls, their offspring, and a few retainers. Many of my comrades are still waiting there drinking, feasting, and fighting.

As I stumble along a row of tents from which clouds of aromatic smoke and carnal sounds are emanating, I ponder my curse, deeply, for the first time. Hel had said I was to be the Spear of God, her spear, yet I still do not know what plans she has for me. Fenrir knows, but he will be more cautious with his thoughts now; I won't learn my destiny until the time comes.

"Asger Agnarson," a voice whispers from the smoke. "I have been waiting for you."

It has been so long since I heard my name, I wasn't sure I'd heard it at all. "Who's there? Do you know me?"

"Yes, Asger Agnarson, I know you. Come in," the voice whispers again.

I enter a tent where a low fire burns in a pit. I am instantly overcome by the smoke, and my head lightens. I see a woman, shrouded in a brightly colored woolen cape, locks of jet-black hair hanging from her bowed head. She must be a Traveler, a Romani, displaced by another war Charlemagne is waging against the Avars to the south. I'd heard of these people, mystics from the east if you believe the legends, whores and thieves if you do not.

"Come. Sit," she gestures to me with a delicate wave of her hand. I comply.

"How do you know me? Is my curse broken?" I ask with great anticipation.

"No, your curse is not broken, but if you complete the task I have for you, it shall be." She speaks my language well, but with a heavy accent.

"What? What is it you'd have me do?" I ask in desperation.

"You must go to the Thing and kill the jarls." Her words seem to float in the air.

"Are you Hel? Have you come to give me my destiny?"

"Hel? No, I am no god and certainly not one of yours. I serve the goddess, Kali. She has heard of your plight and has decided to help you. She can end your curse if you do as I ask. You may return to your wife and children. Your nightmare will be over."

"But why kill the jarls? They have done nothing to your people. In truth, we are fighting against the Franks, your enemies."

"For Travelers, everyone is an enemy. Do not question me further. You must kill the jarls and the sons of jarls. Accept this task or accept your fate. Now, leave."

I have more questions and try to remain, but my body will not do my bidding. I believe the smoke has given the Traveler some power over me. I stand and leave the tent against my will. By the time I return to the olstofa, my body and my wits have returned to me.

I am torn. If I do as the Traveler asks, her goddess will take away Hel's curse. But then, I will likely be executed, for I doubt I would be able to escape. If I do not kill the jarls, my curse will go on and on and on. I decide quickly. I would rather die in dishonor than live anonymous forever. I draw my sword and enter the olstofa.

CHAPTER FIVE

GOD OF MISCHIEF

A bolt of lightning dances on the ground in front of me. I try to follow its path as it zigs and zags, until another bolt cuts across my face and momentarily blinds me. More bolts in the distance glint and flicker in a rhythmic strobe accompanied by abrupt claps of thunder, growing louder and louder as axes and swords strike the shields of my former comrades. I am blinded again and again by sunlight reflecting off those weapons and the shields' umbones. I hang from a post, my hands tied above me, my feet secured at its base.

Jarl Öster raises his hand, and the crowd goes silent. Jarl Svendsen, standing to my right, begins reciting a list of my crimes.

"The villain burst into the room swinging his sword and immediately cut down two of Jarl Vollan's men along with his son, Ragnar, who was his representative," Jarl Svendsen spoke in an even voice. "He proceeded to hack his way down one side of the room, cutting down Jarl Hagar, Jarl

Knutson, Balder Alffson, son of Jarl Alffson, and several of their men.

"He continued his rampage, killing six of the nine jarls present, and severely wounding Jarl Agarson!" With each new atrocity, Jarl Svendsen's voice rose in anger.

"Further, he killed five of seven sons present and more than a dozen men of high standing! In all, twenty-seven of the forty-five men assembled fell to this berserker's sword before he could be subdued! And know that, as is our custom, we entered the Thing without any weapons for our defense."

The men, having been whipped into a frenzy, demand my blood, each wanting to be the one to inflict the killing stroke. I note that Eric's name was not called; I scan the crowd but do not see him. Nor do I see Fenrir. If he truly feared that others may learn of my immortality, that fear is about to be realized. Having left five alive, by my count, I am still under Hel's curse.

"Blood for blood!" cries Jarl Öster. "I call on Bjorn, son of Jarl Jannic, Eric, son of Jarl Halvorsen and Gunner, Jarl Agarson's brother, to come stand with us to pass judgment on this Frankish spy and to draw first blood."

I see two men emerge from the crowd, but neither of them is Eric.

Bjorn cries out, "This beast slaughtered three of my men and many of my friends. I shall draw first blood."

His blade slashes down at my right foot. He clearly intends to bleed me to a slow and painful death. Another blade intercepts the strike with an ear-splitting clank. Eric has stepped from behind me to stop the assault.

"Wait!" cries Eric. "I have not yet passed my judgment. And before I do, I would like to know exactly who he is. Is he a Norseman? A Frankish spy? A Wendish peasant? Can anyone tell me who he is? Can anyone tell me if there are more like him?"

"Who cares who he is," says Gunner. "I'll have his blood for what he has done!"

"But what has he done? Is this truly the man who attacked the Thing? Did anyone actually see him at the Thing?"

There is murmuring among the men. "Is that him? ... the berserker, I remember, he had a shaved head ... No, that can't be him ... the monster was at least seven feet tall ... I've never seen him before ... he is a stranger so he must be the one ..."

"Jarl Svensen? Jarl Öster? Can either of you positively identify this man as the one who killed the jarls?" continues Eric.

"It must be him. No one has seen him before. He's not one of us," says Jarl Svensen.

"Yes. But did you truly see him at the Thing?".

"Well, no. I cannot say that I have ever seen him before," Jarl Svensen replies.

Eric looks at Jarl Öster who merely shakes his head.

Jarl Svensen adds, "But he is the one who was captured, so he must be the murderer!"

"So where is his sword, or did he use an ax?" asks Eric.

"I know not," replies Jarl Svensen, his confusion inscribed on his furrowed brow.

"Can anyone identify this man? Who among you captured him?" Eric asks the crowd.

There is more murmuring, but no one steps forward to claim the deed.

"Well, as no one can identify him as the killer, and since I am the one who brought him, thinking him a childhood friend," Eric says, lifting the crescent moon from my neck with his sword," it falls to me, and only to me, to pass his judgment."

The crowd falls into complete silence.

"I would not have this man killed," says Eric in a strong and commanding voice. "I would have him cast adrift in the sea, without oar nor sail, food nor water. Let Aegir, the God of the Sea, determine his fate. If he is, without a doubt, the one that drew the blood of us who hail and worship Aegir, he has earned a more dreadful punishment than we could mete out. If not, let him drift to a foreign shore to live out his days."

I know Eric is trying to save the lives of these men. He regards me as a demon, indestructible and capable of killing every man assembled. On that second point, he is correct. Though I need only kill the five remaining jarls and sons to regain my mortality, I would need to dispatch the rabble before me first, lest I succeed in ending my curse, but fall to a survivor's sword afterward. I have no intention of dying this day.

"Banishment! NO! I will have justice for my men and my friends. I will have justice for the slain jarls!" screams Bjorn and plunges his sword into my chest.

The familiar blur of blue flashes before my eyes, and Bjorn is torn in half. Fenrir pounces on Gunner before he can pull his ax from his belt. Jarl Öster's sword falls hard on Fenrir's hind quarters, and the great blue wolf howls in agony. The other Norsemen close in, drawing their swords, axes, and hammers. Fenrir leaps from Gunner into the crowd, claws slashing and teeth gnashing, cutting through them like a scythe. The men are aghast, their worst fears about the wolf coming true, his murderous terror befalling them even after they had exalted him as one of their own in the lagoon.

Gunner, uninjured, springs to his feet and joins the fray with Öster and Svensen. More blows land on Fenrir as he bites and gouges in a frenzy. I see blood spewing from wounds on the beast. He is losing his battle. I think, surely, he cannot be killed by us mortals; this is Fenrir, the great Wolf-God, the Bane of Odin. Yet, that appears to be what is happening.

Amid the bloodletting, I feel my head grow light. Smoke and mist fill the square, and I feel like I am suddenly in a dream state. The carnage before me slows to a stop; bloody swords and axes are frozen, mid-swing, in the hands of frozen men. Fenrir emerges from the human statuary with a yelp and trots up to me. He is bleeding from several wounds, and his left hind leg dangles from a thin tangle of muscle and sinew. He looks at me with disgust.

"I will find a way to punish you for this! You FOOL!" Fenrir gnashes at me before wincing in pain and turning to lick his injuries.

"Now Fenrir, that is no way to speak to your companion." A dark figure emerges from the smoke. It is the Traveler; she seems to glide over the ground, her colorful robes flowing, and her jet-black hair swept back by an invisible wind.

"What are you doing here, father?" asks Fenrir.

"Oh! You recognized me," says Loki as he transforms from a woman into a tall, armored warrior with a long green cape and a curved, rams-horn helmet. "I wonder if Asger's children will recognize him so easily. I think not," he laughs.

"I ask you again, what are you doing here?" Fenrir is neither welcoming nor amused.

"Oh, I just want to see how well Asger fared at the Thing last night."

"So, it was YOU who made this idiot mortal kill the jarls. Why would you do that?"

"Do you really have to ask that question?" Loki smiles, making a dramatic open-arm gesture. "Mm... God of Mischief!"

"It is remarkable! I mean, HE is remarkable," says Loki as he runs his scepter through my belly and into the post. He pulls it out, and my injury heals instantly.

I try to speak, but no words escape my mouth.

"Actually, I just wanted to see what he could do. You know, your sister should really learn to share her toys," Loki says as his gaze passes over my body like he is inspecting a horse. "My bargain still stands, Asger. If you kill the jarls, I will release you from your curse." With a quick, circular stroke of his scepter, he cuts the bindings of my hands and feet.

"Don't listen to him," Fenrir says with his thoughts. "He can't do it."

I do not know who to believe, but I pull Bjorn's sword from my chest, walk over to Jarl Agarson, who lies injured and unconscious on a table a few feet away and decapitate him with one blow. This is an easy kill for me. Agarson and I have had a troubled history.

"I told you ... don't listen to him!" Fenrir tells me again, but I pay him no heed. I step into the mass of frozen men and remove the heads of Jarls Öster and Svensen. I feel a twinge of remorse at these killings, as I have a great deal of respect for them both. Theirs were not honorable deaths, but I say a silent prayer that Odin will allow them into Valhalla regardless.

"Very good, Asger. One to go!" says Loki as he circles around Eric.

I approach Eric, one of my oldest friends, someone who, even though he does not remember, is as close as a brother to me.

"Go ahead," chides Loki.

I hesitate, just for a moment, staring into Eric's distant and unaware eyes while I resolve to murder my friend.   I raise my sword and, with a backhand stroke, let it fly.

CHAPTER SIX

THE SORCERER

The perfect silence is broken by a siren's song, faint as a whisper at first, but growing louder. Her voice is high and even, her tone spellbinding to all who hear it, enticing them to follow. My ears fill with sound. I am enchanted, forgetting everything but the placidity of the moment. The unwavering note splits the air, reaching a crescendo as my singing sword stops a hairsbreadth from Eric's neck.

"NO!" I exclaim, coming back into myself. I won't kill him. I am desperate to end my curse, but I cannot end it this way.

"Well, that is disappointing," says Loki with a smirk. "I honestly thought you might do it."

"I won't kill my friend, no matter the consequence," I say.

"Well, you may regard Eric as your friend, but he certainly does not return your affection. In fact, he knows nothing about you except that you are a monster, a monster without honor or sympathy."

35

"That may be true, but Eric is an honorable man, and he deserves better than having me hack off his head." I say these words, but I wonder how true they are, as I still hold my sword to his neck.

"You know, Asger, sooner or later you will realize that having a conscience and being immortal are incompatible," says Loki. Then, turning to Fenrir who is still licking his wounded hip, he adds, "That looks bad, son. Maybe you should go see a laeknir."

With that, Loki vanishes, and the melee continues, at least until the men realize the target of their aggression has disappeared. Eric is, likewise, astonished that I am suddenly free and standing in front of him, my sword at his neck. I pull it away and step aside.

Bewildered mumblings emerge from the Norsemen as they try to comprehend the situation. A moment ago, they saw Bjorn run me through the chest, yet now I am free of my bonds and seemingly uninjured. Blarulf, as they know him, has magically transported some thirty yards away. One of them picks up Jarl Öster's head and lifts it into the air, not knowing if the great wolf killed him or if he fell to a comrade's sword.

"Seidrman!" the crowd begins to shout. They point their fingers at me and continue chanting, "Seidrman! Seidrman!" They all know my secret now, but they believe me to be a sorcerer. This is not a favorable development for me. Though Norsemen fear and respect female practitioners of seidr, or magic, they consider a male practitioner to be ergi, that is, less than a man. To be labeled thus will open me up to ridicule, torment, and probable torture. I may not be able to die, but I can be endlessly tortured – certainly not a fate I desire.

I slowly walk to Fenrir, who has licked his hind leg healthy, leaving no trace of an injury. "You're not the only immortal here," I hear him say. I keep my eyes on the crowd as I move, but I see no one is paying any mind to me. Their eyes are fixed on Eric. They believe he is the sorcerer.

"I knew he was a sorcerer," someone shouts. "Why else would he have that infernal dog. Only a seidrman would have an animal like that."

"And, in the lagoon," another adds, "he abandoned us to save that blue monster."

"Yes! He led us into that ambush intending for us to be slaughtered," cries another voice.

"And now he turns the beast loose on us while he heals and frees the murderer."

"It was Eric. Eric killed the jarls. He bewitched the berserker and sent him into the Thing. Nearly every man there was injured or killed! But HE doesn't have a scratch. TRAITOR!"

It is true Eric's reputation had been diminished by the debacle in the Szczecin Lagoon, but this is something considerably graver. The men are condemning Eric as a sorcerer and a traitor. They have completely forgotten that it was I who brought Blarulf on board. I suppose, having seen the two of them together so much in Peenemunde, the men have decided that Eric is Fenrir's master.

"KILL THEM ALL!" someone shouts, and a rush of armor-clad warriors surround us quickly.

Gunner gets to his feet and makes a run at me. I parry, and he runs his sword through my shoulder to the hilt. I punch him hard in the face, and he stumbles backwards. I catch his sword by the blade as it pulls out and wrench it from his hand. Eric lunges and instantly has his knife at Gunner's throat. Fenrir, hackles up and teeth bared, expels a menacing growl; he is ready for another fight.

"STOP!" Eric shouts. "Another move and I'll cut his throat! With all the jarls dead, Gunner is now Jarl Agarson. He commands you, now." Eric leans in close to Gunner's ear and whispers, "Now command them to lower their weapons."

Eric's words have the desired effect. Everyone ceases advancing on us, awaiting Gunner's orders.

"We must not let them kill Eric," thinks Fenrir. "He is important to us."

"Eric? But, why?" I ask, without speaking.

"You wonder what plan my sister has for us? Well, this is part of it. Eric must live," answers Fenrir as Gunner shouts, "KILL THEM!"

Eric's knife runs effortlessly through Gunner's neck, the latter's face displaying a second of shock before his body drops lifelessly to the ground. A wall of shields circles us and begins tightening like a hangman's noose.

"Meet us at the docks!" Fenrir yells as he grabs Eric by his leather waste belt, leaps over the shield wall, and drags him away from the fight.

"Great!" I think to myself. I flip Gunner's sword into the air, and, catching it by the grip, begin hacking my way through the shield wall, slashing and flailing with it in my left hand and Bjorn's blade in my right. I amaze even myself at the ferocity of my attack. Men begin dropping in front of me. I feel the coldness of their steel and the shock of their hammer blows cutting and crushing my body, but I am unstoppable.

A great warrior, Olaf the Giant we call him because of his immense size and strength, grabs me from behind, pinning my arms to my side where I cannot fight. I struggle against his embrace, but he is too strong for me. He wrestles with me as more men jab and hack at my head and belly. I slide my foot between Olaf's legs and hook his right foot. With all my strength, I push off with my left, tripping him and throwing him off balance. He stumbles backwards, and we crash to the ground. The crushing force of my body on his chest makes him lose his grip, and I roll backwards over his head and onto my feet.

I, finally, hack my way free of the horde and begin running towards the docks. I turn only once to see my pursuers, but there are none. I see only the dumbfounded faces of the disbelieving; they had struck me three score times, yet I emerged unhurt.

I arrive at the docks where Eric has already prepared a skiff for sailing. I jump aboard, grab a pair of oars, and start rowing. Eric captains the sail and rudder. In no time, we are hundreds of yards from shore.

Their shock abated, dozens of warriors pour into two drakkar longships. We may have a lead, but they will overtake us soon enough. Eric swings us around to have the full wind behind us. The maneuver nearly capsizes the boat, and Fenrir topples into the sea. He paddles furiously, barely keeping his head above water. I throw him a line which he catches in his mouth. When the line pulls taut, the skiff slows to a near standstill as we drag the weight of the massive Wolf-God behind us. With all the strength in my back and arms, I haul in the rope until Fenrir is alongside. Then, both Eric and I lay into the gunwales and pull Fenrir back into the boat.

The effort cost us valuable time, as the drakkars are now bearing down on us. Fenrir readies himself to jump onto the closest ship, like he had done in the lagoon. Unbelievably, the longship abruptly turns broadside, the men digging their oars so deeply into the water, that a few of them are flung into the air by the sudden change in momentum. The second ship collides with the first.

I am ecstatic at our good fortune. I guess the thought of Fenrir tearing a murderous path through their ship made them reconsider the wisdom of chasing us down. I watch both drakkars turn and furiously row for land. Our escape secure, I turn to tend the sail. Now, I see what our pursuers were really running from. Ahead is a massive storm of black clouds and a wave so large, I can scarcely see anything on the horizon. Eric cuts hard on the rudder again and faces us directly into the wave. I have no time to pull the sail down securely, so I cut the lines. The siglura drops from the top of the mast bringing the sail with it. The skiff shudders as the yard beam crashes across the bow, barely missing Fenrir's head, but covering him with the sail.

We begin climbing the wave face which seemingly reaches all the way to the heavens. Fenrir hunkers down in the bow, lest we topple over backwards. Eric and I both grab oars and start rowing harder than either of us have ever rowed in our lives. It is as though we are rowing up a mountain. I feel the pull of gravity as I stare at the abyss of black ocean beneath us. Suddenly, we break the top of the wave and slide rapidly down the other side. Eric and I continue rowing, trying desperately to maintain control of our skiff. We fly through the bottom of the wave at an incredible speed and begin climbing the next. Gale winds and sea spray engulf us as we are swallowed by the storm.

CHAPTER SEVEN

KNUCKLEBONES

Long rolls of ghostly white clouds form seemingly from nothing. They start as tiny wisps along the black horizon and then, with a smack of Thor's hammer, are transformed into great walls of white, towering high into the air and stretching as far as the eye can see. The roaring clouds angrily bear down on us, but our lithic ramparts prove their worth as the clouds are broken and dissipated. Wave after wave of the icy Baltic Sea crashes on the rocky beach where we have washed up.

We had fought the storm for endless hours and days, until exhaustion. Now I lie among the stones in the frigid surf. Eric rests a few yards away, still clinging to the last remnant of our skiff. I do not see Fenrir, but I recall him being thrown from the boat, watching him paddle furiously to stay afloat before the waves overtook him. I am not concerned that he drowned; he is, after all, a god. Still, the abject fear on his face as he struggled is an image that will live with me for all my days – my endless days.

I get to my feet, shivering uncontrollably, and go to help Eric. From the angle of his foot, I can tell his lower leg is broken. He is lying face down, so I roll him over to see if he is breathing. Eric's agonized scream answers my question. I lift him as gently as possible across my shoulders and carry him up from the beach, laying him down against a birch tree. He moans while I pull his foot back into position, a muffled pop and a loud expletive letting me know I have successfully set the break. While I splint his leg, Eric grimaces in silence.

I have no idea where we have landed. I survey the area and see we are on the edge of a small, marshy plain dotted with stands of birch and pine that gives way to a low, grassy meadow, and farther beyond, a dense forest. I start out toward the forest. Where there are trees, there must be fresh water. I find a stream quickly, but the water is too brackish to drink. I continue my search upstream where I find a small waterfall of clear, clean water. Cupping my hands, I drink my fill. I wash my face and rinse the saltwater from my hair. Refreshed, I fill my waterskin for Eric and return.

"What need has a god for water?" Eric muses.

"What?" I reply, confused.

"Well, I must be a god, greater even than Thor, for I have drunk in the sea in just one gulp, where it took him three from the giant's horn," Eric laughs, recalling a favorite Norse story.

"Yes, that's true, but I did help you on that score, so maybe we are both greater than Thor," I chuckle. "But here, have some more anyway. This water is not so salty."

"Helped me on that score? Were you caught in the storm, too? I thought, perhaps, you were a local tribesman who found me while collecting mussels."

"We were on the skiff together, along with Fen ... oh, never mind, friend. I was fishing, and my boat went down. Here, drink this." I hand him the skin, and Eric drinks heartily. I keep forgetting that no one knows me.

"So, how did you happen upon our shores?" I ask. If Eric believes me to be a local, I may as well pretend to be one.

"I was returning home from the Battle of the Sees and got caught in a storm."

"The Battle of the Sees? I hear it was a great victory."

"Oh, yes. I don't think Charlemagne will dare cross the Elbe again."

I hold my tongue. I know the Franks will cross the Elbe again and probably already have. The Battle of the Sees was a small victory in a war that is already lost.

"So, were you thrown overboard, or did your ship founder? Where are your shipmates?" I ask, wondering just how much of the last days' events he does remember.

"Well, perhaps Aegir has taken my memory while sparing my life. I remember we were at the Thing in Peenemunde when a berserker burst in and slew many men. I think, perhaps, they thought I had done it, so they cast me adrift, alone. The storm overcame me, and I ended up here," Eric replies. I can see him searching his memory for more detail, but it simply won't come to him.

I pull a strand of blue hair from his belt. "Are you sure you were alone? Where did this hair come from? It is clearly not yours."

"I don't know."

"You know, I have seen hair like this on the large wolves that roam in the east – large BLUE wolves," I emphasize.

"Blarulf ... Blarulf?" Eric looks through me with his mind's eye, scanning a distant horizon where his memories dwell. "BLARULF!"

"Blarulf?" I ask, calmly, though I can barely contain my excitement at the possibility that Eric may remember me as well.

"Yes, Blarulf, or at least, that is what we call him. He is a large blue wolf, like the ones you describe. I think he was one of the spoils of a raid we made on some traders in the Szczecin Lagoon. But why on earth anyone would trade in such beasts is beyond me. Perhaps their fur fetches a nice price. He was quite helpful when we were ambushed by skiffs and barges loaded with soldiers. We made him our mascot, until he went crazy and started killing us. I remember now that they cast me adrift with it. Perhaps I was to be its last meal."

"And no one else accompanied you on your doomed journey?"

"No. It was the wolf and I against the gale. The wolf slid into the sea, and I somehow made it ... ugh ... here," Eric says as he tries to stand.

"Unfortunate for the wolf, but at least you survived," I say as I hand him a forked tree branch to use as a crutch. "What's your name, friend?"

"My name is Eric Halvorsen, seventh son of Jarl Halvorsen," Eric replies proudly as we start walking toward the forest. "And yours?"

"Asger Agnarson," I reply, knowing he'll most likely forget it before we reach the tree line.

"And you live around here? Somewhere close by, I hope," Eric shrugs with his crutch.

"No, actually, I have no idea where we are, but I thought we could follow the meadow heading that way," I answer, pointing to the right.

"Maybe we can find a fishing village or something."

We walk in silence, stopping occasionally to rest. I can tell Eric is in a great deal of pain, but he doesn't let on. After a while, we see smoke rising in the distance. It takes us nearly an hour to reach the source, a small village of fisherman and seal hunters. The smoke we saw was coming from large iron pots in which the villagers were rendering down seal blubber. The stench is overwhelming, albeit blessedly familiar, the smell taking me back to my boyhood village and fond memories of hearth and home.

The villagers warily watch our approach but continue uninterrupted with their chores. Eric sits down on a log while I inquire of our whereabouts. I approach a woman, haggard from her hard life, but who maintains a semblance of her youthful beauty, and ask her where we are. She answers me in broken Swedish. Her words are familiar, but the dialect is foreign. She tells me we are on Dago, an island off the coast of Eistland. I've heard of this place, though, in the many times I have raided in the east, I've never been here. The stories say Norseman have been raiding this island for decades, even building a fort here once. But being here now, I can't imagine anyone thinking Dago had anything worth taking.

I ask the woman where we may get something to eat and drink. She grunts and points me to a long stick and sealskin canopy from which a much more aromatic smoke emerges. Under her breath, but intentionally loud enough for me to hear, she says, "Pathetic excuse for raiders – asking for food – ugh." I can tell by her tone that this village is not too keen on Norsemen. It has probably been raided numerous times, its women raped, its meager wealth seized, and its young men conscripted or enslaved. I collect Eric and go to the canopy. There, we eat a stew of fish, seal meat, and roots cooked in goat milk and lard, along with many cups of ale. The meal is surprisingly good, if you can get past the look of it.

A burly man dressed in animal skins sits down next to us while we eat. "We don't like your kind around here," he says in a displeased voice.

"Well, I didn't plan to be here. I was shipwrecked," says Eric.

"It's a shame you weren't drowned. Both of you," he says.

"Given the ferocity of that storm, I'm amazed we weren't," I say.

"Storm? What storm?" says the man. He looks at me like I'm crazy.

"The storm that raged the last few days. It blew us halfway across the Baltic," I answer, indignantly.

"There was no storm, Norse. You are just bad sailors," he says, spits in my bowl, and leaves.

I make a point of eating my next spoonful, spit and all, before he turns his head. It's not like it's going to kill me if he has some infectious disease.

"So much for hospitality," jokes Eric.

"They're Karelian and Swede. Hospitality is not in their nature," I reply.

"Nor ours," says Eric, and we burst out laughing.

I wonder how the man could not have seen the storm. He may have been lying, but by his face and tone I believe he knew nothing of it. I ask our cook how his village faired in the gale. He tells me they haven't seen rain in more than a week.

I walk down to the beach where their fishing boats are pulled up above the high tide mark and look out over the sea. On the horizon, I see a form, perhaps a boat coming in with today's catch. I squint and raise my hand to my brow. The form begins to take shape, a smudge of azure against the blackness of the sea – Fenrir.

I watch his progress as he swims for land. I have a fleeting pang of fear for these poor villagers. Fenrir does not like getting wet, and he is liable to take his anger out on them. As he gets closer, I see another smudge on the horizon. The distinct tentacles of the Kraken come into focus. Fenrir paddles furiously, but the monster is closing fast. Fenrir is not more than a few hundred yards off when the Kraken ensnares him and drags him under.

I realize now what I had surmised a few days ago. That storm was no ordinary storm. That was Aegir, the God of the Sea, and it was not me he was after; it was Fenrir. The gods do have their intrigues, but they take on a more serious note regarding the great Wolf-God, the Bane of Odin. I do not know if Aegir is doing Odin's bidding, or if he is adding to his own stake in the game. One thing I do know, though, is when the gods are playing knucklebones, the whole of the world is at stake. I wonder, "When will I be wagered, and what will I draw into the pot?"

CHAPTER EIGHT

LOVER'S BARGAIN

The giant lay sleeping, his head resting upon a pillow of mounded earth, his arms folded across his chest. Were it not for the smoky breath escaping his half-open mouth, he would appear dead. The grotesque horns sprouting from his forehead are twisted and broken, and his long beard flows down the hillside like a foss, a waterfall of pink, sweet smelling dogrose spilling over the coastal dune. As I approach, I must step around the remnants of his stone breastplate which lay cleaved and shattered on the ground around him. I enter the once-proud fortress built by my ancestors to find a villager smoking meat in what was once a small courtyard.

The fort is not at all what I expected. I had imagined nothing more than a rotted wooden palisade, but here was a stone and timber fortress which had at least one large tower, now a crumbling ruin. It has clearly been besieged and much of the stone structure has been stripped away by the people who inhabit the island. The forewall is completely gone, except for a few stacks of larger stones. I climb a stack and briefly peer out across the

48

strait, seeing the hazy mainland of Eistland in the distance. I feel a strange connection to my forefathers who came here and established this place to keep watch over the Karelia.

I ask an elderly, long-bearded man in a ragged tunic where I might find the town of Kūk. He grunts and points north along the coast. I leave him to his cooking and walk another half rôst to the town. It is much larger than the village where I left Eric, with a large natural harbor and well-maintained jetties of rock reaching across the entrance, rock no doubt scavenged from the fort. I am weary from the day's journey across the island and search for an olstafa where I may get a drink and, hopefully, a bed.

I find a large building, two stories in height, its doors wide and inviting. The polished stone facade of the first-floor gleams in the late afternoon sunlight, and the second floor of paneled timbers and carved naked bodies tells me this place is more than just a drinking hall. I enter to find several long tables full of men, eating, drinking, gambling, and laughing, as buxom, flaxen-haired women serve them ale and sit in their laps. A burly man stops me and requests I leave my weapons at the door. I show him I have none, having lost mine at sea during the storm. Instantly, an attractive young woman is on my arm, guiding me to a table where another nice woman gives me a cup of ale. I have not felt this welcome since I arrived on Dago. I guess I washed up on the wrong side of the island.

I ask for a plate and am served a platter of assorted smoked fishes, a rosolje of beetroot, potato, and herring, a pirukas pastry stuffed with sliced goat shank, cabbage and carrots, and a loaf of rye bread. The food is delicious, much better than the larded seal I'd been eating for the last few weeks; I eat like it is my last meal, and when that very thought occurs to me, I chuckle aloud and choke on the rosolje.

I pay my silver to the server, who, with a fleeting hike of her skirt, asks if

I would like anything else. I decline the offer, for the moment, in favor of another cup of ale. I am surrounded by fishermen and seal hunters who smell like their work and probably pay in fish or skins. A man with real silver in this place is like a king. It is not long before I am approached by an elegantly dressed older woman, obviously the proprietor, who would like to assist me in choosing my next course from three of her most attractive girls. I am tempted, but my thoughts of Inger stop me from going any further. I still have great hope that she will remember me, and I don't want to do anything that might prevent that. Also, I made her a promise when we married to never lie with another, and though I have had many opportunities, I have never broken that promise. Also, I know that if she does remember me, all she need do is look in my guilty eyes, and she will unman me and tack my parts to the door.

Having finished my meal, I stay to enjoy more ale and to see if anyone can help me with my purpose for coming here – to procure a boat. We will need one that can make the treacherous journey across the Baltic to Lagarvik. I talk to several men, one of which says he knows someone who might sell us a boat. He offers to take me to his friend, but I suspect he'd seen my silver and intends to take me to some isolated spot where he can rob me and kill me. There are many such men in a place like this.

I start up a conversation with a sailor who works on a trading knarr. He tells me the ship's captain is upstairs with orders not to be disturbed but agrees to introduce me to him in the morning to see about booking a passage. I also talk with some local fisherman who offer to take us anywhere we want to sail if the price is right. Having seen a few local fishing boats at the village, I am skeptical that one could make the trip, particularly if there is a storm. However, I plan to go down to the harbor tomorrow and see exactly what is available.

Very tired and a little drunk, I retire to my room. I fall asleep quickly and dream of being home with Inger. We are lying in furs. I can feel the warmth of her body and the softness of her skin on mine. It feels so real. I touch her lovely face, then gently slide my hand down her neck to her breast.

"Again!?" a voice calls out, startling me awake. "You have more stamina than ten men. And I would know!"

I am shocked to find a woman lying next to me. Where did she come from? I am sure I went to bed alone. And what does she mean, 'Again'? Had I made love to this woman? In my drunkenness, had I betrayed my wife? I lurch away from her and fall out of bed.

"What? Don't you like me anymore, Asger?" she asks.

"Wha ... wha ... who are you? Why are ... what are you doing here?" I stutter.

"What do you mean 'What am I doing here?' What do you think I'm doing here? You were surely not asking me that earlier."

"No. I went to bed alone. You ... did I?"

"You went to bed, Asger, but not alone. And, yes, you did."

"NO. NO. I'm sure I was alone. You must have come ... WAIT! You called me Asger!" This woman knows my name.

"Well, that is your name, isn't it? Asger Agnarson?"

"This is a trick. You're Loki! You're trying to trick me again."

"Asger. You insult me. You think I look like my father?"

"Hel." I recognize her now. She is just as beautiful as the first time I saw her, even more so in her nakedness.

"Yes, Asger, it's me. I came to talk to you, and, uh, other things." She says coyly, looking me up and down.

"Say I didn't. Tell me we didn't." I am acting like it would be a terrible thing to have made love to her, but given her beauty, I know it's just an act. I secretly hope I did, and I'm trying very hard to remember if she was as exquisite as her looks promise she would be.

"Yes, as I said, you did. But you were half asleep and kept calling me Inger. You know, Asger, it is beyond boorish that you would call a woman by another woman's name while you are making love to her. Still, it's moving to see how much you love her. Every woman should have someone who loves her that much. It's a pity she doesn't know you."

I feel both ashamed and excited. I want to protest my innocence, but the words escape me.

"Oh, it's alright, Asger," Hel says, seeing the guilt and confliction on my face. "You were dreaming. You thought you were with her. Besides, I am a goddess, so it doesn't count, really. Your virtue is intact."

As she speaks, she emits golden wisps of light, which swirl around her. When they dissipate, she is fully clothed in a gown of silver and blue with her long hair in a braid that runs fully down her back.

"There, better now?" she asks. "Most men would prefer me naked, but then you are not like most men, are you? No mortal men, anyway."

"Why are you here, Goddess?" I have found my voice again.

"Well, it seems you've lost something."

"And what is that?"

"My brother?" She gives me a stern glare.

"Yes, he fell off the skiff during a storm. Later, I saw him taken by the

Kraken."

"So, Aegir has taken him," says Hel with concern. "This is dire indeed."

"Why is that?" I ask.

"Well, as Odin rules the skies through his sons, Tyr and Thor, so Aegir and his wife, Ran, rule the seas. If Aegir has taken Fenrir, it can only be for one purpose – the prophecy."

"Ragnarök?" I ask, though I know the answer.

"Yes, but I do not believe he intends to bring about Ragnarök. He is using Fenrir as a bargaining chip against Odin. I think he wants to expand his dominion to the skies," Hel says. Bands of blue light flash across her gown as she contemplates Aegir's intentions.

"But the storm," I say. "It was unearthly. He must have had help from either Tyr or Thor."

"Tyr, I suspect. He is always so righteous, if not more than a bit naive," she responds with obvious condescension. "Aegir probably convinced him that capturing Fenrir was in the best interests of Odin and the Aesir. Bind the dog; save the realm.

"Asger, you must free Fenrir. This is the purpose for which you exist," she adds.

"Why would I do that, Goddess? Fenrir hates me, and I am not fond of him either," I say. "Besides, you said my curse would be broken by Ragnarök, so what reason do I have to help."

"Because you would be dead and never see Inger or your children again!" she snaps back. "And, as you know, it was you who laid the curse, not me." Her tone softening, she adds," But do this, and I will allow you some relief from your situation."

"You'll lift the curse?"

"You know I cannot do that, but I can, perhaps, allow someone to recognize you."

"I choose my wife and children," I blurt out.

"This is not a negotiation, Asger. I could force you to do as I bid you. But I want you to do this of your own free will, so I will remove your anonymity – for one person only."

Her emphasis on 'one person only' tells me this is a one-time offer.

"Of my choice," I state firmly.

"Yes, of your choice. But not now. Later, you may call upon me to make good on my bargain. But, first, you must rescue Fenrir."

"How am I to do that? He has been dragged beneath the sea."

"You must kill the Kraken. Only that monster has the strength to hold him. Kill the Kraken and my brother will be freed."

"You ask the impossible, Goddess. A thousand men could not destroy the Kraken. Let alone one man."

"A thousand mortal men may not, but one immortal man may," she replies. Her eyes gleam as one preparing for battle. I've seen that look on many men as they sharpen their resolve and their swords. She is sharpening her weapon as well – me.

"But, I agree, you will need help, and I know of one close by who can assist you. You must go to the old fort and consult the Seer. He knows how to summon the only thing that can help you defeat the Kraken – the great World-Serpent – Jörmungandr."

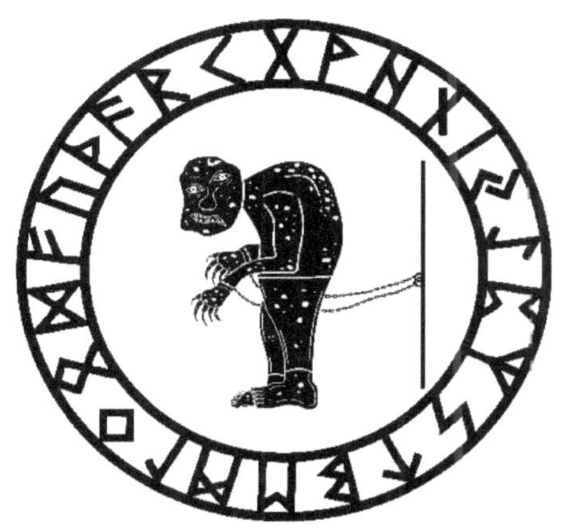

CHAPTER NINE

THE SEER AND THE JÖTUNN

A flock of cranes stands silhouetted in the morning mists, their necks stretching toward the sky. With dawn spreading its orange fingers over the distant horizon, one crane, then another, and then several more spread their wings and take flight over the bay in search of their morning meal. Soon, dozens are winging their way up the straits toward the open sea, as the men of Kūk, their vessels at full sail, begin another arduous day of netting fish and harpooning seals.

I watch them from the docks where I have come to inspect the boats. I admit I was wrong about their seaworthiness. I am quite confident any one of them would be capable of sailing all the way across the Baltic. I find the sailor of the trading knarr I met the night before. He, of course, does not remember our talk, but seems very enthusiastic at the opportunity to make some extra silver. I give him a coin, and he introduces me to his captain. The man is the most ancient of seamen I have ever met, his left leg hobbled and an ear and some fingers missing. I am impressed that a man so aged

55

and crippled would have the stamina to have spent an entire night upstairs at the olstafa in the company of what he tells me was three women. I believe I have found my ship and captain. Clearly, this man has many times survived the rages of Aegir and Ran, and I am quite confident we can come to an agreement on passage. I give him nine pieces of silver with the promise of fifty more. A tenth coin I cleave in half, giving one half to him, and telling him two men will return with the other half coin and the other fifty in a few days. He agrees to take both to Lagarvik.

I make my way along the beach and climb the high, stony mount to the old fort. It looks even more decrepit and foreboding in the morning, the sea mists obscuring the ground around it and making it appear to be floating in the clouds. I approach the old man I had met the day before; he is still smoking meat in his røykhus in the courtyard, the aroma of which makes my belly growl and my mouth water. I see no one else around, so I assume he is the seer I was sent to find. Perhaps he heard my belly because, as I approach, he turns and hands me a hunk of smoked seal meat.

"Are you the seidr?" I ask as I take a bite.

"I may be. Who asks?" he says, his eyes rising to meet mine.

"Asger Agnarson. I have been sent by the goddess, Hel. She said you could help me find Jörmungandr," I say calmly. I had thought of making up some story as to why I was there, but if he is truly a seer, my lie would not have fooled him anyway.

"Hel, hmm?" he grunts. "And you seek the World-Serpent. Why?"

"Fenrir has been taken by the Kraken. I am to free him, and Jörmungandr is to help me."

"Beh! And what makes you think Jörmungandr will help ... you?", he asks dismissively.

"Because Fenrir is his brother!" I exclaim with a brief flash of anger at the old man's attitude.

"Good luck with that, young man. Brotherly devotion is a human construct. Gods and monsters rarely share such affections," he says, shaking his head. "And that goes doubly for the sons of Angrboda."

"But, Hel said ..." I start to respond. The seer cuts me off.

"Why has Hel enlisted you for this? Are you a hero, boy? Do you intend to kill the Kraken?" he chuckles.

"Because I am ..." I catch myself before telling him of my curse. "... I am her servant."

"Only the dead serve the Queen of the Dead. Are you dead, boy?"

"Not exactly," I say, almost jokingly. Suddenly, he grabs my arms and pulls his face in very close to mine, staring deep into my eyes, deep into my mind. After a few seconds, he releases me and backs away, a flicker of surprise crossing his face as he turns his gaze downward and carves off another slab of smoked seal.

"I cannot help you," he says, but I notice the confidence in his voice is gone, replaced by fear.

I decide to push harder for his cooperation. "You must! And you WILL!," I say with conviction. "You will summon the serpent for me, or I will KILL you where you stand!" My voice rises with the threat.

"Boy, you have no idea what you are asking!"

"I'm not asking!" I wrap my hands around the old man's neck. It feels soft and stringy in my grasp as I tighten my grip.

"Very well," he gasps. "Grab that pile of meat and follow me. Have you a sword or ax?"

"Lost in the sea," I respond, as I take up a hundred pounds of sliced, smoked seal across my shoulders.

The seer takes a blazing stick from the smokehouse fire. He groans as he shuffles toward the remnants of the tower. Among the rubble, he finds a rusted sword. It is quite long, very heavy, and ancient. "Here," he grunts.

I take the sword even though it is all but useless. The seer moans as he reaches down for a heavy oaken door that is lying on the ground. Then, with a flick of one hand, he effortlessly pushes it away to reveal a staircase spiraling into the earth. I barely conceal my astonishment at his sudden strength. Just moments ago, I had this man by the throat; I realize, now, he has been toying with me, pretending to be a fragile old man when, in truth, he could have given me a pretty good fight if he'd had the mind to do it. The seer, his torch in hand, descends the staircase. I follow.

We come to a chamber with another large oaken door. It is bolted shut by large metal rods which run vertically and horizontally across it. The seer wraps on the door three times. Beyond the door, a guttural voice responds, "Did you bring my meats?"

"Yes. Step away from the door so I may open it," says the seer.

I hear the sound of jangling chains and something heavy being dragged across a stone floor. The seer unbolts each of the rods and pulls the door open slowly. Beyond it, emerging from the shadows, is a colossal beast, at least twenty feet tall – a jötunn – a giant. It looks almost human but is grotesquely misshapen, slouched over by a large festering hump on its back and shoulder and hobbled by an overgrown clubbed foot, obviously the source of the dragging sound. Its face is so disfigured that one eye droops a foot below the other on its enormous head. I can see that its arms are chained to the wall, but it has full range of the chamber in which it's imprisoned.

The seer enters first, and the giant immediately becomes agitated.

"Where are my meats? You said you brought me my meats!" it yells.

"Now, calm down, Vörnir. I have brought you special meats, see?" the seer says and motions for me to enter. I drop the slabs of meat I have been carrying at the jötunn's feet.

"What's this!?" screams Vörnir. "I don't eat cooked meats! You know I don't eat cooked meats!" The angry jötunn begins thrashing his arms, whipping the chains violently.

"Those are for Jörmungandr," smiles the seer. "The human is for you."

"OOOOO!" whoops Vörnir, rapaciously.

Before I can react, the monster is upon me. He lifts me high with both arms, opens his cavernous mouth, and thrusts me headfirst into it. I am terrified as I slide down Vörnir's gullet into his stomach. The putrid smell of half-digested seal meat is overwhelming. I struggle to climb my way back out, but his stomach is too slippery, and his throat closes tight above me. Digestive acids pour in on me, burning my flesh. My skin instantly heals, but the searing pain lingers on.

I draw the rusted, old sword from my belt and begin stabbing into the walls of Vörnir's stomach. I can hear the faint groans of pain from above, so I continue stabbing and slashing until I open a hole. The contents of his stomach discharge into his abdominal cavity. I feel the monster double over. I continue slashing and jabbing, but my blade cannot pierce Vörnir's skin. I resolve to escape via a different path. I shred his stomach and begin hacking my way through his intestines which explode in a putrid slurry of digested meat and noxious feces, finally reaching the rectum. With the sword, I pry open his anus. The sword breaks off near the grip, but not before I am able to slide through to freedom. I crawl away, vomiting violently as the jötunn wriggles and writhes in his death throes.

"Well done, boy!" cries the seer.

Enraged and terrified at having been swallowed alive, I lunge at him with the fragment of sword. The seer steps aside, and I fall, sliding across the floor as if it were ice. Covered in the slimy, malodorous contents of Vörnir's stomach and intestines, I am unable to regain my feet, continually slipping and falling back down with every attempt. Finally, exhausted, I just hurl several unintelligible expletives at him. Were I able to stand, though, I would beat that old man to death with my bear hands.

"There is no need for such language. You were never in any danger," says the seer.

"WHA ... WHY? WHY DID YOU DO THAT?" I scream. "I'LL KILL YOU!"

"I needed the jötunn dead, and you were just the man to do it," says the seer, calmly.

"ME? WHY ME?" I say, hurling the vestige of my sword at his head. He ducks, but the pummel catches him above the eyebrow, splitting it open. He chuckles as he raises his sleeve to wipe away the blood.

"Because you cannot die, that's why," he says.

"How do you know that? I never told you," I say, my anger subsiding slightly with my small victory.

"I looked at you. I saw you."

"What did you see, old man?"

"I saw a man with no past ... and ... no future. I saw only the consuming flames of Ragnarök, and you standing over the ravaged body of Odin in the Great Hall. You are no ordinary human. You are immortal. Anonymous and immortal. I see why Hel has tasked you with the rescue of her wolfen brother."

"She cursed me. Now I must do her bidding so she will undo it."

"She hasn't the power to curse you like that, boy. No god has that kind of power. No, this was a curse of your own making, and she can't undo it."

"How do you know this? Did Hel tell you this!?" I cry out, but I am afraid to hear the answer. The seer somehow knows the details of my curse, and he has confirmed what Hel has told me – that I cannot escape it.

"She did not. She had no need to tell me anything. I told you, boy, I see you," the old man says as he extends a hand and helps me to my feet. "I see you for what you are."

"So, you say I am truly doomed to remain alive ... forever ... unknown to everyone, even my ... my wife and children?" A vale of darkness falls over me, an overwhelming despair I have never felt before, not even when Hel first cursed me.

"There's always hope, boy. Curses always have conditions. Find the right conditions, and you could end yours. Now, let's go summon the World-Serpent. Pick up the meat."

"Conditions? What conditions?" I think to myself. The old man is toying with me again. He takes away all hope and then offers it back again. It is just a game to him – a sick, sordid game.

The seer turns his back and walks away. I sling the meat over my shoulder and follow, my steps staggered and my head dazed by the events and revelations of the last few minutes. Of all the horrors I've seen in my life, being eaten alive was the worst. I fear I will never sleep again lest I have an eternity of nightmares about it.

"Why did you need me to kill Vörnir? Why not do it yourself?" I ask.

"I couldn't. Vörnir was Hrimthursar. Unlike other jötunn, his skin is impenetrable to any weapon forged by man. The only way to kill him was from the inside. Unless you're a god, of course. You may not be a god, but you are the closest thing to one. I would not have survived long in Vörnir's belly, certainly not long enough to kill him."

"Hrimthursar? Ice giant? I thought they were extinct," I say, surprised by the seer's revelation.

"They are now, boy," the seer laughs. "Well, nearly anyway."

We exit the chamber through another door at the back and descend more spiraling stairs. We come to a cave where the sea has flooded in. As we stand on the shore, the seer chants and throws slabs of smoked seal into the water. I watch silently as the waters begin to ripple, then boil, and then ... part.

CHAPTER TEN

BEGUILING THE SERPENT

A thousand candles shine through the darkness, their delicate flames dancing in the near still air. As a gentle breeze begins to blow, the flames grow and flicker excitedly, becoming frantic as the breeze becomes a wind. The wind becomes a gale, and they become more frenzied, trying desperately to remain tethered to their life-giving wicks. Then, like tree leaves in an autumn storm, the candle flames are blown away and extinguished. The flickering reflections of the torchlight on the surface of the water are pushed away and eclipsed by a giant serpent's head. Jörmungandr has risen.

Jörmungandr, the great World-Serpent, is a sight to behold. The cavern in which we stand is half the size of the isle that contains it, yet only a portion of his head is visible. His eyes are as large as a village, and flash iridescently, the pearly colors of the rainbow radiating outward from his pitch-black pupil. His ebony skin is adorned with colorful, rune-like tattoos which emit their own light in every hue imaginable. He is mesmerizing to

63

look upon. Truly, Jörmungandr is the most frightening of Loki and Angrboda's children, but in many ways, he is the most beautiful, a giant to which even the dwellers of Jötunheimr would pale as a gnat would to a bear.

"Why have you s-s-summoned me, S-s-seer?" bellows the beast, shaking the entire island.

"This boy needs your help," replies the seer. Jörmungandr moves his head so his eye is merely feet from me.

"Help, you s-s-say? What help does he wish and why does he wish it from me?" The cave shakes with every word, and rocks loosen and fall from its walls.

"I need to rescue your ...," I blurt out, but Jörmungandr cuts me off.

"He s-s-speaks without invitation, another ill-mannered human. Take him away les-st I devour him. I may not enjoy the tas-ste as much as s-s-smoked s-s-seal, but at least the world will be rid of him."

"I'm sorry, Great One. He didn't know to hold his tongue until asked to speak," cajoles the seer. "But he does have certain talents that make him hard to be rid of."

"Hard to be rid of you s-s-say? Interes-s-sting. What are these talents-s-s, boy?" the serpent asks me.

"I was cursed by your sister. She made me immortal," I answer.

"And ... anonymous, Great One," adds the seer. "No one knows who he is. No one remembers him."

"And what name does this boy go by, s-s-seer?" asks Jörmungandr.

"He is called ... er ... look at me boy," says the seer, and I turn and face him. "He is called ..." the seer stares deep into my eyes but cannot come up with my name.

"I am Asger Agnarson," I finally respond.

"You s-s-speak again without invitation!" shouts the serpent, "But, as the s-s-seer s-s-seems to have lost his tongue, I will forgive you this one time. Do not dis-s-srespect me again." Jörmungandr moves his head and takes his eye away from me. He seems to have relaxed.

"And the help you as-s-k of me, what is that?" he asks.

"I need to rescue your brother, Fenrir," I reply.

"Fenrir!? HA!" laughs the monster, shaking the cave so violently that part of the ceiling collapses. "Res-s-scue from whom?"

"He was taken by the Kraken. He is the prisoner of Aegir," I answer.

"S-S-So! That is no business-s-s of mine. And I have no quarrel with Aegir. I even allow him to rule in my ocean."

"Your sister thinks he plans to use him against Odin to bring about Ragnarök!"

"More likely jus-s-st as a bargaining chip," reasons the serpent. He is clearly intelligent. "But what would Aegir want in return for delivering my wolfen brother to Odin? A realm of his own, perhaps-s-s?"

"Or perhaps more power in this realm?" I offer.

"Yes-s-s, of course — the s-skies-s-s. Well, that s-s-seems like a good trade. Aegir is clearly more cunning than I gave him credit for. S-s-so, immortal mortal, why would I help you thwart Aegir's plan? I s-s-see no benefit for me."

"Not even the destruction of the Kraken?" I ask, rhetorically. "The Kraken has become the most feared thing in the sea, more feared even than you, Great One."

"Nothing is more feared by gods-s-s or men than I am," booms Jörmungandr.

"I would not be so sure of that. The Kraken instills fear, taking ships and drowning men at his leisure, while you merely swim around, growing thin off your diminished reputation."

"LIES-S-S!" cries the serpent, causing the cavern to shake violently and more of the ceiling to collapse. I begin to worry if I will not be buried alive.

"Besides, Great One, if Aegir succeeds in claiming the skies for himself, where will that leave the sons of Odin. They will be idle. And you know what idleness does to a god, especially one that is as prone to bluster and waywardness as your mortal enemy, Thor."

That did it. The World-Serpent thrust his head upward with such force, the ceiling split open all the way to the surface, raining rock and debris all over the island and flooding the cave with sunlight.

"THE KRAKEN MUS-S-ST BE DESTROYED! I WILL KILL IT!" cried Jörmungandr in outrage. I felt the entirety of the earth shutter. Then, suddenly, the monster calmed, as if coming to some sullen realization.

Seeing his mood cool so quickly, I ask, "What is wrong, Great One?"

"I cannot kill the Kraken," he answers, almost dejected.

"Of course, you can!" I say, "You're Jörmungandr, the great World-Serpent."

"Yes-s-s, I am the World-S-S-Serpent, and I can crush the bones of anything with my coils-s-s. But alas-s-s, the Kraken has no bone-s-s. It can s-s-simply flatten its body and s-s-slip away from me, or even if it cannot, it will use its million tentacles-s-s to pes-s-ster me, while it continues to s-s-sink ships-s-s and imprison Fenrir. I will be nothing more than a nuisance to it."

"Couldn't you eat it?" I ask.

"Yes-s-s, but it would take millenia to s-s-swallow the body and all the tentacles-s-s. I may s-s-still be trying to finish it off when the world ends-s-s."

"Perhaps if you encircle only the tentacles holding Fenrir, I can cut them off, freeing him."

"You will need an enchanted blade. The Kraken's s-s-skin is as impenetrable as Vörnir's," offers the seer.

"Angurvadal or Skofnung?" I ask.

"They have been lost to time," says the seer.

"What about Dains-s-slief?" asks Jörmungandr.

"Yes, Dainslief would do well; it's said that even a scratch from its blade is fatal, though I'm not sure that would apply to the Kraken. And there is one who knows the location of the blade," answers the seer.

"Who is that?" I ask. Considering what I went through to summon Jörmungandr, I'm dreading what I will have to endure to secure Dainslief. According to the legend, King Högni lost the sword battling giants in Jötunheimr, some saying the king himself had his heart carved out with it.

"Vörnir," replies the seer, seemingly forgetting that Vörnir was dead, a fact of which I reminded him with such great mockery, that even Jörmungandr chuckled.

"Vörnir need not be alive to tell us the location of Dainslief. I will simply read his entrails. Odin attest, you certainly pulled enough of them out of him when you escaped," the seer says with a snicker. I wretch at the thought causing the seer and the World-Serpent to explode in jovial laughter.

The seer and I return to the chamber where Vörnir's body lies. It is half collapsed, and we must move several large stones to reach the jötunn. The seer collects the entrails, pulling more from the jötunn. They are shredded and come out in pieces. I ask if they are in good enough condition to read, but the seer just grunts. We return to the surface where the few standing remnants of the castle and the seer's røykhus have been leveled by Jörmungandr's outburst. The seer throws the entrails on the still burning fire and they begin to smoke and shrivel. The rancid smell forces me to move away lest I begin vomiting again.

The seer chants over the burning entrails for an hour or more. Finally, he stands and shuffles over to me. "Though the entrails were immensely damaged, I was able to discern the location of Dainslief. It rests in the Savonian Forest near the borderlands of Jötunheimr."

"Savonian Forests?" I whisper to myself. It is a very dangerous place consisting of dense forest, lakes, marshlands, and tribal warfare between the Karelian, Swede, Rus, and Lap peoples that make their home there. And then, of course, there are the Jötunn – the giants. Few Norsemen have ventured there since King Högni's legendary betrayal and defeat. But if I must go, I will need a guide, someone who has been there and knows the territory. Fortunately, I know of such a person – Eric. And though I am obliged to keep him alive for a purpose I don't yet know, I will have to risk his life to acquire Dainslief. I wonder if it is for this reason that Eric needed to remain alive – to be my guide.

I return to Kūk to find a blacksmith. Though I seek Dainslief, I do not have it yet, so Eric and I will need weapons for our journey. The people are wandering the streets in shock and many buildings lie in ruins. Jörmungandr's temper has devastated the town, and as I walk through, I begin to get looks of fear, suspicion, and hatred. I understand why. A catastrophe has occurred, and now here I am, an outsider, a Norseman, strolling through. It doesn't take long for an angry crowd to form and start following me.

I find the smithy's forge, which, too, has been nearly destroyed, the blacksmith frantically fighting a fire that had broken out. I assist him with buckets of water and together we manage to extinguish the flames. I hope that helping the blacksmith will gain me some goodwill with the mob, but I am wrong. They close in on me with accusatory slurs and finger-pointing.

Three large men surround me, pulling knives and axes. I grab two axes from a nearby pile and make ready for an attack. Though these axes are made for felling trees rather than fighting, I swing them swiftly through intertwining arcs, showing everyone that I am a warrior with expert precision and causing one of the men to have second thoughts and flee. The other two begin circling, looking for an opening in which to attack. One jumps in from behind me, and I quickly spin and parry the blow from his ax with one of my own. I swing the other, but he jumps back, barely escaping a stroke that would have spilled his guts. The other comes in with his ax, but I duck, swinging my leg around and kicking his feet out from under him. He falls hard, flat on his back. I jump on him and chop down with a killing blow. At the last moment, I deflect, burying the ax in the ground next to his head. I yell that I do not want to harm anyone, that I am not responsible for the destruction of the town.

The crowd falls silent and the man I spared gets to his feet, staring at me with a look of fear and thanks as he moves back into the mob. "It wasn't me," I yell again. "I did not do this." I hold out my arms and turn in a circle in a display of submission I hope will quell any further violence. I barely catch a glimpse of the rock out of the corner of my eye before it strikes me in the head, and everything goes black.

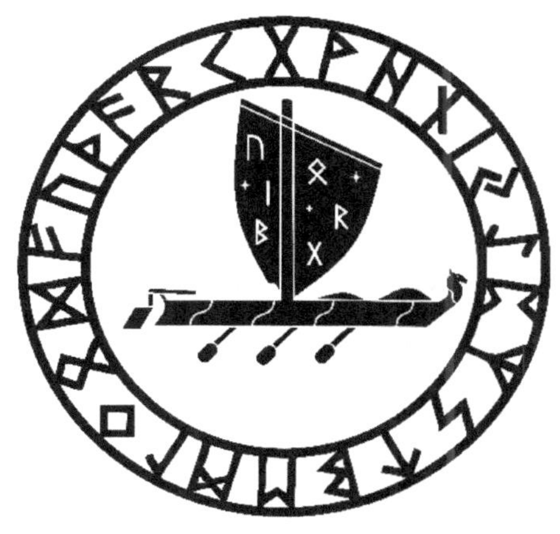

CHAPTER ELEVEN

PASSAGE TO VYBORG

A solitary dog heralds the coming of morning, his bark echoing hauntingly through the brisk dawn air. Soon he is joined by others, their voices becoming a cacophony reminiscent of a crowded market. Above the din, a frightening squeal rings out, a sound of terror and pain. Panicked screams quickly overtake the barking as the bob of seals, who are gathered on the harbor jetty are clubbed and harpooned by hunters in a pre-dawn harvest.

I watch the carnage from a cage which stands in the ebbing tide off one of the piers, just my head yet above water. I had been placed here last evening to determine my fate – a trial by drowning. If innocent of the destruction of Kūk, I will have survived the hours submerged by the high tide. If guilty, I will have drowned. Though it can be argued that I am in fact guilty, as it was I who angered Jörmungandr to the point he quaked the island, I have survived the ordeal, thus proving my innocence.

Some fishermen arrive. I recognize them as the men who locked me up.

Having forgotten he put me here, one of them asks what I am doing in the cage.

"You put me here ...," I answer, "last night." I give him a malicious glare. "You accused me of destroying your town."

"Last night? You've been here all night? At the high tide?", the man asks in confusion. "I can't believe it. No one's ever survived before. How did you do it?"

"Simple," I say, "I'm innocent. Now, let me out."

The two men are completely dumbfounded, mumbling to each other about how drunk they must have been to not remember putting me in the cage. But, holding true to their tradition of justice, they comply with my request.

Free of my watery prison, I politely ask them to sail me back to the village where I left Eric. They agree, even though it means they will miss an entire day's fishing. They claim it is to make amends for falsely accusing me, but I can see they have just realized that the trial by drowning is senseless. Only someone with God-like power could survive the drowning, and a person with that kind of power could be capable of anything – even leveling a town. It is fear rather than tradition that motivates them.

One of the fishermen accompanies me back to the blacksmith to complete my purchase of weapons – four knives, two axes, and two hammers, each of exquisite quality. None of them were designed for battle, but all are quite capable of killing efficiently in the hands of people like Eric and I who know how to use them. Upon our return to the dock, the other man has readied their vessel, and we set sail.

The day's journey is uneventful. The sun shines in a clear sky and the waters are flat and calm. It takes most of the day to sail around the island, but still much less time than walking. I talk sporadically to the fishermen, but they have no interest in having a conversation. They continue to mumble to each other in whispers and give me occasional glances of awe and suspicion. They clearly do not know what to make of me but have decided to remain on my good side. It helped that I sliced open my hand with a knife while one of them was looking. Seeing the wound heal instantly, the man almost fell out of the boat trying to get as far away from me as possible.

We arrive at the village. I tell the men to remain in the boat while I collect Eric. I am confident they will not sail away. Fear will be their anchor. I find Eric has taken up with the woman we met when we arrived on the island. Apparently, she either doesn't hate Norsemen as much as she intimated, or she is just a fool for Eric's legendary charm. Either way, she has taken good care of him, and his leg is mending well.

"Eric, I have secured us a boat. We can leave the island," I say.

"Who are you, and why would I want to leave," he says, laying his head on his lady's ample breast.

"I'm Asger. We were shipwrecked together. You suffered a fractured ankle, and apparently, also a head injury as you seem to have lost your memory." I scratch my neck, making sure to 'accidentally' catch the crescent moon charm with my finger so Eric can see it.

"Oh, yes. Sorry, I think you're right. Maybe my memory did fail me. But at least I haven't forgotten everything!" he says, pulling the woman in close to him and kissing her hard on the mouth. She responds with a big smile while she grabs his groin. "Oh, this is Katye."

"Hello, Katye," I say, "I'm sorry but I must take your man away. He is needed elsewhere." I can tell she is confused, but I grab Eric and start half-walking, half-dragging him toward the boat.

"What, I don't even get to say goodbye?" says Eric. I realize now, he is very drunk, which is why he isn't resisting or complaining about his leg hurting.

We reach the boat, and I make brief introductions. "This is Eric. Treat him as you would me. Eric, these are fishermen who will be taking us to Savonia.

"Savonia? I don't know if you know," Eric slurs, "but it's landlocked."

"I know, but you've been there, and I need to go there. So just tell these fishermen where to put us ashore."

"Why would you want to go to Savonia. It's dangerous there, and there's virtually no treasure. Even the women are ugly, un ... unless you're going after one of those Jötunn women. I hear they are extremely attractive ... and tall, very tall ... but worth the climb."

"I am going to get Dainslief!"

"Ooohhh, Dainslief! It's been lost for centuries. How're you gonna find it?" Eric burbles, drunkenly.

"Let's just say, the entrails of a Hrimthursar jötunn told me where it was and leave it at that."

"Hrimthursar entrails? How'd you get'em out?"

"Leave it!"

"Well, then, we could go to Vyborg, but that's in the heart of Karelia. There are rivers and lakes we could navigate, but we'd most like be killed by Karelians before we ever get to Savonia. Or we could sail north to Vassa. It's a longer journey inland, not as much navigable water, but we may actually survive that way," says Eric in a besotted ramble. The ale in the

Dago fishing village is certainly strong. I've known Eric my entire life, and I have never seen him this drunk.

"Could you make the journey inland from Vassa on your leg?"

"I don't know. It'd be hard," says Eric as he stands to test his leg. He stumbles, and I catch him just before he falls out of the boat.

"Alright, Vyborg it is. I'm not concerned about dying at the hands of the Karelians."

The fishermen hear me and start whispering to each other again. "You heard the man!" I call out. "Sail us to Vyborg."

After almost two days at sea, we put ashore a mile west of the Vuoksi river. I ask the fishermen to take us upriver, but they've had enough. It may not be a suicide mission for me, but it would be for them. I give them five silver each, which I insist they take, and thank them for their service. I am not sure what they thought of me and my immortality, but I know they were glad to be rid of me. I'm sure it will make for a very good tale when they get back to the olstafa in Kūk, but as no one remembers me being there, I doubt anyone will believe them.

Eric and I grab our supplies and move inland, avoiding the town that guards the inlet. Eric has sobered up and is excited about our adventure. The chance to reclaim Dainslief and, possibly, a sizable treasure rumored to lie with it is motivation enough. But the chance to reclaim his reputation is what is really driving him. He laments that we do not have Blarulf with us. "I may not like that dog," he says, "but he would certainly give us an edge if we encounter any Karelians." I don't tell him that our ultimate mission is to free the great, blue wolf.

We encounter the river several miles upstream. Eric's leg is hurting him badly, but he doesn't complain at all. Still, I know he must rest his leg, or we will never reach the Savonian Forest. I find a place to camp and gather wood for a fire. I stalk and kill a small doe, and Eric and I enjoy some venison for dinner. Eric tells a few of his stories, highly embellished to be sure, but it passes the time, and reminds me of the days when we used to raid together. I laugh and urge him to tell more.

Eric begins a story about raiding a Swedish harbor town during a particularly wet spring. I recall he and I broke into a storehouse full of very high-quality bear, elk, and reindeer hides, along with smaller game. We found a sled and loaded it up with hides, but it was too heavy to pull back to the boat. So, we levered it over into a runnel of fast-moving mud, and in a driving rainstorm, slid downhill on it all the way to the harbor. Of course, we couldn't stop and skipped out into the bay sinking the sled with all the pelts. We salvaged a few soggy bear and elk skins. Our friends gave us a lot of good-humored grief for our failed escapade, but we just laughed along with them. Eric still has that soggy bear skin, I think. Of course, in Eric's version, he did this all alone. The memories are somewhat painful now, since it is only I who remembers them, at least the way they really happened.

Long after dark, I leave Eric asleep and go down to the river. I travel back toward town, making sure to stay out of sight. When I reach the inlet, I commandeer a river skiff and row away quietly. As I head upriver, I look for the glow of our campfire, but the embers are dying, and I can't see where to pull ashore. Not sure how far I've rowed, I find a small gravel beach and land on it. As I didn't see this gravel beach when I left camp, I assume I missed our campsite and am somewhere upriver from it. Rather than trying to find my way back in the dark, I decide to stay with the boat. I stretch out in it and go to sleep.

When I awake the next morning, I am drifting in the middle of the bay.

I had forgotten this is a tidal part of the river, so when the high tide came in, it floated the skiff, and the river current dumped me in the bay. I slap myself in the head for not having pulled the boat to higher ground. The bay is starting to fill with Karelian fishing boats and skiffs. I am hoping that no one notices me in a stolen boat. I begin calmly rowing toward the river inlet, not rushing, trying to make it look like I belong there. Unfortunately, I see three other skiffs rowing urgently on an intercepting path between me and the inlet.

CHAPTER TWELVE

SHADOW

A dragon's breath rolls across the water, shrouding everything in a billowing cloud of foul-smelling brimstone. From the smoke, rises the great dragon's head, spewing fire and death over the town of Vyborg. Reaching the sky, the dragon's head explodes into a dark, deformed aureole, to be instantly replaced by another head and another as plume upon plume of black smoke erupts from the burning city.

My pursuers closing quickly, I row my skiff into the choking smoke. I believe I have escaped them when I am suddenly rammed, my skiff capsizing and dumping me into the water. Unable to get my bearings, I start swimming toward a hazy glow, the funeral pyre of the once proud city of Vyborg. I am slapped by an oar and nearly lose consciousness. A hand pulls me into a boat, but I cannot see my rescuers ... or are they captors ... I do not know.

"I told you he wasn't Karelian," a voice says in a distinctive Norse accent.

"But this is not Eric Halvorsen," decries another. "You owe me two silver!"

"Ha! You can deduct it from the five you owe me for firing the entire wharf with just my knife and flint."

"Not fair, Knute. I didn't see the barrels of seal blubber."

"Or the straw, Stigr! A kick and a flick was all it took!"

Knute? I recognize the name and the voice. He was one of the men drinking with Eric at the olstofa where I first found him after the Battle of the Sees; a kinsman, I believe. I do not remember Stigr, but he may have sailed with us to Peenemunde. I would need to see his face to know for sure, but my head is still spinning from the blow and the thick smoke is making my eyes tear up.

"Are you looking for Eric Halvorsen?" I ask groggily.

"Yes, he is our cousin. Have you seen him?" Knute asks with a combination of excitement and suspicion.

"He and I are camped upriver," I say. "We were shipwrecked together on Dago."

"Dago? Stigr, I told you we should have gone there."

"But there's nothing there, Knute. Why would Eric go there?"

"Are you deaf? He was shipwrecked!"

"How was I supposed to know he was shipwrecked?"

"It was a powerful storm. We fought it for days," I interject. "Eric broke his leg, but it is mending well. Head upriver, and I'll take you to him."

"Right ... wait ... how do we know you aren't lying to us to save your own skin?" asks Knute.

"Eric sailed with Blarulf, did he not?" I know they won't remember me, but they should remember a blue wolf.

"He did. Is that murderous hound still with him?"

"Lost at sea," I respond.

"Well, that's good!" says Stigr. "He killed about forty men!"

"Forty men that were trying to kill Eric," I remind him. "Forty men who thought he was a sorcerer."

"Well, that's true. Still, better the beast be drowned."

I man an oar and help row. I see that there are about a dozen other river skiffs and larger boats with us. I ask Knute how many men came with him to look for Eric. He tells me only he, Stigr, and three others, but that they fell in with a band of raiders, mostly Swede and Rus with a few Karelian and Lap mixed in. It was a 'join or die' proposition. I am surprised at the variety of tribes in the band, knowing the hatred that exists between them. It seems, though, that this enterprise is strictly for profit, each man receiving an equal share of the spoils and paying no tribute to any jarl or king.

Knute explained that he and Stigr used the raid on Vyborg to look for Eric, thinking he may have been captured by the Karelians. "We never could have entered the town by ourselves, but as part of a large raiding party, it was easy to get in, look around, and get out. And it seems we were successful. We found you, and you are taking us to Eric." We row a few miles and I see smoke rising from the campsite. We pull ashore and find Eric stretched out gnawing marrow out of the bones of the deer we ate the night before.

"Eric!" cries Knute.

"Cousin! Come to rescue me?" jibes Eric. "As you can see, I need no rescuing."

"This man said you were shipwrecked on Dago," says Knute, pointing at me.

"Yes, I was. But some fishermen were kind enough to sail me here. I'm glad you're here. We will need more men where we're going."

"Where's that?" asks Stigr.

"Dainslief!" Eric responds, a big grin creasing his face.

"That's a myth," says another of the band.

"No myth, my friend. It is in the Savonian Forest. And he knows where." Eric points at me.

"And you believe him?" asks Knute.

"I do," says Eric, staring at me with a familiarity I have not seen since my curse began.

"So, what's your name, friend?" Knute asks, turning to me.

I hesitate to answer, knowing that he will soon forget my name, just as he has forgotten ever meeting me, sailing with me, or fighting beside me. I hearken back to Fenrir's words, 'You may be the Spear of God, the Immortal Soldier, the Twilight Warrior, but now is not the time to foster that reputation.' I decide now is the time. "I am Helsvein, the Drengr Røkkr," I say.

"THE DRENGR RØKKR?!" laughs Knute. "He's a bit full of himself, isn't he?"

Stigr joins in the amusement. "Of course! He's the TWILIGHT

warrior, the servant of HEL! I wonder why I didn't recognize him sooner."

"You shouldn't laugh," says Eric calmly. "He is exactly who he says he is."

I am dumbfounded. Eric has remembered me – well, not who I am, but at least, what I am.

"Ha!" laughs Knute. "I think Eric is drunk or ate something he shouldn't have."

"Show them, Helsvein. Convince them like you did those fishermen," says Eric. I look inquisitively at him. "I heard them talking," Eric answers my unspoken question. "They called you 'the undying demon' – said you destroyed their town."

"I ... I didn't destroy Kūk," I say.

"You know, I met a demon once," Eric continues. "He couldn't die either."

In an instant, a knife appears in my chest. When it comes to throwing axes and knives, Eric is quick and deadly accurate. I pull the blade from my chest and throw it back, sticking it in the ground a hairsbreadth from Eric's broken ankle. I can be accurate, too.

Knute, Stigr, and the rest of their band stand slack-jawed. Stigr spins me around and puts his hand on my chest. There is no blood, no wound. He looks at me with disbelief, then slowly staggers backwards. He shows his bloodless hand to Knute, but never takes his eyes off me. Knute, thinking it must be a trick, comes to me and stabs me in the belly. He pulls out his bloodless knife and feels for a wound.

"Demon," he whispers. "Demon! DEMON!" His voice rises with each accusation.

"I am no demon!" I shout. "I am a man – a CURSED man, but still, a man!"

Some of the men begin returning to their boats, wanting no part of what is transpiring before them. Others of a more curious nature remain.

"Eric, come with us, away from this demon," says Stigr.

"No. I am going with him to find Dainslief. Cousins, you are welcome to come with us. And your men, of course."

"They're not my men," says Knute. "They don't really have a leader."

"Well, then," says Eric turning to the men, "Any man who would drown himself in silver and gold, come with us. A great treasure awaits, and there will be an equal share for all."

The old Eric has returned. He is not the brooding, mistrustful Eric of Peenemunde, nor the drunk I picked up on Dago. He is the bold commander, full of charisma and bravado, ready to lead men on the adventure of a lifetime. He is in his element.

"But Eric," decries Knute, "remember what happened in the lagoon."

"You would begrudge me a chance to regain my honor, cousin?" Eric glares at his kinsman.

"No, of course not. I will follow you anywhere," says Knute.

"As will I," says Stigr.

"And what of the rest of you, hmm? Would you be rich beyond your dreams?" cries Eric.

There is murmuring among the men, as Eric's words are interpreted for those who don't know our language. Many point at me, shake their heads, and leave. The rest, thirty-eight men by my count, decide to stay and travel with us. I hadn't planned on an entire raiding party, but they will be very useful if we get into a fight.

We row upriver all day until we come to the shallows. There is a clearing on the bank where we make camp for the night. Tomorrow, we will make a portage to an inland lake and sail north toward Savonia. The men eat heartily from the foodstuffs they took in Vyborg. Everyone is in good spirits. That may change, I think, the closer we get to our objective.

When night falls, I volunteer for the first watch, as do two of the others, a Swede and a Rus. We take up positions around the encampment, the Swede near his kind, and the Rus near his, each keeping an eye on the other's sleeping men. A band of raiders they may be, but there is clearly still mistrust between them. They are supposed to be watching out for Karelians, not for each other.

As I contemplate my mission, my mind drifts, as it always does, to Inger. Hel promised to allow one person to know me. I know now that my curse is permanent, but if Inger will remember me, I will be able to bear it. And all I need to do to accomplish that is to find Dainslief and free Fenrir.

"Helsvein," a low voice calls, bringing me out of my thoughts. It is Eric.

"Eric. You should be resting. We have a long hike tomorrow and a difficult one, especially with your leg," I say.

"I can't sleep. Not now anyway," he says as he sits down beside me.

After a long silence, I ask, "How did you know I wouldn't die when you threw your knife?"

"Oh, I didn't. Not really. It's just that, well, you're a shadow."

"A shadow?"

"Yes. I mean, I can see your face, right now, but I don't know if you are real."

"I'm real," I say. "So why do you think me a shadow?"

"When I woke up this morning, I was alone. But I knew where I was, and why I was here – to find Dainslief. Except, I don't know where Dainslief is. So why would I be venturing out to find a mythical sword, when I don't know where to look? Simple, I say to myself – someone else is with me, I just can't remember who.

"Then it occurs to me. There was a shadow on the boat that brought me here. Someone I know had to be there, but that I just can't remember."

"I was on the boat with you, Eric. Do you remember me taking you away from Katye?"

"No, actually, I don't. But I know it happened. Were you also on the boat I took from Peenemunde? Were you the berserker that attacked us at the Thing? Were you the man whose life I spared?"

"No, Eric, you didn't spare my life. My life needs no sparing," I say jokingly.

"True," laughs Eric. "Still, I think you were in Peenemunde. I think you have been with me a long time. I do not see you in my memories, but you are there. The gods have bound you to me. You are my shadow, and as long as I have you, I am destined for great things. I shall find Dainslief and the treasure and return to Lagarvik a hero, a warrior of the highest praise – finally the man my father never thought I could be."

"We all want to be the men our father's never thought we could be, Eric. But you won't be returning to Lagarvik with Dainslief. Dainslief is mine. I need it."

"What does the Drengr Røkkr need with an enchanted blade?" Eric scoffs.

"I have to kill something that can't be killed," I say, turning my gaze to the forest.

"Well, Shadow, after you kill yourself, may I have the blade?"

"It's not for me. It's for the Kra..." I stop myself. I hadn't thought that Dainslief might be the way to end my curse. Is that what the seer meant when he said 'curses always have conditions – find the right conditions, and you could end yours'?

The brief silence is broken by the snap of a twig. Both Eric and I jump to our feet, pulling our axes. We tune our ears for any sound and peer squint-eyed into the darkness of the forest. Another twig snaps to our right, then another to our left. Instantly, black figures emerge from the tree line, rushing at us. Eric shouts a warning, and we ready ourselves for battle.

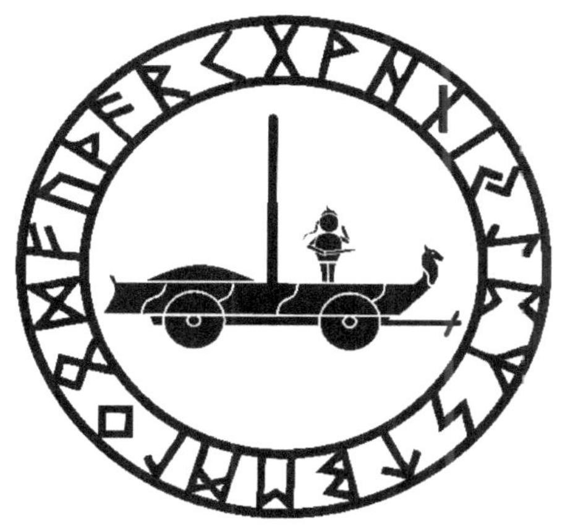

CHAPTER THIRTEEN

THE AMBUSH

A beautiful flower blooms in a vast field of gray, its center expanding as petals open wide around it. Soon, more flowers begin blooming until the whole field is alive with them, moving, shimmering, and fighting for space. With each drop of dying sunlight, a new flower is born. Our boats glide through the rippling flowers, as we make our way across the lake in the gentle rain.

Though the rain dampens our clothing, it does not dampen our spirit. Everyone has a full belly from the boars that Eric and I killed the night before – five in all. I have no trace of the bites and gorings I took, but Eric is nursing a rather severe gash on, what was until now, his good leg. A Rus by the name of Pavel is particularly good with a needle and thread and stitched the wound tight. He is a dumpy fellow, shorter by half than anyone else in our company, but an excellent surgeon and of a jovial spirit. He speaks only his native language, but through his friend, Ivor, he tells us that Eric should be fine in a few days, and he gave Eric a dram of some

87

medicine for the pain. It seems to work well; Eric appears happier than I've seen him since Dago.

What was a simple rainstorm is becoming a torrent, large drop stinging the backs of our necks as we row northwest into a wicked headwind. The boats with sails are forced to drop them. The choppy, windblown waves make the going very difficult. Water sloshes over the gunwales by the gallon. Everyone not rowing is baling water.

The journey across the lake should have taken just over a day, but since the storm came up, it may be at least another day before we make landfall. Everyone is working in silence, except for the Rus; they are singing. I guess they enjoy the miserable weather. It probably reminds them of their miserable lives in the Ruslands. I have raided in the Ruslands on many occasions. I have found the people to be hearty, but sad. Certainly, I had never heard them sing, nor had I ever expected to. However, their singing keeps everyone in a good humor despite the storm.

Knute and Stigr are baling water in my boat and betting on who can bale the most. They are always betting on something. I've been with them for only two days, but between them, they've laid enough bets to open a gambling hall. But I notice, no money ever changes hands. They just deduct their losses from what each believes the other owes him. I can appreciate the comradeship. These two will bicker and bet with each other, but they will never cross swords – not for money, not for women, not for anything. They are closer than brothers.

I remember a time when Eric and I were close, too. But, after I met Inger, Eric and I drifted apart. We were still good comrades, and there was no one either of us would rather have at our back in a fight. But, when we weren't raiding together, we really didn't see that much of each other. I think Eric found me boring, a settled man with a wife and children. Eric is not the settling type. He needs adventure and values only his own reputation. Wife, children, family – those things are not for Eric. I look at him guiding the rudder, and I feel almost sad for him.

"Don't tell me you're bothered by a little rain," Eric says. He must have noticed my pensiveness.

"No. I was just thinking," I answer.

"That's a dangerous thing to do," he quips. "A man who thinks too much can't be trusted."

"Are you saying you don't trust me?" I fire back.

"Well, I don't NOT trust you."

"That's not the same thing."

"I know, but it's the best I can do, Shadow."

I don't like Eric calling me 'Shadow'. Still, it is better than not remembering me at all, I guess. It really isn't the name I take issue with, but the connotation. He says I am bound to him, like he owns me. And, knowing Eric as I do, he means it. There is no doubt in his mind that the gods gifted me to him so that he may achieve greatness. I guess I can't blame him for his belief. For my part, I see Eric as the best chance I have of ending my curse, so I have essentially bound myself to him. And, for reasons I still don't know, I am tasked with keeping him alive. That, I suppose, is what irks me the most – the fact that even in his ignorance and arrogance, Eric is probably right – the gods have bound me to him. I wonder if this is how Fenrir feels about being bound to me. "No," I laugh silently to myself, "I only feel mild resentment for Eric, whereas Fenrir has abject hatred for me."

Mid-afternoon the next day, we arrive on the distant shore of the lake.

We set camp and build fires to warm our cold bodies and dry our clothes. Tomorrow we will begin a tough, two-day portage of boats and supplies to another lake further north. There is a connecting river, but in many places, it is too shallow to navigate. The portage track is well worn which means it is used quite often. That also means we will, almost certainly, encounter others on our journey, most likely Karelians who will surely want to kill us. I wonder if having a small army is such a good idea. These are hard and seasoned fighters, but if we get into a battle with hundreds of Karelians, I don't think we will prevail. Perhaps stealth would be a better strategy, but that would mean Eric and I heading out alone through the woods in tough terrain. I'm not sure Eric could make it with two bad legs. Besides, now that he is in command of these men, stepping into the role of leader without any opposition, he would never abandon them. He would rather die fighting than slink away silently, even if slinking away would mean achieving our goal of finding Dainslief.

We break camp before sunrise and start moving. The previous day's downpour has left the path muddy, and progress is very slow. The good morale of the men is gone, and I hear much grumbling in the ranks. Eric tries to quell the unrest, but only a few of the men understand our language, so his efforts have limited success. There is a nervousness enveloping our group as we make our way. Every one of us has the feeling we are being watched. Eric sends a few men into the woods on both sides of the track to act as pickets, but the denseness of the forest and underbrush makes it difficult to keep up with the rest of us. After a while, they all return reporting that they have seen nothing.

"We're walking into an ambush," Knute tells Stigr.

"I know," Stigr replies.

The fact that Knute and Stigr didn't make any bets as to the when and where of the ambush or how many Karelians each would kill tells me that we are in a very grave situation.

"Eric," I call out, "I need to talk to you." Eric hobbles up from the rear of our column. I know he'd rather be leading, but he can barely walk.

"What do you want?" Eric snaps. He must be in a great deal of pain.

"Two things," I answer, ignoring his mood. "First, you need to stand in the first boat."

"I don't need to be carried, Shadow. I can walk." Eric is a true leader, never expecting his men to do something he wouldn't do himself.

"That's not what I mean," I say. "You know the Karelians are watching us from the woods. Having you stand high in the front would give you, as our commander, a better view of what's ahead." He knows I am making an excuse for him, but he needs to get off his feet, or at least stop walking for a while, which is why I suggested he stand rather than sit. Anyway, it does make tactical sense.

"What else?" he asks.

"We need to position fighters to the front and rear. I suggest we use the Karelians. There are seven of them, so we put four to the front of the column, and I will take the other three with me to the rear. Perhaps if the Karelians see some of their own leading, they might be inclined to leave us alone."

"I doubt they'll leave us alone, but it's a good idea. At least it'll show them that our Karelians are fighters, not slaves. Why do you want to be at the back?"

"Because, when the ambush comes, they will concentrate their forces to our rear to cut off our escape and use their forward forces to drive us back into them. I need to be where the bulk of their forces are. They'll never expect what I'm capable of."

"True. But take Knute with you. I'll send Stigr and Hals to the front. I want my own men in place in case those Karelians decide to rejoin their tribe."

Eric gives the orders as we move to the front of our column. I help him climb into the skiff, which is being wheeled on a cart and pulled by six men. They grumble in confusion until they see him stand and start looking around. From there, Eric can see over the next rise. He tells me the path narrows significantly, barely enough room for one boat to pass through.

If there is going to be an ambush, that is where it will happen. A narrow passage means fewer men able to establish a shield wall, and the rest of us will be strung out, with no way to concentrate our forces. They won't strike, however, until we are all in the narrowest part of the path, and they will use the rise we are crossing now to hide their rear forces.

I see Eric call Stigr and give him a message which, running quicker than a spring buck, Stigr delivers to me. "Eric has a plan. We take two boats into the narrow path to make it look like we are unaware, then we stop while the others catch up. We move the boats as close together as possible, side by side if we can. Once the attack comes, we upturn the boats on the sides of the path, creating walls we can fight behind."

Eric is truly a brilliant strategist, and his plan works perfectly. When our enemy sees us stop and wait for the rest of our column, they decide to attack before we are all in the narrows. To them, it looks like we are in disarray, when in actuality, we are preparing for battle.

The first wave comes in the front, perhaps forty Karelians. We drop our boats in the narrows and retreat to where the path widens. Now we have the advantage as their numbers are constrained by the narrowness of the path. It will be a slaughter.

Moments later, attacks come from both sides. On cue, we upturn our boats and form walls down both sides of the path. There are many gaps, of course, but the obstacles force our enemies to attack us through those gaps, again, giving us the advantage. And we will need every advantage we can get, as, by my estimation there are nearly a hundred Karelians attacking us from the front and flanks. If I am correct, that means there are at least as many to our rear beyond the rise.

With no time to watch the incredible defensive battle, I take the lead and go over the rise into the heart of the Karelian forces. Ten men follow me, forming a shield wall. They advance, pushing into the enemy, while I, in front of the shield wall, hack my way deep into their ranks, my axes flying furiously. Men are falling like autumn leaves on a windy day. I am stabbed and slashed numerous times, but I am not slowed a bit. I am the Drengr Røkkr, the Spear of God, and I am invincible.

The battle rages for another twenty minutes before our adversaries finally withdraw. The looks of horror on the Karelians' faces, as I absorbed blow after blow, but continued fighting is a sight I'll not soon forget. An accounting of the battle shows we have five dead and seven wounded, two of those severely. The enemies' dead is astounding. Sixty-three in all, once we put the wounded they left behind to the sword.

It is a great victory, but the men do not celebrate. They go about the grim task of collecting their dead. I am intrigued by the death rites of the different tribes. Some bury their dead, others burn them. Still others make a mat of twigs and leaves and cover the body in stones. We have similar rituals, depending on a man's station in life. Warriors are often burned in their boats, while jarls and kings are sometimes buried with their wealth. As the funeral pyres rage, I search for Eric. He is not among the dead or wounded, but I cannot find him among the living either. My heart sinks. Eric has been captured.

CHAPTER FOURTEEN

THE TOMB OF HÖGNI

The light of a thousand stars trespasses on the pitch of night. We are surrounded by them, as if we have made camp in the heavens. The rainbow revealed by the passing of an afternoon rain and the coming of twilight must have been the Bifrost which we unwittingly ascended, passing unknowingly and unnoticed into Asgard. The stars glow an eerie green; they must be utangard, that is to say, they reside beyond the veil of Asgard in the realm of Jötunheimr. I walk to the edge of the veil and plunge my hand through it. I grasp a star and find that it is just goblin's gold, the luminous moss that grows on the gnarled trunks of trees and in the dank places of the Savonian Forest.

The mysteries of the Savonian Forest are revealing themselves. I know I am on the path of King Högni. I can feel the presence of Dainslief. It is near. After weeks of harsh travel and battles that have reduced our ranks, we have arrived at the very place that Vörnir described, or rather, that his entrails described.

Eric's knowledge of the Savonian wilderness has been crucial. I know that, without him, I would have been lost here forever, which for me, truly is forever. I think back to the ambush, and how relieved I was to find him lying under the skiff he had been riding in, which had overturned and trapped him during the attack. It was at that moment I realized I valued him more as a guide than a friend. Had he actually been captured, I would have sought out his captors and freed him, not because he was my best friend and someone to whom I owed more than my life, but only because I needed him to help me find Dainslief.

That realization still troubles me greatly, but now, as I stand on the precipice of achieving that which I seek, I push it from my mind and focus on the task at hand. With the dawn, a white runestone will be revealed in the depths of the forest which can only be seen from above. While my comrades sleep, I ascend the tallest tree, marked by a lightning strike that pierced it and left it hollowed out all the way to its roots. I enter a hole at the base and climb through the narrow passage to the very top of the tree, and there I sit waiting for the sun to rise.

I fight the sleep that threatens to overtake me until the first glimmer of light appears on the eastern horizon. I scan all around, searching for the stone, but I do not see it. Knowing the stone will only be visible for a few seconds, I want to fix my gaze on the horizon where I have the greatest view, but I know the stone will be much closer. I frantically turn my head side to side, spinning around in my perch, hoping something will catch my eye. I see the sun is fully above the horizon now and wonder how much higher it needs to climb in the sky before it will reveal my treasure.

I begin to despair. Perhaps this is not the spot. We have passed numerous trees that had been scarred by Thor's hammer. Why would this tree be any different? A sudden gust of wind blows me from my perch. As

I am thrown forward, I grab a branch to keep from falling, peering straight down the trunk of the tree. A glint of white flashes from a branch below. My eyes instinctively snap to it. It is oval in shape, perhaps three feet long and two feet wide, and it appears to be embedded in the branch. I squint, and I can see markings on the object – runes. After a few seconds, the runestone disappears into darkness again.

I mark its position and climb down to the branch. It amazes me how well hidden the runestone is. No one could ever see it from the ground; it is only visible very briefly from above. I am literally sitting on top of it, my face mere inches away, yet I can barely make out the markings, which blend seamlessly into the rough bark of the branch. I can read some of the runes, having learned the skill from my mother. It says, "Here lies Högni, son of Gjúki, bane of the Jötunn, betrayed of Gunnar." There are other markings I don't know, and I think, perhaps, they are directions or a map to the burial mound.

As I try to decipher the other runes, a question arises from the back of my mind. Why would someone place a runestone so high in a tree? It occurs to me that it may not have always been so. As ancient as the legend, so too, is this tree, which would have been a mere seed or sapling in the time of Högni. This great tree has grown from the burial place of King Högni, fed by his flesh, and even Thor's lightning could not fell it.

I scamper quickly down the tree, falling the last thirty feet in my excitement. The impact with the ground knocks out my breath, but I quickly recover. The sound of the impact, however, has stirred my comrades who ask why I had climbed the tree to begin with. I am loath to tell them that the Niflung Hoard lies below their feet. I, myself, am leery of the legendary treasure, for which Högni and his brother, Gunnar, who betrayed him to the Hun, Atilla, in hopes of securing his own freedom,

Högni's crown, and a half portion of the hoard, both died. It is said that Högni's body and the treasure were then spirited away by dwarfs. I have always believed another legend that says he died fighting giants in Jötunheimr, perhaps betrayed by Gunnar, and that the Niflung Hoard never existed. But now, standing upon the burial site, I don't know which legend, if either, is true.

One thing I am sure of, though, is that if there is no treasure, the men will kill Eric, Stigr, Knute, and Knute's three Norse companions. And they will attempt to kill me as well. When the blood dries, I will be left alone in the Savonian wilderness with no way of getting back to Inger. I decide to tell them a clue to the location of the treasure lies buried here, and that I climbed the tree to make sure we weren't about to be attacked. I figure if there is a treasure, they'll be pleased, and if not, I will make up some story based on the runestone that the treasure lies further north. Then Eric, his kinsman, and I will slip out under cover of darkness and return here to find the sword.

Fueled by greed, the men begin digging in earnest, with spade, ax, and even their hands. Some, thinking the hoard lies within, attempt to fell the tree, but their axes are worn dull after only a few chops, and the tree remains unscathed. I tell them I have already inspected the tree and found no treasure, but I encourage a Karelian to climb to the top from within, as I had done, to satisfy him that I spoke the truth. Finally, when no one is looking, I crawl back into the hole beneath the tree and dig. Eric sees me, and knowingly comes and stands beside the tree, obscuring my labor from the others.

A few feet beneath the tree, I encounter a crypt cover. It is carved in the likeness of King Högni and surrounded by more undecipherable runes. There is no way to move the stone away, so I hit it with my ax, again and again and again, until the ax breaks. A large war hammer drops from above, a gift from Eric, who had procured it from an unknowing Swede. With a few whacks of the hammer, the stone cracks beneath me, and I drop through a hole, falling at least twenty feet. I find myself in a pitch-black cavern with the barest thread of light streaming in from above. The walls are wet and covered in tree roots. I call to Eric, and within minutes, a fiery torch drops through the hole. A moment later, so do Eric and Knute.

"I have Stigr covering the hole from above," Eric says. "And Knute's retainers are seeding the ground several paces away with silver and gold to keep our 'friends' occupied."

We look around and find a narrow passage leading away and downward. Holding the torch, I take the lead, followed by Eric and Knute. We walk perhaps fifty yards before coming to a chamber. A stone crypt lies in the middle, covered in runes, the largest of which spell out "Högni". The walls of the chamber are adorned with the images of men, small and ruddy, and caked with earth, as if they were buried alive alongside the king.

I hand the torch to Eric, and Knute and I try to open the crypt. We wedge our ax and sword under the capstone and lever it up. Knute continues to hold up the stone while I slide it away. There, in the torchlight, I see the skeletal remains of the great King Högni holding his enchanted sword – Dainslief. I speak a soft prayer for Odin's forgiveness as I desecrate the king's tomb and remove the sword from his bony fingers.

Suddenly, the walls of the chamber begin moving, the images therein coming to life. We are surrounded by a host of dwarfs, axes and shields at the ready. Eric and Knute close ranks, standing back-to-back, while I advance on a dwarf standing near me, swinging Dainslief. The dwarf counters my attack with his shield, and I am instantly subdued by three more.

"Who dares to disturb the rest of Högni the Jötunn-slayer?" asks the dwarf who I attacked.

"I am Helsvein," I say. "And these are Eric and Knute."

"And you have come to steal Dainslief, forged by the renowned dwarvish blacksmith, Dain, himself, and wielded by the great warrior-king Högni? Ha!" he laughs. "Perhaps you've heard the legend of the sword's enchantment, and you have come to claim it as your own? You should know, then, that it is useless to you. Only one worthy of Dainslief can wield it. For all others, a strike from its blade would be as that from a feather."

"How does one prove his worthiness?" I ask.

"Simple! One must use the sword on himself. If he is worthy, then Dainslief will be as a feather tickling his skin, but if not, a single scratch will doom him."

"What if I use it on you, instead?" I ask, grimly.

"I have nothing to fear from the blade, menskr. It must be tested before it can kill, tested on the one who would wield it." The dwarf looks at my disbelieving face and pulls aside his armor, exposing his breast. "Kill me. Go on. Pierce my heart. Kill me!"

I thrust the sword into his chest, but it folds away like sackcloth, refusing to enter his body.

"See. I have nothing to fear. But, as you hold the sword, you must now test it on yourself. If you are worthy, you will live, as will your companions. But if you die, so will they."

I think back, again, to the words of the seer – "curses always have conditions – find the right conditions, and you could end yours". I had concluded some time ago that the sword may be a way to end my curse, but I had not thought that I would need to test that theory in order to obtain it. I look over at Eric, knowing that we will either leave this place together, alive, or we will meet each other in Valhalla. He nods and whispers, "Go on, Shadow." I plunge the blade into my heart.

CHAPTER FIFTEEN

THE RAINBOW ROAD

The sun chariot, driven by Sól, rising in the east is met by a second, rising in the west. The two drivers lock eyes and begin their battle. Who will shine brighter? Sól drives her horses, Arvak and Allsvinn, high into the sky, shedding her light across the nine realms. The second sun-driver captures her light and radiates it back with greater splendor. The sun goddess drops her shield, Svalinn, allowing her sun to burn even brighter. Her adversary matches her brilliance, then bests it with a sparkling display of white light and shimmering rainbows. Sól, beaten and shamed, retreats behind the clouds, as we gaze upon the Niflung Hoard, a blinding pile of gold and silver as tall as a jötunn queen, her crown adorned with the largest, most magnificent diamond anyone had ever seen.

I was wrong about its existence. The Niflung Hoard is greater than even the legends foretold. The band is ecstatic with the haul, but none more so than Eric. Strangely, he only takes two things from the pile: the diamond, which he names Sólmeir, and Andvaranaut, a ring that allows the wearer to find gold and silver, or even to create it.

The story of the ring is well-known. Cursed by the dwarf, Andvari, the ring eventually came into the possession of the dragon, Fáfnir. When the great hero, Sigurd, slew the dragon and possessed the hoard he gave the ring to his lover, Brynhild, as a promise he would return. However, he forgot his promise, some say by magic, and married Gudrun, sister to Högni and Gunnar, instead. Later, Gunnar, married Brynhild, but before he did, Sigurd took back the ring and gave it to Gudrun. The ring worked its curse upon the family, costing Brynhild her first and only real love, and costing Gundrun, the lives of her husband, Sigurd, her son, Sigmund, and both of her brothers. I remind him of the ring's curse and urge him to take a greater portion of the hoard instead.

"You claimed an enchanted sword; I claim this enchanted ring. And with this ring, I can find more gold and silver, a mountain more than I see before me, here. Let the rest have these scraps. I will have a greater treasure than this," Eric asserts.

"That ring brings only sorrow and death," I say. "Think of the heartache it brought to Brynhild, the loss of her only beloved, and to Gundrun, the annihilation of her clan."

"Perhaps to women, it brings tragedy. But to men, it brings riches."

I am regretting my decision to share the treasure. When the dwarf, Brokkr, revealed the treasure to us, he said it belonged to the one who wields Dainslief, to me and me alone, to do with as I pleased. No other may touch it, lest they be burned alive. I, having no need for treasure, took only what would fit in my pockets and released the rest to my comrades. Watching their greed overwhelm them, seeing them fight each other for a larger share, is beyond my comprehension. Not a single man among us can carry more than a fraction of the treasure, be it on his back, in a cart, or in a score of carts. Yet, each man's desire to possess more than another is driving them to insanity.

While the rest of the band fights over the treasure, Eric collects his kin and their retainers, and we slip away quietly with but a single cartload of gold and silver. It is heartening to see clan loyalty in the face of so much greed. Eric guides us on a weeks-long journey back to the coast. I am quite surprised that we are not attacked along the way. I think, perhaps, Andvaranaut is saving the misfortune it has in store for us for a later time.

We purchase three sailing skiffs in Vyborg, good, strong boats able to sail the breadth of the Baltic, even in the foulest weather. I encourage Eric and the others to return to Dago with me, but they refuse. Eric, especially, is keen to get back to Lagarvik and reclaim his reputation. He believes he no longer needs his 'Shadow', as I have brought him the wealth and acclaim he believed I would. He even proclaimed, "before gods and men, I release you of your bond to me" as if that statement, with all its air of ceremony, meant something or would make any difference. I extract promises from Knute and Stigr to keep Eric alive until we meet again before setting a course for Dago – alone.

Upon my arrival in Kūk, I go immediately to the ruined fortress. I find the seer has rebuilt his røykhus and is dutifully smoking his meat again.

"Still smoking seal, I see." I announce my presence.

"The World-Serpent must eat. Did you find the sword?"

I tap the scabbard on my belt.

"And let me see the scar," he says, reaching for my breast and tugging at my tunic. I snatch his hand away and pull down my leather breastplate and shirt to reveal I have no scar.

"Why did you think I'd have a scar?"

"I saw it in the entrails. You plunged the blade into your heart."

"That was a test. Only one worthy of the sword can wield it. If you are unworthy, a mere scratch is fatal, but for the worthy one, the blade will melt away, refusing to penetrate." It suddenly occurs to me the seer remembers me, not as a shadow, but as a man. "How is it ..."

"That I remember you?", he interrupts, knowing my question. "You are constantly in the smoke, the embers, my dreams. You are very difficult to forget."

"Maybe for you, but not for everyone else."

"Well, that's a start, eh?" he chortles. "Come! Time is short. We must summon Jörmungandr and get you on your way. Now!"

"What's the urgency? I've been gone for months. And, given my curse, time is not something I'm concerned about running out of."

"The bargain is struck. The Aesir have acquiesced to the sea-god's demands. In exchange for the wolf, they have agreed to give Aegir control of the skies above the waters. I believe it may be a trick. Odin gets Fenrir, and then Thor takes back the skies by force. It will be a war between skies and seas. Midgard will be the battlefield and all of us will perish in the struggle. You must free Fenrir before the exchange is made."

"Well then. I guess I will have to be the savior of Midgard. Let us go and greet my destiny," I say, flippantly.

"You do not greet destiny, boy. You make it! You get the destiny you choose."

"Very strange words, coming from a seer," I say, recognizing the irony of his words, given his vocation.

"Yes, they are, aren't they. Come!"

We descend the stairway as before, past the rotting corpse of Vörnir, and into the cave of Jörmungandr. The seer throws slabs of smoked meat into the water, and we wait. And we wait. And we wait.

"Does he always take this long to come?" I ask, exasperated by the urgency of the seer and the seeming aloofness of Jörmungandr. I have traveled a long way to get to this point, and I am beginning to question the wisdom of what I am about to do. To say I am pleased to be partnered with yet another of Hel's brothers would be an utter misstatement. I feel as though I have been adopted into a family of erratic, perhaps insane, self-serving delinquents, without care or conscience.

After nearly three days, the serpent finally emerges. He is just as beautifully adorned with colorful patterns and iridescent eyes, but I am not as impressed as before. Perhaps I'm just weary, but in truth, I would prefer not to be here. I relish neither the mission I have been assigned nor the assistance of this monster. But I do have a bargain with Hel, one in which I feel I may have been cheated. It is true – desperate men often enter into contracts that do not serve them well. However, I intend to make the most of this bargain. Perhaps I can use it to my advantage. If what the seer says about destiny is true, whatever plans Hel may have for me, having both Fenrir and Jörmungandr bound to me in some way will give me immense power, something far beyond the mere promise Hel made me.

"Does he have Dains-s-s-lief?" the World-Serpent asks the seer.

"Yes, Great One," the seer responds, in reverence.

"Let me s-s-see?"

I draw the sword and hold it out, its point mere inches from the snake's great eye.

"You wish-sh to poke me with it, boy?"

"I wish-sh to get this-s-s over with-th," I say.

"He mocks-s-s me!" screams Jörmungandr, the island shuttering from his voice.

The seer is astounded at my insolence. He attempts to speak, to temper the serpent's rage, but I cut him off.

"The seer says it is imperative we act now, lest Aegir deliver your brother to Odin in exchange for the skies. Yet, you kept us waiting – for THREE days. That is not a 'well-mannered' thing to do. What took you so long?"

"I am well aware of the bargain, boy, and I need not explain my tardiness-s-s to you either. But I agree, I could have made my lateness-s-s known to the s-s-seer." Jörmungandr's tone softens and seems almost contrite. Perhaps my expression of perturbation caught him by surprise. I am sure no one has ever spoken to him that way.

"And I am sorry for mocking you, Great One. I would blame my weariness, but in truth, there is no excuse," I offer.

"Yes-s-s. All is-s-s well. We mus-st be about our work then, you and I," the serpent says. "I have found the pla-c-ce where the Kraken keeps-s-s Fenrir. It is-s-s deep beneath the s-s-sea, too deep for even you, I fear."

"I spent an entire night submerged. I think I can handle it," I say, cockily.

"Can you s-s-swing a s-s-sword underwater?"

"I only need scratch the beast to kill it. A full swing won't be necessary."

"The Kraken is-s-s a magical creature – part Hrimthurs-s-sar it is said. Even Dains-s-slief may not penetrate its-s-s flesh-sh eas-s-ily without s-ssignificant force. I mus-s-st bring the beas-s-st to the s-s-surface, where you may cut away the tentacles-s-s impris-s-soning my brother. Have you a boat?"

"I do," I answer.

"Good. Then follow me to the pla-c-ce in the s-s-sea. We will des-s-stroy the Kraken and free Fenrir." Jörmungandr descends beneath the water.

I return to my skiff and set sail. I follow the brilliant rainbow colors of Jörmungandr's skin, laid out for me like a curvy road, shimmering just beneath the surface. My thoughts trail back to my beloved, Inger. I remind myself, I do this for her, so she will know me. But I think I may gain more than just that. Is my destiny truly, as the seer says, of my choosing? I am not sure, but I do know my destiny awaits me beyond the horizon, and the horizon is looking very dark indeed.

CHAPTER SIXTEEN

BELLY OF THE BEAST

A dreadful darkness creeps over the horizon, dulling the battle line between Odin's sky and Aegir's sea. The Jötunn, crouching in the darkness, begin to emerge and join the fight. One by one, they stand, their huge bodies silhouetted against the blackening sky as they rush into the fray. Thor strikes hard against the giants, his hammer, Mjölnir, sending lightning and thunder crashing through them, yet they continue undaunted. Aegir sends his nine daughters into the battle, raising huge waves against the sky. I sail my skiff toward a great tempest of high seas and immense, thunderous storm clouds.

The storm surrounds me, a prison of sea, sleet, and boreal wind. The ocean spray is like a swarm of hornets, stinging my face with their icy venom and forcing me to turn my head away, lest I be blinded. I am buffeted by huge waves that crash over the bow and drench me in bitter cold seawater. My clothes are encased in hoarfrost, icicles clinging to my hair and beard. The cold stabs me like an Ulfberht sword, penetrating deep

109

into my body, turning my heart and blood to ice. Yet, I persevere, secure in the knowledge that I will triumph over the Kraken, free Fenrir, and win my reward.

I have lost sight of Jörmungandr, yet I believe I am sailing the true course. In the many days I've been at sea, and through the fairer weather of those days, his gleaming rainbow skin led me north. I expected to make landfall in the Lapland two days ago, as I had passed through the Haparanda Islands in the Bay of Bothnia. However, a strange fog overtook me, and I continued sailing through ever colder waters, strewn with glacial sheets of ice, guided only by the colorful illumination beneath my skiff. I wonder if I am still in Midgard or if I have sailed into another realm.

In the high seas of the storm, the large sheets of floating ice, treacherous enough in calm waters, have become battering rams, smashing my small boat and splintering the wood. As seawater flows in, I realize I must abandon my skiff soon.

I spy an island not far off, appearing and disappearing as the waves pass. I steer for it, hoping I can land before I sink. I hold the course as best I can, but the island appears to be moving. When I get within fifty yards, two ice sheets converge on my boat and crush it between them. I climb the mast as the boat founders and jump onto one of the ice sheets. It is then I notice that the island is not only moving, but glowing. Even through the driving rain and sleet, the electrifying colors of the World-Serpent blaze like the midday sun.

"JÖRMUNGANDR!" I yell. "JÖRMUNGANDR!" I fear the ferocity of the storm has muted my words.

The ice sheet tips violently, threatening to throw me into the sea. I draw Dainslief and plunge it into the ice to keep myself from sliding off. The sheet hurtles toward the rainbow serpent, riding what I believe to be a huge wave. Suddenly it stops and rights itself, as an enormous tentacle bursts from the sea and towers into the sky above me.

"S-S-STRIKE IT! NOW!" Jörmungandr's voice booms above the din.

I pull my sword from its icy sheath and slash at the Kraken's monstrous arm. A fiery gash opens up as the blade passes through, the intense heat of it easily winning its battle with the frigid air. My hair and eyebrows are singed, and I am momentarily blinded. I step back a few feet and watch as a pillar of fire engulfs the tentacle.

The burnt appendage falls away, and from the wound, I see two new tentacles emerge. One dives back beneath the waves, while the other challenges me to a duel. It attacks like a snake, thrusting and recoiling as I dodge and parry.

"DON'T DANC-C-CE WITH IT, BOY! CUT IT OFF!" I hear Jörmungandr cry.

I jump quickly to my right and go into a shoulder roll. As soon as I regain my feet, I turn and cut down hard on the tentacle. It erupts in a glorious blaze as did the first, and likewise, is rapidly replaced by two more. Thankfully, both retreat, giving me a momentary reprieve in the battle.

"HAVE YOU FOUND FENRIR?" I ask.

"HE IS DIRECTLY BELOW ME. I AM TRYING TO PULL HIM UP BUT THE KRAKEN HAS-S-S ENTANGLED HIM IN DOZENS-S-S OF ARMS-S-S. WHEN I DO S-S-SURFACE HIM, YOU'LL HAVE TO ACT QUICKLY."

"IT'S NOT WORKING. THE KRAKEN KEEPS GROW..."

I feel the ice sheet below my feet shutter violently, and I am flung onto my back, my breath knocked out of me. Three tentacles rise toward the heavens, carrying with them a twisting rainbow. The ensnared World-Serpent struggles against his captor, managing to wrap his coils around one of the arms. With a mighty squeeze, the tentacle bursts into flame. The charred remnants come crashing down on my ice sheet, shattering it. I am thrown into the sea, but, just as quickly, am lifted out again by another tentacle. I cut clean through it and am consumed in a funeral pyre. I drop as a flaming meteor back into the sea.

Extinguished, I swim toward the island that is Jörmungandr's head. I climb onto him, gale force winds blowing me across his slick skin like an ice sled. The great serpent raises his head just before I slide off his snout, and my momentum slows to a stop. Another tentacle rises and attempts to grab him. I slash it off, but again, it is replaced by two.

"THE KRAKEN – IT KEEPS GROWING NEW TENTACLES. TWO AT A TIME!" I yell.

"WHAT?!"

"WHEN I CUT ONE OFF, TWO GROW IN ITS PLACE!"

"THAT IS-S-S UNFORTUNATE. WE SHALL NEED A NEW PLAN."

I cut off another flailing tentacle. Jörmungandr's eyes flash iridescently in the ensuing flame.

"THE FLAME. THE KRAKEN IS CAUTERIZING ITS WOUNDS-S-S," yells the serpent. "TRY CUTTING IT AT THE WATERLINE. PERHAPS THE S-S-SEA WILL S-S-SNUFF OUT THE FLAME BEFORE NEW TENTACLES-S-S CAN GROW."

I do as I am directed, leaping into a trough between two great waves and swinging Dainslief as a tentacle bursts through the surface. My aim is true, carving off the appendage just as the wave passes over it. The tentacle does not burn, but the water surrounding it is instantly infused with a black, foul-smelling liquid – the Kraken's blood. I am covered in it, and it burns like acid. As the wave passes, the stump of the beast's bloody arm is again exposed above the sea. It spontaneously combusts, igniting the blood floating on the surface and on me. Tentacles sprout from the burnt stump like spring grasses.

I am quickly concluding that we may not win this battle. As Jörmungandr continues struggling with the monster, I swim to another ice sheet and climb atop it. Battered by wind and waves, I watch the spectacle of the two giants engaged in a death bout from which only one will emerge victorious. I know I must get back into this fight, but even with Dainslief, I can make no headway against the Kraken. In fact, every blow I strike makes it stronger. And the sword itself is not having the desired effect. I was hoping a scratch would kill it, but that, apparently, is a trait that Dainslief reserves only for humans.

Still, I penetrate the flesh of the beast, which is something no ordinary sword could do. I just need the wounds to remain open. It occurs to me that the Kraken is much like I am. Its injuries heal instantaneously, making it difficult to kill. But whereas I am immortal and impossible to kill, the Kraken is merely a monster, a jötunn not unlike Vörnir. In the depths of my brain, a thought begins to form, a thought so horrible that I try to suppress it with every fiber of my being. That thought, however, proves too powerful, and I find myself yelling, "BRING UP ITS HEAD!"

"WE DO NEED A NEW PLAN, BOY, BUT I DO NOT THINK THAT IS-S-S IT!" Jörmungandr replies. "WHAT ARE YOU GOING TO DO? POKE IT IN THE EYE?"

"NO! BRING ITS MOUTH TO THE SURFACE!" I hear the words coming out of my mouth, but I cannot believe I am saying them.

"THAT MOUTH CAN S-S-SWALLOW TEN LONGSHIPS-S-S AT ONCE. IT WILL MAKE SH-SHORT WORK OF YOU!"

"THAT'S THE IDEA!"

"THAT'S-S-S INSANE, BOY. THAT'S S-S-SUICIDE."

"NOT FOR THE DRENGR RØKKR!"

"AAAHHHH!" booms Jörmungandr. Then, his head disappears beneath the waves.

The World-Serpent's great body continues to twist and fight with the Kraken's tentacles. As I am able, I cut them off, unconcerned about how many new arms it grows. The idea is to keep the thing busy while Jörmungandr goes for its head.

Time passes slowly, the minutes seeming like hours. Unfortunately, the lag allows me time to think about my decision. My mind slips back to the terror of being swallowed alive by Vörnir. I am filled with dread at the thought of it happening again. My resolve is failing. I may be immortal, but I am not without fear. My stomach turns over, and I wretch.

"Think of something else," I tell myself. "Think of Inger. Think of how good it is that she loves you and will remember you. She is why you are here. Do this for Inger." Thoughts of my wife prove to be the distraction I need. I feel my courage returning to me, filling me as strong ale fills a cup. I am newly emboldened. Dauntless.

Jörmungandr returns, the great head of the Kraken in his coils. It is as high as the cliffs of Preikestolen with a single, massive, black eye. Jörmungandr rolls the monster over, exposing a lamprey's mouth the size of a fjord, thousands of hairlike teeth standing like trees around its gullet. The seer is correct. My destiny is of my choosing, and I choose to go into the belly of the beast. I leap into the cavernous maw of the Kraken,

Dainslief held high and gleaming.

CHAPTER SEVENTEEN

GODS AND MONSTERS

As my eyes adjust, strange forms begin to emerge from the darkness. The skeletons of giants lay strewn about, hundreds of them, as from a battle fought long ago. Their ribs are exposed, their spines split and shattered, their heads deformed into monstrous shapes. The acrid bog they lie in glows an eerie blue, casting grotesque shadows which add to the spectral horror of this place. I climb atop one of the skeletons, a drakkar longship, its mast snapped in two, its hull stripped and mangled, its carcass dripping with merituli, a strange, luminescent algae the gives the stomach of the Kraken its mystical azure aura.

Except for the putrescent smell reminiscent of Vörnir's belly, this place looks more like a cemetery, one that has been desecrated in a most heinous way. Like anyone who'd ever taken to the seas, I'd heard stories about a graveyard of ships, but I never expected it to exist in the innards of a Kraken. I walk along the spine of the longship until I come to the spot where its back was broken. There I find a large splinter of wood impaling

116

the skeleton of a Norse warrior, his bony fingers still gripping his sword. It was a battle he could never win. Nonetheless, he'd fought valiantly and died an honorable death. I can see him in Valhalla, feasting with his shipmates, exclaiming that for a sad turn of fate, they would have defeated the Kraken and been hailed as heroes. I take his arm and his sword and fold it across his chest. "Rest easy, friend," I say. "I shall have your vengeance."

I make my way through the flotsam and jetsam of broken ships until I reach the side of the Kraken's stomach. The creature must be of enormous size to have such a large belly, maybe not as big as Jörmungandr's, but certainly a size beyond comprehension. I plunge Dainslief into the spongy wall. The black, noxious blood of the beast begins flowing from the wound. I stab at the stomach again and again and again, each time opening a bloody wound but realizing the futility of it. I am but a gnat, stinging the Kraken for a small trickle of blood on which to feed. I cannot hurt, let alone kill it by slashing away at its stomach. I must find its heart.

I make a torch of merituli and an oar and climb the mast of a nearby ship. I carve out a hole and slip through into the cavity of the beast. Having cleaned and eaten many an octopus, I hope the anatomy of the Kraken is similar. I navigate through the pulpous tissue surrounding the stomach, finally coming to the cecum. With my sword, I open a yards-long gash, spilling massive quantities of digestive fluid as I do. The monster quakes violently as the acid begins burning through its musculature and organs. I have the Kraken's attention now.

I move slowly along my path toward the heart, trying to keep my feet as the Kraken continues to shudder every few minutes. It appears I have given it quite a bad case of indigestion. After a while, the shuddering stops. I think, perhaps, the pain is abating, so I quicken my pace. Just as I reach my objective, I am deafened by a gurgling sound. The whole of the monster shakes like a massive earthquake as it ejects the contents of its stomach into the world outside. I am thrown dozens of yards, losing my torch. When I am finally able to regain my feet, I am in pitch darkness, the sound of rushing water surrounding me.

Thinking I must be near the Kraken's siphon, the organ it uses to draw in water, I follow the sound until I reach the creature's gills. The feather-like spines are like tall pine trees, and I stumble through them as I would a forest on a moonless night. I know the heart is close now because I can hear the faint thumping. As I amble along in the dark, I stab and slash at the branchial hearts it uses to pump blood through the gills, silencing each one in turn. If I am unable to kill the beast quickly by destroying its heart, perhaps I can suffocate it to death. Of course, a monster this size may take millennia to die that way, so I keep moving toward the beating heart which grows louder and louder with every step.

Glowing in the distance, I see my torch. I retrieve it and raise it above my head, bathing the gargantuan organ in ghostly blue. With Dainslief, I split the heart open. Instantly, a fountain of blood shoots through the hole, followed by another, and another in rhythm with each beat. I must get to the center of the heart, but I will not be able to move against the force of blood spurting from the gash.

As I did with the cecum, I cut a laceration twenty yards long, around and back again. A substantial hunk of muscle falls away and putrid, black fluid begins pouring out like a waterfall. I cut two more such openings, the last one draining enough blood for me to enter. The Kraken's cavernous ventricle is ribbed with bands of sinew that contract and stretch with every heartbeat. Despite the blackness of the blood, the interior walls of the heart have an orange hue, which like the skin of the World-Serpent, emits

its own radiance.

I estimate the size of the heart to be that of a small city, one in the midst of a springtime flood. Slogging through the rushing blood is extremely difficult, but I take my time, using Dainslief as a walking stick, driving it into the floor of the ventricle and pulling myself along. Finally, I reach the valve to another chamber of the heart. It is split into wedges, like the slices of a pie, which fold back to allow blood to pass through. I carve off one of the wedges, the flesh peeling away, allowing a great quantity of blood to flow through, unstaunched. I cut away the rest of the valve's wedges, stabbing Dainslief into the heart wall each time to avoid being washed away by the discharge.

I feel the Kraken convulse again as I enter the next chamber. I am close to the center now. I need only cut into the thick muscle there and sever the nerves. Then the heart will stop, and the beast will die. The interior muscle proves to be very stout against my blows, but eventually I arrive at a yellowish nodule buried deep in the center of the heart. With the fury of a berserker, I cut out the nodule and repeatedly stab it. The deafening thumping ceases. In the heart of the monster I stand, Dainslief held high in victory. I have vanquished the Kraken.

I make my way back to the siphon and exit the lifeless creature. I swim for the surface, and upon reaching it, am met with an astonishing sight. The hundreds of ships once in the belly of the Kraken are now strewn across the seas and ice sheets. Among them, wrapped in a hundred silent tentacles, is a gigantic blue wolf, twenty times the size I had known Fenrir to be. As he struggles to free himself, Tyr and Thor descend from the heavens, and Aegir and Ran emerge from the sea.

"Which of you has killed my Kraken!" bellows Aegir, a wall of water breaking forth against the sons of Odin. "We had a deal! You have your prize; why kill my monster!"

"We did not kill your beastie, Aegir," Thor responds. "Perhaps this abomination did it."

Thor flies toward me, swinging Mjölnir overhead with a killing blow. I wince as the great hammer comes down. I have survived hundreds of wounds from mortal men's weapons, but I don't believe I can survive a blow from Thor. I hear a crash of thunder and lightning fills the air around me. Yet I am alive, uninjured. In fact, I felt nothing, not so much as a feather tickling my skin. I open my eyes again and realize I was not Thor's target. I see him, instead, wrapped in a deadly struggle with his greatest nemesis – Jörmungandr.

Tyr, with Gungnir, the Spear of Justice, begins prying the Kraken's arms from Fenrir.

"Give me my skies, Tyr, before you take the dog!" booms Aegir.

"You shall have your skies, once I have the Bane of Odin," Tyr replies, continuing to peel away the dead monster's tentacles.

"We'll have the wolf and the skies as well, Aegir," cries Thor. "You shall have nothing, for you accused us falsely of murder." Thor strikes Jörmungandr but directs the lightning bolt at Aegir. Ran counters with a waterspout that rips Thor from the great snake and hurls him skyward. Thor extricates himself with a crash of thunder and lightning.

"Our father has promised the skies for Fenrir, Thor," says Tyr. "We shall not go against his wishes."

"Go against his wishes, brother? Do you think you know the All-Father's mind better than me? Why do you think I am here?"

"Odin would not renege on a promise," Tyr replies. "Especially not to a god such as Aegir."

"But Odin didn't make that promise, did he?" asks Thor rhetorically. "You made that promise. You thought bringing the Wolf-God to Odin would put you in better standing with him. But, as usual, you have shown your weakness, entering into a bargain that you could never fulfill."

"LIES! LIES AND DECEIT!" screams Aegir, realizing he has been taken for a fool. "I will have my skies, or I will have your lives. Tidal waves of incredible size materialize out of nowhere and crash down on Tyr, knocking him away from his work.

Thor counters, swooping down from the sky and smashing an ice sheet with his hammer, sending blocks of ice infused with lightning against the waves, freezing them instantly. As Tyr attempts to pry more tentacles, Jörmungandr wraps his coils around him. Aegir, meanwhile, enraged by the death of his Kraken, forms a sharpened disk of ice and hurls it like a spinning ax at Jörmungandr, slicing deep into the serpent's side and causing him to release Tyr.

Thor swings Mjölnir at Ran as she attempts to wrap him in another typhoon. Aegir defends his wife by hurling an iceberg at Thor. Thor turns quickly, throwing his great hammer at it. The iceberg explodes and shards of ice rain down like daggers. Aegir redirects the shards at Tyr, who is forced to counter, spinning Gungnir like a baton, creating a shield against the icy blades.

I am witnessing a great battle between the gods, one in which no clear battle lines exist. Thor not only fights with Aegir and Ran, but with Jörmungandr. And as Tyr continues to try to take Fenrir, he fights against the World-Serpent, and against Aegir, while also trying to appease him. And through it all, the brothers continue to argue, occasionally slinging lightning bolts at each other. It is quite a spectacle to behold, but through the confusion, my mission has not changed. I am charged with freeing Fenrir. He will be leaving this battle with me, and no other.

Amid the thunder and lightning, rain and waves, I swim to an ice sheet and climb up. Tyr has almost freed the Wolf-God from his cephalopodic prison. The god has in his hand, a loop of silvery ribbon, Gleipnir, the dwarven chain with which he intends to bind Fenrir. If he succeeds in ensnaring the great wolf with it, he will have won. I must act quickly.

I fly across the ice with Dainslief held above my head. Tyr is too focused on Fenrir to see me. As Fenrir struggles against the binding, I come down hard on the wrist of Tyr, severing the hand that holds Gleipnir. A shout of anguish such as the world has never heard bursts from Tyr's mouth. The very skies are cleaved open, and the sun and stars are peeled away as the God of Justice ascends from the battle. I manage to get a loop of Gleipnir wrapped around a toenail of Fenrir's front left paw as a brilliant white light envelops everything around us. I am blinded and knocked unconscious.

CHAPTER EIGHTEEN

BREAKING THE CHAIN

The sky stretches out before me as I ascend to Valhalla. Shy, wispy clouds pass beneath my feet while braver ones billow up to meet me. I glide through them as a jötunn walking through a field of grass, my eyes searching for a horizon that doesn't exist. The sun shines brightly behind me, casting my shadow infinitely into the blue. I pause a moment and look down to see my face staring up at me. This northern ice shelf is polished to perfection, a mirror so reflective that no distant line exists between earth and sky. If not for snow blowing into small drifts on its surface, or the scrapes of snow buried inside it, I would believe that, indeed, I have left Midgard for a higher realm.

The sun sinks low but does not set. I am very far north, but I am not sure where. There are no trees or grasses, only frigid desolation as far as the eye can see. After the flash that rendered me unconscious, a lightning bolt from Mjölnir, I think, I woke up in this frozen desert. I have been traveling south for days, sucking on ice chips to stay hydrated. I am

123

famished, but I have found nothing to eat. I try cutting a hole in the ice for fishing, but it is too thick. My only hope is to continue southward until I find land and food.

My thoughts hearken back to recent events. I had known the gods since childhood. I'd heard the stories of their heroics, their failures, their pride, their humility, their violence, and their tenderness. I learned the lessons those stories teach, and I honored the gods and their importance to my people. Inger and I passed those stories on to Gyda and Brant so they may also know their place in this world and what is expected of them. Yet, the display of jealousy, power-lust, deceit, loathing, and resentment I had just witnessed makes me question whether the gods are worthy of our reverence. They behaved more like spoiled children fighting over a toy than noble beings deserving of our admiration.

"They're not who you thought they were, are they? Now you know why we don't have anything to do with them," says Fenrir, reading my thoughts and responding with his. He has returned to normal, that is the twice-sized wolf I have known him to be rather than the gargantuan god he truly is.

"I've seen some of the same things in you," I say. Since his rescue, I am not sure how many days ago, Fenrir has not communicated with me. I had hoped he'd express some gratitude, but thus far, he has not. I wonder if he is even capable of it.

"Loathing, yes. Resentment, most definitely," Fenrir responds. "But jealousy? Deceit? No. I have never deceived anyone, and I certainly don't covet what others have, nor do I seek to wield power over anyone. I only wish to be left to myself. But my sister has bound me to you, so ..."

"Your sister?", I interject. "It is not your sister that binds you to me. It is this infernal chain!" I give a hard tug on Gleipnir, which is still looped tightly around Fenrir's paw and, unfortunately, my wrist as well. I had tried to pull it off, bite it off, cut it off with Dainslief, all to no avail.

"I told you; you need to cut off your hand. That's how you got it away from Tyr. You're just afraid to do it," sneers Fenrir.

"I was swallowed by a Kraken – WILLINGLY! I am not afraid of anything."

"Then chop off your hand!"

I do as Fenrir suggests, but I know the outcome before I land the stroke. Dainslief melts away and refuses to cut. "See! The sword won't work."

"Grr! Let me try!" snaps Fenrir.

Before I can respond, the Wolf-God chomps down on my arm and yanks. He comes away with a mouthful of blood, but my hand remains attached, the wound healing even as his teeth were tearing through my flesh. Frustrated, Fenrir jerks his paw and sends me flying. As I crash to the ice and slide, the chain pulls taut. Fenrir's leg is yanked from under him, and he falls, sprawling out on the ice. The thin, silver thread connecting us appears to be unbreakable and irremovable. The thought of being chained to the Wolf-God for all eternity is enough to make me wretch.

"DWARFS!" barks Fenrir in anger.

Dwarfs are very skilled at forging things that have powers beyond the elements. Dainslief has the capacity to kill anyone but the person who wields it and powerful enough to kill a Kraken. Yet, it cannot cut Gleipnir, a thin silver chain also forged by dwarfs and made for the specific purpose of binding Fenrir, who had broken every other chain used on him. But Fenrir's angry outburst gives me an idea. We need to find a dwarf.

"Do you have any idea where we are?" I ask as I scramble back to my feet.

"Niflhiem, I think, somewhere beyond Jötunheimr," says Fenrir, as he struggles to right himself.

"So, we're not in Midgard?" I ask, somewhat depressed by the revelation.

"The realms don't exist separately. They intersect, endlessly, each realm surrounding and surrounded by the others," Fenrir responds.

"I don't understand."

"Think of it like a den of snakes, twisted and twirled around each other. It is impossible to tell where one snake ends and another begins."

"Well, wherever we are, we need to find Nidevellir, the realm of the dwarfs," I proclaim.

"Are you thinking a dwarf could untie us?" asks Fenrir, skeptically.

"Well, it's abundantly clear neither of us can. So, unless you want to spend eternity chained to me, we need to find a dwarf."

We continue walking across the ice for several weeks. Exhaustion and hunger are taking their toll on my mental state. I start seeing things: forests, animals, towns, even my family who disappear when I call to them. Finally, Fenrir claims to see smudges of black on the horizon. Though his eyesight is much keener than mine and despite his assertion of never having deceived anyone, I doubt he sees anything, believing he may simply be trying to give me focus and hope. But Fenrir proves to be truthful, for two days later, I also see smudges, and they are not mere figments of my imagination.

We finally reach the tundra, frozen ground with sparse grasses. The tree line of the forest is still quite far away, but at least we are no longer on the ice shelf. I gather some grasses and ground beetles for a meal, but they do not assuage my hunger. A polar bear wanders up, thinking he'll make a quick meal of us. Instead, Fenrir and I, with the help of Dainslief make a meal of him. Raw polar bear is chewy and gamy, but you can eat anything if you're hungry enough.

Upon reaching the forest, we immediately start looking for caves and hollows where we may find an entrance to Nidevellir. Fenrir sniffs the air for any scent of dwarf, which as I recall, is quite earthy and pungent. I tell him the story of the dwarfs in Högni's tomb, and how they appeared to be part of the cave walls. He wasn't surprised, saying, "Dwarfs are quite good at concealing themselves. Hiding from trouble is what they do best, even better than forging accursed weapons and chains." It is clear Fenrir has no love of dwarfs or their craftsmanship and for good reason. Every weapon the gods have used against him, from Mjölnir to Gungnir to Gleipnir has been forged by a dwarf.

After several days plodding through the forest, the ground begins to rise into foothills and mountains. If we are going to find Nidevellir, this would be the place. We follow a river into the mountains, much of it covered in ice. In a canyon, a frozen waterfall, some two hundred feet high, blocks our path, and even Fenrir cannot jump that high. As we look for a way to climb the steep sides, we find a cave hidden behind the wall of ice. Fenrir's hackles bristle as he immediately smells the distinct odor of dwarf.

We enter the cave and descend deep underground. In the pitch black, I am at the mercy of Fenrir's eyes, following along as a blind man on a leash. Before long, I smell brimstone, and I see a flickering red light. We have found a forge. To our surprise, none other than Ivaldi, whose sons famously created Skidbladnir, the ship of Freyr, and Gungnir, the spear of

Odin, is the forge's smidr – its blacksmith. Ivaldi is aged beyond words, gaunt and weathered, his beard so long that he braided it with gold bands around his body and wore it as a tunic.

"Wolf-God, what business would you have with me?" the raspy voiced Ivaldi asks.

"I would have you remove this wretched chain and this human with it," Fenrir responds, trying very hard not to show his disgust, but failing.

"Hmm." says the wretched old dwarf. "What would you pay me for the service?"

"What is your price?" I ask.

"The heads of Brokkr and Sindri. They have shamed me and my sons, forging weapons and rings that the gods say outshine our creations. It is because of Brokkr and Sindri that I have been banished here, no longer a blacksmith to the gods."

"The gods lie," says Fenrir. "Nothing they have created is worthy of praise. I have seen Odin's ring, Draupnir, and Thor's hammer, Mjölnir. Neither is as exquisite as Gungnir. We have just fought with Thor, yet here we are to tell you Mjölnir is no more than a feather, and its lightning no more than a dying ember."

"Is this true?"

"Yes, it is true," I say. "And see here, I have Dainslief, a sword that can only be wielded by the worthiest of people, and by it, I swear Fenrir speaks the truth. We embarrassed both Thor and Tyr in battle. I even severed Tyr's hand."

"A great feat, indeed, if it is true," says Ivaldi, doubtingly.

"It is true, I assure you. And now we come to you, the greatest smidr in all the realms, to rid us of Gleipnir," I say, hoping to cajole him into cutting our chain. "How may we convince you to do as we ask?"

"I told you. Bring me the heads of Brokkr and Sindri," Ivaldi snaps, unswayed by my flattery.

"Forget it, Asger. We are wasting our time. This old fool has neither the desire nor the skill to help us. He thinks by killing Brokkr and Sindri, he and his sons can regain their former glory. Yet by asking us to do the deed, he admits that they are superior blacksmiths. I say we seek out Brokkr and Sindri and have them remove the chain," chides Fenrir.

"Are you saying I am incapable of severing that chain!?" decries Ivaldi. "My skills are second to no one!"

Fenrir's coercion works. The dwarf grabs the chain and inspects it. He then goes to his forge and fashions a tool, so tiny and delicate, that a spider might use it to mend his web. He hangs the tool on a loop of hair from his beard, drops it into an infinitesimally small hole on Gleipnir, and gives the loop a twist. The chain falls away. Ivaldi's skill is truly magnificent. I doubt any dwarf could have crafted such a petite and elegant work of art, not even the dwarfs that made Gleipnir.

"A small imperfection in the chain – just needed some jostling – very shoddy craftsmanship!" exclaims Ivaldi.

"We thank you for your service, Ivaldi," says Fenrir. "If the Aesir cannot appreciate your genius, I know many others who will. I shall let them know that your skills are unmatched."

"You do that," says Ivaldi. "And if you come across those two charlatans – kill them."

We leave Gleipnir with the dwarf. He says he wants to fix it, and I believe he will, though I hope to never see it again.

Once we exit the cave, I say to Fenrir, "You told me you never deceive anyone, yet you just manipulated Ivaldi into giving us what we wanted. You played on his pride. That was a masterful deception."

"I did not deceive him. I spoke of the battle with Thor and Tyr, one in which we emerged triumphant. For all Thor's strength and Mjölnir's power, he could not defeat us."

"Yes, but when you threatened to go to his enemies for help, you knew he would do our bidding. That was deceptive."

"Again, I did not deceive him. I would have gone to Brokkr and Sindri to break the chain."

"You're splitting hairs. He did what we wanted, and we did not have to pay. That was deceptive."

"But we did pay him. We gave him back his sense of worth, a greater reward than simple revenge."

"I can see you'll never admit your deception."

"If I deceived him by telling him truths, can you really say that I deceived him? Perhaps he was deceiving himself, and I merely made it possible for him to see the truth."

"You are truly your father's son, Fenrir. Anyway, it is good to be free of you," I say jokingly.

"I wish I could say the same," he responds, unamused. "I shall never be free of you. I am bound..."

"You're free," I interject. "I release you from your bond." I chuckle to myself remembering how foolish that sounded when Eric said those words to me. "You owe me nothing."

"Owe you? For my life? Should I owe you? Was rescuing me of your own doing ... or did you make a deal with Hel?"

"I did. And as I rescued you, I expect her to keep her word."

"Then you do not know Hel. What did she promise you? To end your curse?"

"No. Only that one person would remember me."

"Small compensation," Fenrir responds, his brow furrowing with confusion.

"It means a great deal to me."

"I can see that. So, you have accepted your fate – your immortality – your anonymity?"

"I have accepted that I make my own destiny. I am not bound to your sister; I will not do her bidding. Quite the contrary, she is now bound to me, for I will hold her to her promise."

"Be wary. She's the deceitful one. She may honor her promise, but there will be consequences you do not expect." After a long pause Fenrir adds," And ... thank you." Though he speaks to me with just his thoughts, I can imagine Fenrir choking on those last two words.

As we continue our southward journey, I am keenly aware that my disruption of this affair of the gods will bring their ire upon me, and they may opt to seek their vengeance upon my family. But I will have the children of Angrboda as my allies, Fenrir for his life, Hel for her promise, and Jörmungandr for my deed, and I pray that will be enough to keep the Aesir at bay.

CHAPTER NINETEEN

FOUNTAIN OF PAIN

A lonely dragon roars in the distance, his guttural moan filling the frozen valley and shaking the icicles from the tree limbs. His forlorn cry goes on for hours, as if from a single breath, growing louder as we approach his den. As the dragon's lamentation reaches its deafening crescendo, we break out of the forest and gaze upon its source – a huge waterfall a mile high and two miles wide flowing into a giant pool from which many rivers flow outward. If there truly exists a paradise, this is it.

High above the waterfall erupts a lustrous fountain spouting untold miles into the air, its waters feeding the falls and the pool below. Fenrir and I have come to the Spring of Hvergelmir, one of the springs that feeds Yggdrasil, the cosmic tree that connects the nine realms. It is said the spring flows from the antlers of the stag, Eikthyrnir, who stands upon the roof of Valhalla, eating the leaves of Yggdrasil and dripping water from his rack. I feel suddenly at peace with myself, awed by the beauty of this place, but more so, connected to the universe and the nine realms. Fenrir, I can

132

see, feels the connection, too, but rather than being at peace, he seems extremely agitated.

"We need to keep moving," Fenrir says, his voice no more than a whisper inside my head but spoken with true urgency.

"Where?" I ask. I think I know where I am, but I have no way of knowing where to go.

"It doesn't matter," says Fenrir. "Just pick a river and sail it."

"Sail it? We don't have a boat!" I exclaim, losing my inner peace, Fenrir's apprehension infecting me like a disease.

"Then we build one. There – that tree – that'll do for a boat." Fenrir points a paw at a fallen oak lying near the side of the pool.

I hadn't even noticed any fallen trees, having been overcome by how pristine this place is, with its great waterfall, crystal-clear pool, and vibrantly colored rainbows that dance in the mists where the two meet. Now I see dozens of them, some dead and gray, others appearing to be recently felled. The fallen trees' roots and trunks appear gnawed, and I wonder what could have wrought such destruction. In my mind, I picture a jötunn-sized beaver, but the image is quickly whisked away when I think of its ridiculousness.

I take an ax from my belt and begin hacking away at the branches of the fallen oak, but its blade dulls before I've pruned away even one of them. Not wanting to dull its blade, too, but seeing that I have no other choice, I draw Dainslief and chop down on a large branch. The sword cleaves deep into the limb, and two swings later, the limb falls away.

Meanwhile, Fenrir has busied himself cleaning off roots and gouging out the trunk into a keipr, a dugout canoe. He is moving ferociously fast with his teeth and claws, digging and tearing at the trunk like a galinnulf, a mad dog. Though I have known Fenrir only a few months, I have never seen him afraid, not even when we battled with Thor, Aegir, and the Kraken. But now, I can smell his fear; he clearly wants to get away from this place as quickly as possible.

I finish pruning the branches and begin carving a wedge-shaped bow. It is hard enough work when you have the right tools, but a sword, albeit an enchanted one, is assuredly not the right tool for fashioning a boat.

"We don't need a bowpiece!" growls Fenrir. "Just cut a wedge and be done."

Of course, I have no intention of carving a bowpiece, but the desperation in his voice causes me to hasten my effort. It normally takes days to fashion a keipr; we finish this one in less than an hour. It certainly doesn't have the clean lines and craftsmanship of a proper canoe, but it is seaworthy enough for our purposes. As a final task, I fabricate an oar and long pole.

"Get in. Let's go!" says Fenrir.

I jump in, and the Wolf-God starts to push us into the water. He is stopped in his tracks by an ear-piercing shriek. We are momentarily thrown into darkness as a large shadow passes over us. Fenrir drives his head hard into the stern of our keipr, pushing it into the water with such force, it almost capsizes. Fenrir leaps into the stern and begins paddling with his front paws.

"ROW!" he screams as another shriek erupts, and a shadow engulfs us from above.

I hesitate for a moment while I look up. I see a huge dragon, its black body so large that it blocks the sun, its tail a long, twisted mass of snakes, its head displaying a mouth with a hundred rows of tiny, razor-sharp teeth, and its crown hideously adorned with a thousand hissing snake heads.

"What's that!?" I yell as I drive my oar into the water and start paddling.

"Nidhöggr!" answers Fenrir in a panic.

Nidhöggr descends on us at great speed. I slap at the protruding snake heads with my oar as the dragon passes over us, narrowly avoiding a bite. Fenrir crouches low into the canoe, barely avoiding another snapping snake head.

"Don't let it bite you!" screams Fenrir. "It's deadly."

"Deadly? We're immortal. How deadly can it be?" I ask as I swipe away at the dragon making another pass.

"Nidhöggr is the deadliest creature in the nine realms! The snakes secrete a venom that will immobilize even the greatest god or jötunn while causing unimaginable pain. Then, the dragon will feed on you for a thousand years, killing you slowly. No living thing, god or mortal, can survive it. It is the most agonizing death."

"I thought it only fed on the roots of Yggdrasil." I realize now that it is Nidhöggr, not some giant beaver, that has felled all these trees, trees which are actually the roots of Yggdrasil.

"It does. But Yggdrasil can sustain itself against Nidhöggr by growing more roots. You and I cannot do that."

I draw Dainslief and sever many snake heads on the next pass. I also manage a thrust into the beast's open mouth, hoping that the curse of the blade will kill it. Sadly, the blow does not kill the monster, but the dragon does shriek in pain from the cut and whips its tail violently at me. I am knocked overboard, but Fenrir snatches me back into the boat before I hit the water.

"You must stay out of the water. It is filled with more of those snakes."

I wish, now, that we were not in a canoe. At least on land, we could move around, flee, hide, or strike from cover, but out on the water, we are completely exposed and unable to maneuver. I understand Fenrir's desire to leave this place, but his haste has put us in the gravest of situations, facing an unbeatable monster with nowhere to run or hide. What's worse, Fenrir has no protection against this threat and is completely useless in the battle.

Another pass of the beast nearly capsizes the canoe. I am paddling as fast as I can, but we have a long way to go before we get to a river, and hopefully, an avenue of retreat from this battle. I glance back, and Fenrir is on his back kicking and baying as Nidhöggr swoops overhead. If only we had another canoe to use as a canopy, we might be able to fend off the dragon.

That fleeting thought gives me an idea. If we turn the boat over, we could hide underneath it. Of course, then we'd be in the water with the deadly snakes. Still, I think, I can handle a few snakes, whereas it is only a matter of time before Nidhöggr gets lucky and nails one of us.

"Get back on your feet," I yell to Fenrir. He does as I say without question.

"Let's capsize the canoe and use it for cover!" I say.

"But there are snakes in the water, too!" Fenrir cries.

"Let me handle the snakes. You dig into the canoe with your claws and stay low. You can use your back feet to paddle while I hang on your tail and fight off the snakes!"

Fenrir looks at me like I am crazy, but another pass of Nidhöggr makes his apprehension moot. The keipr flips over, throwing me into the water.

Fenrir, however, digs in his claws and clings frantically, upside-down, to the boat. I swim underneath the capsized canoe and come up.

"Fenrir, you'll have to paddle!" I command.

At first, he looks at me in anguished fear, but then regains his composure.

"Don't let me be bitten, or we both die slow, horrible deaths." Fenrir drops his feet and tail into the water and begins paddling.

I dive under the water, grab onto his tail, and wait for the snakes. Thankfully, the water is crystal clear, and I have hundreds of yards of visibility. We can hear Nidhöggr continue to shriek and dive on us, but for now, it seems my plan is working. Below, I see the water in turmoil as a nest of snakes disbands and begins swimming to the surface to attack us.

Swinging Dainslief underwater is extremely difficult, just as Jörmungandr had warned. Luckily, the sword's enchantment works against the snakes. Even if I barely knick one, it curls into a ball and sinks to the bottom. As Fenrir paddles blindly beneath the keipr, I keep the snakes at bay with Dainslief. I kill perhaps a hundred of them before their assault is driven back. I take the brief respite to surface under the canoe.

"We're doing great. The snakes, for now at least, have been driven back," I say confidently.

"I cannot see where we are going," says Fenrir. "We have to get to a river."

"I'll go up and steer us toward one. You keep paddling."

On the surface, I see no sign of Nidhöggr. He must have gotten bored or thought we'd drown. I look across the surface of the lake, but I cannot discern where the rivers are. I climb atop the capsized canoe and stand up so I can see further. There is a river nearby, but we must make a quarter turn to line up with it. I am just about to dive back into the water when Nidhöggr appears out of nowhere. I am barely able to defend myself against a dozen snakes that snap at my head, one of which strikes me on the cheek. Lucky for me, it was just the top of its head that hit me, but one of its fangs gets caught in my beard and breaks off as I am dragged from my perch.

I dive underwater and swim to the other side of the canoe. From here, I push the bow around until we are aligned with the river. I yell to Fenrir, "paddle as hard as you can."

By then, the water snakes are making another attack. I return to my position on Fenrir's tail and start fighting back. I am amazed by the speed at which Fenrir is paddling. I think he must have been a bit hesitant before. The turbulence of his kicks makes it difficult for me to both hang on and cut down the snakes, but somehow, I am able to manage.

I feel our speed increasing, and it's not from Fenrir's frenzied kicking. We are entering the headwaters of the river. I slash a few more snakes; they curl away harmlessly. We are home free. I believe we may just escape with our lives. Suddenly, I feel a sharp pain in my left thigh, a pain that instantly overtakes my entire body. I go limp. I drop Dainsleif and fall away from Fenrir, my body taken by the flow of the river, tumbling in the rapids like a dead log.

The pain from the venom is so overwhelming that I do not feel the shock from the rocks that my body is dashed against. I am rolled into an eddy near the bank, where I am continuously swirled around, colliding with a huge boulder over and over and over again. I am powerless to stop it. I am at the mercy of the river.

After uncountable revolutions in the eddy, I find myself being dragged onto the bank. Fenrir has pulled me from the river. "Where were you bitten!?" he asks, excitedly.

"AAHHH ... my thigh ... I think ... AAHHH!" I scream out in pain.

Fenrir rolls me over face down in the mud and opens the bite wound wide with his claw. He places his mouth over it and tries to suck out the venom, but the wound closes quickly, sealing the deadly poison in my body.

"AAHHH," I scream. "Do something. This is agony."

"I know!", howls Fenrir. "But there is nothing I can do."

"But you are ... a god! There must be some ... AAHHH!"

"Wait! Let me try something," says Fenrir. He leaves, returning a few minutes later with a mouth full of green weeds with yellow-petaled flowers.

"Chew on this," Fenrir says as he drops a few into my mouth.

"What ... what is it?" I cry, barely able to move my jaws enough to chew.

"Hensbane. Stinking nightshade," answers Fenrir.

"They're POISON ... AAHHH," I cry out.

"Only if you swallow them," Fenrir responds. "... So don't swallow them."

I begin chewing the hensbane, the poison-infused saliva trickling down my throat. Within minutes, the pain is half of what it was – still agonizing, but bearable.

"I am going to leave now and find help. There is an antidote for the venom. Hopefully, I can find a laeknir who knows how to make it," says Fenrir.

With that, he bounds off into the woods leaving me alone with my agony. I chew on the deadly flowers, praying for relief from the pain, or death, or both. I wonder if Fenrir will return as he said, or if he will abandon me to my fate. Strangely, at this moment, I realize that Fenrir isn't just a snide and spiteful sidekick, a sharp-tongued, angry, blue wolf who despises me as much as I despise him; he is also my friend. I hope he feels the same way about me.

CHAPTER TWENTY

VISIONS

Disciplined and ordered, a column of soldiers advances up the steep, uneven terrain. Forward scouts locate the objective and communicate its location back to the leaders. The army movement increases to a double-time step, fanning out and encircling the enemy with stealth and precision. The order given, the army attacks from three sides, driving the enemy into a fourth where it is swarmed upon and destroyed. The ants lift the grasshopper, still kicking in its death throes, and begin carrying it back to the mound.

I watch as the tiny ants effortlessly hoist the giant grasshopper up my leg and bring it down the other side. I am nothing but an obstacle to them, a mountainous presence to be overcome in their quest for food. Though hundreds of individuals, they move, act, and react as one unit, each knowing the job it must perform and supporting its comrades in theirs – a perfect display of military rigor. As a soldier, I can't help but be impressed. I think we can learn a lot from watching ants, their selflessness, discipline,

141

and complete focus on the task at hand.

I have been lying, immobilized, for I don't know how long. I am delirious with pain, though the hensbane I am chewing is taking the edge off. Suddenly, I feel movement, as if my body is being lifted, the sky and trees around me swirling as I am carted off. I see my arm covered in ants. They seem to be directing the others where to take me. I am brought along the riverbank to a gap in the forest where the ants carry my limp body over some rocks and into the woods.

I am laid to rest against a tree next to a mound as large as a longhouse. Ants, much larger than the ones that brought me here, emerge from the mound and begin the grim task of breaking me down. In no time, I see sections of my legs carried to the mound, disappearing through a hole that serves as the entrance. Next, my arms are drawn away, followed by my torso and organs. Strangely, though my body has been ripped apart, I can still feel the pain in every part of it. When they come for my head, I cry out, "STOP", but the ants ignore my plea and dutifully bear my head to the hole and deposit it.

The sensation of falling a great distance overcomes me, and I am nauseated. I start to vomit, the remnants of masticated hensbane scattering in a flurry of green, yellow, and white. My head lands with a thud upon a sandy mound, surrounded by large ants, the heads of each bearing a resemblance to my fallen comrades from the Battle of the Sees.

"Asger Agnarson! You are a disgrace to your people. You cheated your death for a life of disgrace. You begged the gods to save you. You dishonor those who fought alongside you," booms a voice, echoing around my head like a bell.

"Dishonor! Disgrace!" chant the Norseman-headed ants.

"It's not true!" I cry. "I was cursed. Hel cursed me!"

"Hel did not curse you. You begged for your life. You begged to be immortal" the voice says. From the shadows, Tyr emerges, his bloodied stump held high. "How dare you? Gods are the only immortals! Now feel the hand of judgment!"

Tyr's enormous, severed hand descends on me, lifts me high in the air, and hurls me. My head lands in a pit of fire, orange flames burning all around me. I see demons feeding the parts of my body to a jötunn of incredible size, his hair and beard a mass of flames, his body blackened and smoldering like the embers of a dying fire. I know it is Surtr, the fire-giant who rules Muspelheim, the realm of fire.

"Welcome Asger! We've been waiting for you," says Surtr, a blue-flame smile crossing his face. "Your arrival signals the start of Ragnarök. Your immortal body has made me impenetrable. Now, you and I will assault the Aesir and bring them down."

He gallops forth on his reindeer with flaming antlers, plunges his sword into my head, and holds me out at the tip. I see Asgard in flames, overrun with jötunn, the gods battling demons. Freyr charges forward on his boar, Gullinbursti, carrying an antler instead of a sword. Surtr flings me at the antler, and I am impaled on it as Surtr cuts Freyr down.

"Well done, Asger!" cries Surtr. "You have served your purpose. Now to Midgard to claim it in flame!" I hear him say as he snatches Freyr's antler bearing my head and throws it into the burning remnants of Bilskirnir, the great hall of Thor.

The burning is excruciating. I try to pat out the flames, but my arms have been eaten by Surtr and are now part of his armor. Suddenly a splash of icy water envelops me, and I am shocked back to reality.

"You're burning up, dearest," says Inger, gently. "Here is a cold rag for your head."

My head is aflame and my body aches. "Inger," I gasp.

"Don't try to speak, love. You are very ill. Just lie here quietly."

Despite the pain, I am ecstatic. I am home. It has all been a terrible dream brought on by a fever. Inger takes my hand and lightly kisses it, the warmth of her lips soothing my pain.

"Is father going to die?" I hear Brant ask, as Gyda weeps in the background.

"I don't know, Brant. He is very sick. But he did wake up just now and say my name. That is a good sign."

"I don't understand. Father was recovering from his war injuries. Why is he so sick now?"

"Sometimes, no matter what medicine we have, a sepsis will take hold. All we can do is keep him cool and comfortable and wait for him to get better. You may want to pray to Eir for healing, too. You and your sister can both pray. I'm sure that will help most of all."

I hear the children whispering their prayers through their sniffles. If I die now, I will die in complete joy. I am in the bosom of my family and my beloved Inger remembers me. But I don't want to die. I am going to fight this with every ounce of my strength. I have not been through all that I have been through, whether it be real or the machinations of a fevered mind, to die now. I reach deep into myself, past the memories, past the pain, and I find the strength to live.

"Did you think you could lay such a curse upon us, and we would allow it?" Hel's voice surrounds me. I open my eyes, and I am on the battlefield, my life's blood spilling out of me.

"Goddess, I laid no curse on you. I have not spoken a word. I have only, just now, regained consciousness," I say, wondering if I am having another fever-born dream in my bed at home, or if I am really on the battlefield, my mind addled by my impending death.

"True. You said nothing. Still, you have a strong desire to live, stronger than any I've witnessed. And, because you will not die, because you will not accept the honorable death the gods have given you, the Valkyries have abandoned you. So, I have come to collect you, but as you have no intention of drawing your last breath, I cannot do that. Asger, you have condemned yourself to an eternity of pain and suffering, pain that will worsen every moment, forever. But should you choose, I can take away your pain. I can give you the life you desire above all else – above riches, above fame, above family – a life free of attachment, free of pain. All you need do is say yes."

"NO! I WON'T! NO!" I scream. "You are lying to me again. I will not be your spear. I will not be the Twilight Warrior!"

"But Asger – you are the Twilight Warrior. You have always been the Twilight Warrior."

"NOOO! Go away and let me DIE!" The pain wraps me like a death shroud, squeezing ever tighter until I feel my breath stop.

"He is certainly in a bad way," a distant voice whispers from the darkness. "It's a good thing you gave him the hensbane else the pain may have driven him stark, raving mad by now."

"He was already stark, raving mad," Fenrir replies, the timber of his voice echoing faintly inside my brain.

"Well, we have all the ingredients – elder, angelica, and of course, hensbane – well, almost all the ingredients. Do you have a snake head?"

"No, we were unable to procure one."

"Well, I cannot make the potion without the snake head. I need some of the venom."

"Can't you get it from his blood? It should be full of venom by now."

"That's not how this works, Fenrir. I need pure venom or else the potion is useless. You'll have to go back and catch a snake. Try not to get bitten."

Fenrir growls and then bounds into the river.

"Wait! What's this? Fenrir, come back. I think I have what I need. See here ... a fang caught in your friend's beard. Perhaps it will have enough venom to do the trick."

Fenrir returns with a sigh of relief.

"Okay. Let me just grind this up. There. And now a fire," the voice says, followed by the sharp sound of a knife striking flint. "Now we cook it a bit ... there, it's ready. Open his mouth. He'll have to swallow all of it."

I feel the claws of the Wolf-God pry my jaws open and hot, rancid liquid enter my mouth. Then, my mouth is closed shut and my head shaken. I instinctively swallow. The fluid hits my stomach like a gut punch, amplifying my pain a hundredfold. My body convulses uncontrollably. The fog of my dreams is lifted, my eyes fly open wide, and a blurry vision of an old man and a wolf slowly come into focus.

"It's working. See. His eyes are open. Can you hear me young man?"

I start to answer, but instead, a final violent convulsion causes me to vomit. The agonizing pain subsides quickly. I raise my hand to my mouth, and it responds. I move my legs, and they, too, are working again.

"HEL!" I yell.

"No, young man. This is Fenrir, her brother. And I am Birger," says an ancient little man with a beard as long as his body and as gray as a rain cloud. "You were bitten by a Nidhöggr snake from the Spring of Hvergelmir. Do you remember?"

"Yes. I remember," I say, my faculties returning to me.

"You have a good friend in the Wolf-God, young man. Fenrir saved you from a slow and agonizing death."

"Death? I dreamed I died. But Hel wouldn't let me. She said I begged for immortality. Tyr said I begged for immortality."

"Well, that certainly is a strange dream, even for hensbane visions. You were hallucinating, my boy. You are not dead, at least not yet. And I can assure you, you are quite mortal."

"Well, not exactly, Birger. He is the Drengr Røkkr, the immortal Twilight Warrior," says Fenrir.

"Are you sure you haven't been chewing hensbane, Fenrir," laughs Birger. "I can understand if you have a taste for it. It hasn't been but forty years since I had to give you this potion. I am surprised that you would venture into the Spring of Hvergelmir again after the last time."

"We didn't have a choice," says Fenrir. "Thank you for your help, Birger."

"Anytime, Fenrir. I am always at the service of the children of Angrboda," Birger responds. "Now would you like to come to my hovel and rest before you continue your journey? I am sure the Drengr Røkkr could use some sleep."

"Thank you, but no. Asger's had enough sleep already. We must get moving."

Birger grunts and waddles off into the woods. I am becoming aware of where I am and everything that has happened. My dreams were just that — dreams. I was never in Muspelheim or Asgard. And I was never home with Inger. With that last thought, I feel a deep sadness cut through me, causing me more pain than the snake bite ever could.

"I think this is yours. I found it in the river," Fenrir says, holding Dainslief in his mouth.

"Thank you," I say, taking my sword and sliding it into its scabbard. "And thank you for saving me. I guess this makes us even."

"Not even, just ... ," Fenrir doesn't finish his thought. "Besides my sister, and dying, or, rather not dying, did you dream anything else?" Fenrir asks with true empathy and curiosity. I am taken aback. It is certainly not like Fenrir to ask such a deep, personal question, especially one with such concern.

"I dreamed I was home with my family. I was sick, and my wife was taking care of me," I respond trying to keep my emotions at bay.

"You know, they say the visions of hensbane are not just dreams. They are a view into your soul, your deepest fears, your deepest desires. And your deepest regrets," Fenrir says solemnly. His eyes take on a distant look, like he is remembering his own hensbane journey.

"I think that's true, Fenrir. Certainly, my deepest desire is to be home with my family, and my deepest fear is Inger and my children not knowing me," I say.

Fenrir nods. "My deepest fear is ... well, I guess you already know my deepest fear," he says, surprising me with his openness.

"Nidhöggr," I answer, quietly.

"Yes. You have no idea of the ..." Fenrir pauses. "And your deepest regret?"

"My deepest regret is this immortality. That because of it, even if I do get home, I'll not be able to stay."

"It isn't good to regret something that hasn't happened yet," says Fenrir, profoundly.

"The truth is, I am not so sure that it hasn't," I say, wondering what my true reality is. Am I still dying on the battlefield, sick in bed with a fever being nursed by Inger, or am I really here with the Wolf-God trying to get back to Midgard?

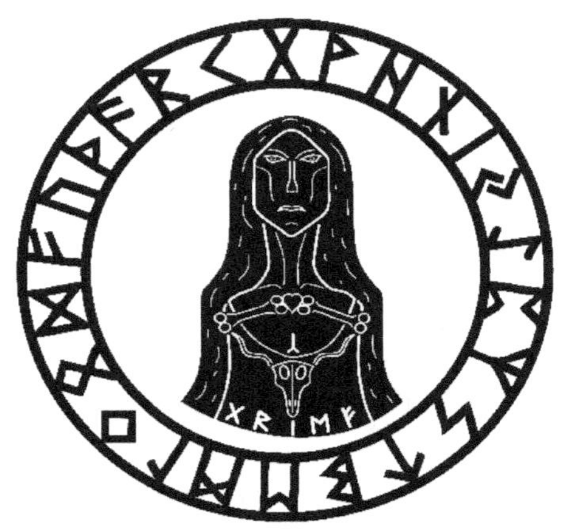

CHAPTER TWENTY-ONE

MOTHER OF MONSTERS

The autumn sunset lingers on the horizon, emblazoning the indigo sky with streaks of reddish-orange and amber yellow. Dark clouds billow in the distance, threatening a storm of great consequence. For hours, we float down the river, yet the twilight refuses to yield to the dusk, instead filling more of the sky, as if time has reversed and dawn is again brightening the earth for a day that will have no end. At a bend in the river, the forest gives way to a plain which stretches out for miles and is covered with thousands of funeral pyres, burning corpses of jötunn and human alike, the flames of which reach to the heavens, the acrid smoke choking us as we pass.

"I wonder what ... cuhk ... happened here," I cough.

"A battle, I think," Fenrir replies without speaking.

"Where do you think we are?" I ask, wondering where such a battle would take place.

"Jötunheimr, perhaps, though I am not sure why so many humans

150

would be here. There hasn't been an incursion like this in more than a thousand years. Even Hogni's foray into this realm was small by comparison to this."

We pull our keipr ashore to inspect the devastation. Besides the piles of burning bodies, the ground is littered with boulders and broken trees, some snapped off at their trunks, others, hundreds of feet high, uprooted and strewn across the field.

"What could have brought about such destruction? Why would humans risk invading Jötunheimr?"

"Odin and the Aesir caused this." I was not expecting an answer, especially one from a voice that was distinctly feminine – and dreadful.

"Mother," says Fenrir, "It is nice to see you."

"And you, my lovely," says Angrboda, bending her giantess form over to kiss her eldest on the head.

My blood runs cold. An overwhelming sense of sadness floods over me, and I feel myself drowning in despair. The power of the Mistress of Grief is legendary, and her very presence is enough to overcome a man's will to live.

"This is Asger, my companion." Fenrir politely makes an introduction.

"Yes, I have heard of your great feat – slaying the Kraken and freeing my son," Angrboda says. "You have done my family a great service. We are in your debt."

I try to speak, but my mouth cannot form words. Tears well up in my eyes as hope is drained from my soul. All I can manage in acknowledgment to her words is a slight nodding bow that leaves my eyes staring at my feet.

"You say Odin did this?" Fenrir asks his mother.

"Yes, he sent Thor and Tyr to Midgard to raise an army. They came into the Ironwood and attacked us."

"Why? What did they want?"

"They were looking for you, my love. Tyr is exceedingly angry with you since you bit off his hand."

"Is that what he said? It was Asger that took his hand, not me. Tyr fancies himself to be the God of Justice, but he's just another liar like the rest of them. He couldn't even bring himself to admit that he was bested by a mortal."

"Ha ha ha ha ha," laughs Angrboda, her mirth so disquieting that I fall to my knees. She takes no notice of my anguish. I suppose she is quite used to it. "What weapon has he that could slay the Kraken and maim a god?"

"Dainslief, Mistress," I mumble, drawing the sword and turning the blade to my belly.

"Remarkable. I know of its power to kill mortals, but I had no idea it would be so effective against gods and monsters," says Angrboda. "May I see it?"

As she reaches for the sword, I am overcome and plunge it towards my belly, the blade turning slack and refusing to enter my body.

"Come, now, Asger. You know you can't die," she says, her sweet voice like a dagger in my ears. I raise my arm slowly and hand her the blade. "A fitting weapon, indeed, for the Twilight Warrior, capable of laying low all who oppose you. And you, Asger – immortal, invulnerable, unstoppable – you are a true instrument of death. I am pleased to have you serve us in this battle. My daughter has done well to have created you," she adds, handing Dainslief back to me.

Her words ring of ownership, like I am a possession to be used at will. Rage suddenly fills my body, sweeping away my despondence. "NO!" I clap, rising to my feet.

Angrboda steps back, a mild shock rippling across her beautiful face.

"I do not serve you, Mistress, nor any of your children. My destiny is my own. And as you have said that you are in my debt, I would keep it that way."

Her shock flashes to anger, and then, to stoicism. "As you wish, Asger. Your life is indeed your own. But I think you will find that you will have to choose a side in the coming conflict, and that your choice, whichever side you choose, is your destiny. So, you see, in reality, you have no choice in your destiny."

"I can choose not to choose!" I proclaim.

"Choosing not to choose is still a choice, Asger, and that choice will lead to another and another and another. Eventually, as I said, you will have to choose a side. There is no other way. And when the time comes, I know you will choose us, because it will be the only choice you can make."

"You lie!" I hiss.

"You should watch your tongue. My mother is not one to be trifled with," says Fenrir. "You may be immortal, but as you have already seen, you can still suffer greatly. And believe me, that snake venom would be a gnat bite compared to what she could do to you."

I want to respond, but I do as Fenrir says and hold my tongue. My rage subsides, and I feel the sadness returning. I fight against it, but it threatens to overpower me again. Strangely, at this moment, I think of Inger and my children, and it strengthens me, helping me find a balance between my anger and my fear.

"It's alright, my lovely. I have been called many things – Witch of Ironwood, Bringer of Doom, Mistress of Grief, Mother of Monsters – I think I can tolerate being called a liar," Angrboda says, calmly.

"For a man, you really are quite unique," she says to me. "None has ever been able to so much as stand in my presence, let alone speak from their heart as you have. There is an odd power in you – a defiance – a refusal to accept things as they are or shall be. You curse and defy the gods, you deny yourself an honorable death, and even now, deep down, you still believe you can regain your mortality. Many men want to live forever, but you ... you simply want to live. And, this power you have, it is not because you are the Drengr Røkkr. It is what made you the Drengr Røkkr. I see now that my daughter did not choose you. You chose this."

My hensbane-fueled visions flow back into my mind – my encounter with Hel – she said I have always been the Twilight Warrior. Now Angrboda says I chose this for myself. Could it be true? Could I really have made myself the Drengr Røkkr? No! Hel did this to me. She cursed me. I have accepted what she has made me, but that does not mean I have accepted the hidden role she would have me play. I refuse to accept the things Hel may have me do ... accept the things Hel may ... accept things ... accept things as they are ... or shall be? Angrboda's words sear into my brain, and I am wracked with confusion. In the midst of my internal chaos, a moment of clarity bursts through like the sun on a cloudy day, and I start laughing.

"Heh heh heh heh. I can't believe it," I laugh. "You are worse than Loki. Is that why he partnered with you? Because you are a better trickster than he is?"

Angrboda gapes at me strangely, scowling, glaring, trying everything she can to stare me down, but her power no longer affects me.

"You would have me believe that I created myself, the immortal Drengr Røkkr? You, Hel, my visions – they are all a great deceit. You have planted these things in my mind to make me feel hopeless, a prisoner of a fate that you decide. You are right, I do have a power inside me. I have the power to see that you are afraid of me and what I can do. You would trick me ... make me question my ability to choose my own way so you can control me. You need to control me; Hel needs to control me. I will not be controlled. The seer is right. I can choose my own destiny!" I exclaim, fully confident that I have seen the truth, that they were trying to manipulate me into doing their bidding.

"As I said, Asger, you are quite unique," Angrboda says. "But I can assure you, I am not trying to deceive you, even as you are right about my consort. I am the better trickster. How else could you explain my offspring?" she adds with a laugh.

"I am satisfied. You are free to pursue your own destiny. My children and I will not interfere in any way," she continues. "Further, as we are indebted to you for what you have done, we will be there when you call on us. But, be assured, once that debt is paid, you may not greet any of us again as a friend.

"Take him back to Midgard, my lovely," she says to Fenrir. "And please take care. The Aesir and mortals are out for your blood."

"I will, Mother," says Fenrir. "Will you be alright here in the Ironwood?"

"Of course, dear," answers Angrboda, a sly smile crossing her lips that sparks a dread inside me I am barely able to contain, even with my newly found spine.

The Mother of Monsters leaves us, walking hurriedly back into the smoke-filled forest. I cannot believe that I have not only met Angrboda but have survived the encounter. It is true that no man can resist the urge to take his own life in her presence, even as I had tried to do. Somehow, though, I overcame her power, and now I truly feel invincible.

Fenrir and I return to our keipr. I look back on the smoldering piles of flesh and know the answer to the question I posed when we arrived. It was not Odin and the Aesir that caused the desolation. True, they may have brought an army to the Ironwood, but it was Angrboda that brought about the slaughter. I can see it now, thousands of men and hundreds of jötunn gathered on a field of battle when Angrboda strides in, bringing depression and despair to all. The battle plays out, not as a strategic encounter where one side fights and maneuvers to defeat the other, but as a mass suicide where both sides run headlong onto the swords of the other.

"Your mother is truly terrifying," I say.

"Yes, she is," says Fenrir. "She is quite impressed by you, though. No mortal has withstood her, let alone, said the things to her that you said. I will tell you this. She wasn't lying to you or trying to deceive you. She believed every word she said. And, you were right, too. She is afraid of you."

"Really?"

"You know I wouldn't lie to you, Asger. I never have, and I never will." After a long pause, he adds, "And I won't abandon you as a friend, no matter the debts we owe or pay."

"I don't know if I can get used to you being so friendly. It seems unnatural," I laugh. "I rather liked you better when you hated me."

"Who says I don't hate you," growls Fenrir as he pushes me off the boat.

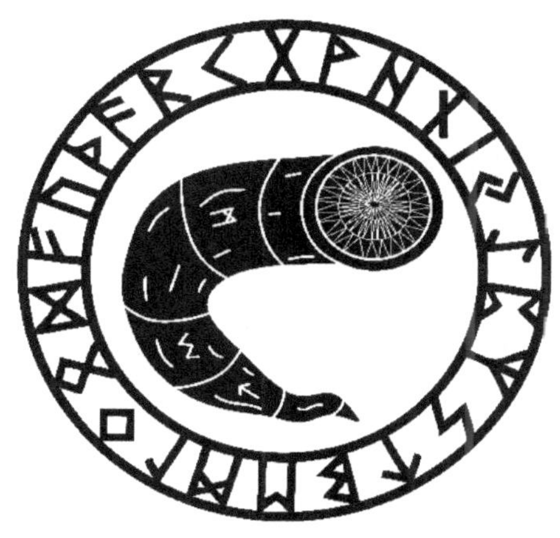

CHAPTER TWENTY-TWO

THE MISTLANDS

A malodorous aroma corrupted an otherwise pleasant autumn day. The stench of rotting death permeated the air, an attestation of a great calamity that has befallen this part of Jötunheimr, a rapid plague that has laid low the giant inhabitants. A field of colossal plants with heart-shaped leaves and fluted yellow flowers feed on the corpses of the dead, creating a scene of tranquility that disguises the unpleasant reality beneath. We enter the field expecting to step lightly over the bodies of dead, but we find none. It is as if the flowers themselves have fully consumed the fallen, the fetid tang of which has infected their bouquet, giving them a fragrance quite contrary to their beauty.

"Birthwort," says Fenrir, recognizing the scent.

"Birthwort? Aren't those the plants brewed and given to expectant mothers to induce labor and calm the pain?" I ask, covering my mouth and nose to avoid vomiting. I am amazed that anyone would drink anything

157

smelling of death, let alone a woman in the throes of childbirth.

"The same. We are at the border of Jötunheimr and Midgard. The jötunn have planted this to mark the boundary," says Fenrir, somehow immune to the overwhelming smell of the place.

"Why?" I ask, but by the smell, the answer is obvious, or so I think.

"To keep my brother in Midgard and out of Jötunheimr. He hates this stuff. Some call it snakeroot."

"Jörmungandr? Why would the jötunn care if your brother was here?"

"Because they are afraid of him ... of us. You see what the mere thought of my presence here has wrought, how the gods inspired the mortals to attack. Well, Jörmungandr is as reviled and feared, and maybe more so, as I am. The jötunn are content to keep us in Midgard or Helheim or ... well ... anywhere but here."

"The birthwort doesn't seem to affect you, though," I say. "What would the jötunn do to keep you out?"

"Capture me and take me to Nidhöggr," replies Fenrir with a shiver.

I realize now why Fenrir hates this place so much. He's had terrible experiences here, the worst imaginable given what I myself have undergone in my brief time beyond the realm of Midgard. I never thought about it. I always assumed he'd be welcome in Jötunheimr because he is, in reality, a jötunn, the son of a jötunn and a god. In truth, he is a half-breed, unwelcome in the realms of the gods and despised in the realm of giants.

"Is that what happened the last time you were in Jötunheimr?" I ask.

"Jötunheimr was my home, but as I grew, so did the hatred of my kind. They dragged me to the Spring of Hvergelmir and gave me to Nidhöggr. I barely escaped. I left Jötunheimr and went to live in Midgard. The mortals hate me, too, but at least they leave me alone for the most part. I've not been back here since. I was still a pup, then. I am more formidable now."

The anger and pain of Fenrir's thoughts take a physical presence in me as well, and I feel the heat of rage burning in my chest. Something has changed. I could always hear his thoughts, but now, I can feel what he is feeling, a much greater depth of connectedness than simply being bound to one another by necessity and deed. I wonder if he senses the same thing.

Beyond the field of stinking birthwort, is a dense forest suffused by an even denser mist. I am loath to enter, remembering the last time I encountered a mist like this, I ended up in another realm battling Thor, Tyr, and the Kraken. Fenrir assures me this is the way to Midgard, so I follow, but cautiously.

In the misty forest, I hear strange sounds, howls of lonely wolves, grunts and bleats of solitary deer and elk, and the cries of men and giants in languages I can scarcely understand, but know by the sound, that they are in fear and longing. These are the midlands, also known as the Mistlands, separating the realm of men from the realm of jötunn. I have heard stories that you will lose yourself here and go mad. I trust that Fenrir knows the way and we will not get lost like these other poor souls.

I wonder how Högni led his expedition through these lands, or that army of men that passed through quite recently. How many of those men am I hearing now? And I wonder how long it will take for us to pass through.

"A day or two," says Fenrir, sensing my unasked question. "The mists move and grow and shrink so it is impossible to know for certain."

"That is not reassuring," I say, not wanting to remain a moment longer in this place.

"And I don't know where we will come out – maybe in Karelia, maybe somewhere else," Fenrir adds, familiar with my previous adventure in the borderlands in search of Högni's tomb.

"Well, in that case, I would like to come out in Lagarvik!" I say laughingly.

"You don't get to choose, but it will most likely be a place you've been before," responds Fenrir, unamused.

I did not expect that kind of an answer. I have been many places in my life, some of them very, very far from Lagarvik. I start thinking of all the places I might end up, and I feel lost. I begin to feel a madness coming over me as I contemplate the possibilities.

"Don't overthink it. Just know that you won't be lost when we escape the Mistlands." says Fenrir, sensing my anxiety. I am certain now that Fenrir feels the same connection to me as I have to him. We can not only read each other's thoughts but feelings as well.

We come to a small clearing where three ragged jötunn are feasting on a reindeer and what appears to be the remains of a man. One of them jumps up, wielding an enormous hammer and swings down on us, barely missing as we jump out of the way. I draw Dainslief and slice the tendon on the back of his leg. He topples over, unable to stand, dropping the hammer, which strikes one of his comrades on the head, knocking him unconscious. The third grabs the remains of the reindeer and runs off into the forest.

I approach the fallen giant, intending to slit his throat, but Fenrir begs me off. I am unsure why he would want to show mercy to one who would torment him, but I do as he wishes. As we leave, however, I slice the tendon of the other leg. Fenrir may have spared that jötunn, but he will live out the rest of his days on his hands and knees.

Many hours pass in silence. Finally, I ask, "Why did you not let me kill him?"

"Death binds you to a place like this. To kill a thing here is to lose part of yourself. You will become lost like those you hear all around us."

"So, these men and giants have all killed someone in the Mistlands?"

"Not all of them ... not at first, at least. But desperation leads us to do things we regret."

I am intrigued by Fenrir's change in mood. He is suddenly somber, a state in which I have never known him to be. We once discussed our fears and regrets. I know Fenrir's greatest fear is Nidhöggr, but I realize now, he never mentioned his deepest regret. I sense that it is related to this place, so I ask him about it. He growls softly but does not answer.

Weary, we decide to make camp by a bog. The smell is awful, but not nearly as bad as the field of birthwort. We fall asleep quickly. Normally in a dangerous place like this, a watch would be set, but being a god and an immortal, neither of us need keep watch over the other. My dreams are disturbing, hearkening back to the visions I had under the influence of hensbane. I wake often, sweating and out of breath. I've not had a good night's sleep in weeks. I wonder if it is just the lingering effects of the hensbane, the snake venom, the cure, or something else altogether. But I know something is not right with me.

Unable to sleep anymore, I wake Fenrir, who growls and nearly takes my arm off. Apparently, the adage about not waking sleeping dogs applies to wolf-gods as well. Though I would rather not, we wade through the bog; Fenrir says it is the best path. We emerge from the filthy, stagnant water covered in leaches. Fenrir, particularly, has hundreds of them all over his body, and as they draw his god's blood, they grow to enormous size, some over a foot long and as fat as a greylag goose. It is quite a chore to remove them. I put each to the sword, lest they breed and make more jötunn-sized leaches.

Late the next day, the mist seems to be subsiding, and I can make out more of the forest. It is not the spruce, birch, and pine of the Savonian forest that I was expecting, but mighty oaks and other hardwoods that are native to the southern Baltic, the lands of the Saxons and Wends. I would hate to think that I have come all this way, months of wandering and fighting in Midgard and other realms, only to end up back in Pomerania where my journey began.

We emerge from the misty forest into a great field near a lake. The sharp sound of steel-on-steel echoes all around, augmented by the shouts of the combatants and the screams of the dying. I am back at the Battle of the Sees, the place where I died, or rather, the place where I didn't die. I am dumbfounded. How could this be?

"Time passes differently in other realms," says Fenrir, again, sensing my thoughts. "In some realms, time passes so quickly that months would be no more than a second in Midgard, others so slowly that a second would be years in the realm of men."

"I don't ... I don't understand," I say, the situation well beyond my comprehension.

"I believe time in Niflhiem may actually move backwards," says Fenrir.

"That makes no sense!" I shout.

"Do you think all the realms bare the same existence? They don't. It would not make sense that they would. Do the honored dead in Valhalla know the time of day? Do they even care? Of course not. They are there for eternity. Time means nothing to them. The only time that matters to anyone in any of the nine realms is the end time – Ragnarök. At that time, everything ends everywhere."

I would like to contemplate what Fenrir has told me, but I am approached by a man bearing a jarl's crest who orders me into the shield wall. I recognize him. He is Olin Halvorsen, Eric's older brother, who died in Peenemunde the day before Eric and I arrived there. Yet here he is, alive, and leading his men into battle. I look for Eric, but do not see him.

"We must join the fighting now, or all is lost!" Olin shouts.

I blindly set aside my confusion and follow Olin into the field. Unsheathing Dainslief, I cut into the Franks like a berserker, turning the tide of the battle.

CHAPTER TWENTY-THREE

RETURN TO PEENEMUNDE

The bellows rise and fall rhythmically, expelling puffs of air, each time giving the dying fire life. The sound is like a creaky siglura atop the mast of a drakkar longship as wind fills the sail and retreats again. I watch silently, focusing on two embers as they shift color from stone gray to brilliant blueish white. Despite the rush of air, over time, the embers begin to fade. At last, Olin takes his final breath, the light in his eyes extinguished and the bellows of his lungs ceasing for eternity.

Emerging victorious in the Battle of the Sees, again, I am now back in Peenemunde, my life taking a circular track, but somehow running a bit ahead. I, along with some of his men, have brought Olin here in hopes the healers may save his life. At first, it seemed he may survive, but overnight, a sepsis formed in his wounds and made quick work of it. I am greatly saddened by his passing. I have known Olin my entire life, as he is Eric's brother, and I have always looked up to him. But, to see him in battle, his strength, his courage, his leadership, and his sacrifice to save his men from a rout is beyond anything I have ever witnessed. I once questioned the existence of Valhalla, but if anyone has ever achieved that reward, it is Olin. I imagine him sitting at the head of Odin's table, glasses raised as the Allfather declares "Here is Olin, the greatest among us!"

I retire to the livery where Fenrir and I have made our beds. Though it is only early evening, he is already fast asleep. The last few days have been a whirlwind of events, and I have been caught up in them. I have not had the time or inclination to think about how I came to be reliving my life, or at least, passing through the same occurrences a second time, but from a different perspective. Now, as I await Eric's arrival, which if things continue as they had in the past, should be tomorrow, I have time to consider my situation and what it means.

I wonder, had I remained on the battlefield instead of leaving with Olin, if I may have found myself lying among the dead and dying. I do not see how it could have been plausible, but given the strangeness of my life, I cannot deny the possibility. I am, after all, the Drengr Røkkr, so perhaps I am no longer Asger Agnarson. Perhaps Asger Agnarson did indeed die in the Battle of the Sees, and I am merely an image of him, a creature suffused with his likeness and memories, but none of his humanity. The thought is more than I can bear, so I put it from my mind. I decide to accept my situation as it is, that I am Asger Agnarson and I am the Twilight Warrior, and that everything that has come to pass up until this point in my life is real, albeit, confusing. But the thoughts still nag me from the back of my mind, and I wonder if my precognition of things to come, having lived them before, will work to my advantage or disadvantage.

Eric arrives the next day, as expected, but he is severely injured. He only has about a third of his men, having lost the rest in his ill-conceived foray into the Szczecin Lagoon. His kinsmen, Knute and Stigr, both wounded as well, bring him into the olstafa which has been transformed into a makeshift hospital and lay him on a table. Eric's leg is broken just above the ankle, and he has a deep laceration to his chest just beneath his right arm, the result of being stabbed with a sword, no doubt. I quickly realize that Fenrir and I were not there to influence the battle, and so, it went very badly for Eric and his comrades, even worse than before.

The laeknir gets to work on the sword wound, scraping away the dried blood and cleaning it with ale. He cuts away some of the flesh, widening the hole, which is oozing bubbling blood as the air in Eric's right lung escapes. Knute, Stigr, and others hold Eric down, putting a knife handle in his mouth to bite down on, while the healer takes a red-hot iron rod from a nearby fire and inserts it into Eric's chest. Eric convulses and lets loose a muffled scream as the flesh inside his body is seared, cauterizing the wound and staunching the flow of blood. The smell of burning flesh reminds me of the field in Ironwood where I witnessed a mass of funeral pyres just a few weeks earlier. Or will it be some time in the future? I ignore my mind and approach Eric with some hensbane I procured on my journey. It should ease his pain for a while; I only hope his visions will be more pleasant than mine were.

After two days, Eric is able to sit up. His wound is healing nicely – no sign of infection – and his leg is set and splinted. It is, surprisingly, or maybe not so surprisingly, the same leg I splinted when we were shipwrecked on Dago. One of the barmaids has taken a shining to Eric and is taking very good care of him, waiting on him, changing his dressings, feeding him by hand. She bears a striking resemblance to Katye, but when I call her by that name, she corrects me, saying her name is Raina. Still, the similarities of Eric's injury and a woman attending to him are not lost on me.

With Eric better able to represent the Halvorsen clan in Olin's place, the Thing has been planned for this evening. I want to talk to Eric before it happens. He has been moved to Raina's sleeping quarters, where I am sure she has been tending to his every need. I knock before entering and find Eric sitting up in bed with Raina's head in his lap. She sits up abruptly, her face flush red with embarrassment. Eric bursts out laughing. "It's not what it looks like, friend!" Then with another wail of laughter he adds," Well, maybe if you'd come in a few minutes later."

I stand at the door, unable to speak, but Eric's laughter is infectious, so I start laughing as well. "Well, if it's NOT what it looks like, then I'm NOT sorry for the interruption."

"No ... heh, heh ... she was just tying off the straps of this brace with her teeth. It should allow me to walk with a crutch without reopening my chest wound."

"Oh, is that all ... too bad," I laugh, approaching the bed. I inspect the leather brace and strapping. It is quite ingenious. The crutch is held in place at the hip, relieving the pressure on the shoulder and arm, and thus, not adding undo stress to his chest injury.

"I came up with it myself," Eric boasts, proudly. "I can't wait to try it out."

"I'd like to talk to you, if I may," I say.

"Sure. You are welcome, friend." Eric motions for Raina to leave, which she does so, quickly, her head still bowed in shame.

"Do you know me, Eric?" I ask, as I have asked numerous times in the past.

"Yes. You are one of the men who fought with my brother and attended him while he died. I am grateful to you for that. Tell me, did he die well?"

"He did, Eric. He fought bravely and sacrificed himself to save his men. He was a true leader, and at the end, he gave no cry of fear or pain." I speak the truth about Olin, even though I know Eric has no affection for him.

"Well, then, I suppose his legacy shines even brighter – a glorious death to match his glorious life. Come, let us drink to my brother," Eric says.

I can't tell if he is being serious or facetious. I pour two cups of ale from a pitcher on the table.

"To Olin. May he live forever in Valhalla," toasts Eric.

"To Olin," I say, "a great man and leader of men. Long may he sit at the head of Odin's table."

Eric drains his cup, throws it down, and snatches the crutch beside the bed. "So, what would you have with me?" he asks as he straps on the crutch and struggles to his feet.

There are so many things I want to talk to him about, like where he was during the battle. I expected him to be at Olin's side, but he was not there. I want to know what happened at the Szczecin Lagoon, or if he had even gone there. I had assumed he was wounded there, but it occurs to me that no one actually mentioned the lagoon or a battle. Mostly, I want to know if he remembers any of our adventures together after the Battle of the Sees, adventures that are in my past, but may be in his future. 'How could he remember something that hasn't happened yet?' my mind interrupts. I am confounded.

"Do you remember the 'Clan of the Crescent Moon'?" I ask, not knowing what else to say. I pull the crescent shaped charm on the chain around my neck and display it.

"Of course," says Eric, doing the same.

I am completely overcome, my bewilderment spreading across my face like a sheet. Hanging on the chain next to the crescent charm is Andvaranaut, the cursed ring of Andvari taken from Högni's tomb. But how could he possess the ring? We have not yet been to the Savonian forest, or at least I don't think we have. I compose myself before asking, "That is an interesting ring. How did you come by it?"

"It was part of the Niflung Hoard," he says, holding it up, more to gaze upon it with his own eyes than to show it to mine. I procured it from Högni's tomb many years ago."

"How is that possible?" I ask, still trying to reconcile how something I believe will happen in the future has somehow already come to pass.

"Högni's tomb? The treasure? I assure you, both are real," explains Eric. "And I found it. Well, not just me ... I did have a little help from my shadow."

"What?" My head is spinning.

"My shadow. Oh, you probably know him better as Helsvein, the Drengr Røkkr, servant of Hel, destroyer of men, slayer of the Kraken, bane of the gods. I hear he joined the Battle of the Sees and slaughtered the Franks giving us a great victory. He and I found the tomb and the treasure."

"How long ago?" I ask, still trying to wrap my brain around what I am hearing.

"Seven ... no eight years," replies Eric.

I recognize the time. Eric first ventured into the Savonian Forest eight years ago. It was why I chose him to guide the expedition to acquire

Dainslief. He had been there before and knew the area. Now, he is telling me that, not only did he find Högni's tomb on that trip, but that I was with him.

"Do you know a man by the name of Asger Agnarson?" I ask.

"I've never heard that name before. Is he a friend or a foe?"

"He's nobody – just someone I met once who said he knew you. So, this man you speak of, Helsvein you called him, is he a friend of yours?"

"Do you not know Helsvein? He is the Drengr Røkkr, the Twilight Warrior. He is the most famous warrior of our age. His feats are legendary."

I am astonished to learn that I am so well known, a legend in my own time. Well, Helsvein is, anyway. "Well, I would surely like to meet your friend, Eric. How would I recognize him?"

"He carries an ancient sword – Dainslief – King Högni's enchanted sword, said to kill any man by the merest of scratches."

"You mean, this sword?" I ask, drawing Dainslief from its scabbard.

Eric is amazed. "SHADOW!" he cries out. Regaining his composure, he says, "It has been too long, my friend. Have you come to bring me good fortune?"

"I've come to find out why you were not with Olin in the battle," I say, ignoring the strangeness of this encounter for the moment.

"I was with King Dragowit of the Wends, ensuring payment for our services against the Franks," he says, smiling.

"And your injuries? How did you come by those?"

"Dragowit refused to pay. He escaped into the Szczecin Lagoon with our silver. I went after him. There was a brutal battle. The Wends are better fighters than we give them credit for. But, in the end, I secured our bounty. I even got a little extra ransoming Dragowit back to his people."

I had always known Eric to be daring, but this is simply out of character. True, he is a self-serving man of adventure, but not the sort that would betray an ally or engage in extortion. Not that those things were taboo to our culture, but rather, his honorable reputation means more to him, or at least, it did.

"You know, Andvaranaut is certainly powerful in filling a man's pockets, but it doesn't, as the legend says, create gold and silver. It merely helps a man find it," Eric says, sliding the ring and chain back under his tunic. "And, as yet, I have not been affected by its supposed curse."

"Curse? You were severely wounded – almost killed. You have lost most of your men. How can you say the curse has not affected you?" I ask.

"Because, in the end, I get what I want – riches, fame, women. Who wouldn't want to get everything they want?"

"But the way you acquire what you want is dishonorable," I say. "The Eric I know values his honor more than anything. As a Halverson, you should know your honor is the only thing that has true value. Olin understood that. Are you telling me you don't?"

"Yes ... well ... Olin is dead – killed by his honor. And now I will be jarl, so if you'll excuse me, Shadow, I must go to the Thing and represent my family. With that, he hobbles past me out the door without a backwards glance. I hear him clonking down the narrow, cobblestone hallway as shouts and screams of terror erupt from the room beyond. I almost knock Eric down as I run to the meeting hall where I catch a glimpse of a great, blue blur making a slaughterhouse of the olstafa.

CHAPTER TWENTY-FOUR

EAGLES

The eagle lay upon the ground, its wings folded, its head down. The great bird screeches and clamors, as if longing for a lost mate. Suddenly, it spreads wide its wings and takes flight, its cries growing shriller and more anguished, piercing the ears of all who bear witness. Blood runs down the eagle's legs and drips from its talons as it freezes in the air a few feet above the ground. It takes Gunner Agarson several minutes to die as he hangs from a post, his back split open and his lungs pulled out like wings.

A blood eagle execution is a rare thing, reserved for high-born traitors. I have never seen one, myself, but find it to be both grotesque and fascinating. Even as Gunner has been put to death for crimes he did not actually commit, I am not at all sad about his passing, as I have had a long-standing feud with his father and clan. Now, the only clan leader left is Eric Halvorsen, son of Jarl Halvorsen, all the others having either been killed in the mayhem that occurred at the Thing the night before or executed this morning. There are three other posts next to Gunner with the bodies of

172

Jarl Öster, Jarl Svendsen and Bjorn Jannic hanging on them, their ribs likewise cut away at the spine and their lungs pulled out like an eagle's wings.

Unlike last time, none of this was my doing. I did kill Jarl Agarson, removing his head during the initial melee as I had done before, but the rest of it played out without me. It was Fenrir that attacked the Thing, inflicting the exact injuries and deaths that had previously befallen the attendees. When I questioned him about it later, he said they were conspiring against Eric and his retainers, intending to eradicate the entire Halvorsen clan, those here in Peenemunde and the rest in Lagarvik when they returned home. Their reasons were sound; Eric had essentially stolen the bounty from King Dragowit that was intended to be divided among the clans in proportion to their contributions of men and material for the Battle of the Sees. But, as Fenrir has often reminded me, Eric is to be kept alive for some purpose that I have yet to discover.

Following the carnage at the Thing, fights broke out between the clans, each blaming the others for what had transpired, and several of them banding together to attack the Halvorsens. During the fighting, Stigr was mortally wounded, a death I am sure to mourn. Though Eric has become unrecognizably greedy and duplicitous, Stigr and his cousin Knute have not changed a bit, still making bets with each other and, in general, remaining very loyal and happy in spirit.

Eric was masterful in ending the squabbling before it took more lives. He put his knife to Jarl Öster's throat, threatening to cut it if the fighting did not stop. With the grave injury to Agarson, Öster had become merkis, the leading general, and commanded a great deal of respect from the men. Öster ordered everyone to stop and sheath their weapons, and the men complied without question.

"Now, it is true that I pursued Dragowit into the lagoon to procure our fortune," Eric announced, his blade pressed so hard against Öster's neck, blood began to trickle, "but I did not do this for my own enrichment. My brother, Olin, learned of a plot by some of the jarls to abscond with the bounty after the battle. For his part, Dragowit would gain some of the contested lands of the Obodrites, allies of the Franks, north of the Elde and west of the Warnow rivers and would occupy the forts being built there."

"Those forts are being built on the Elbe, not the Elde," decries Öster. Eric slips his blade a fraction, causing a slight gash to open on Öster's neck.

"We bleed with the Wends against our common enemy, yet our jarls and the Wendish king conspire against us to gain lands and deny us our payment," Eric continues.

There had been rumors that Dragowit had his own designs and was using the Frankish incursion as pretext to gain control of the eastern portion of the Obodrite territories, thus gaining complete control of the Baltic coast between Warnemunde and Peenemunde. From there, Dragowit could control navigation and trade in the southern Baltic, which would enrich him and the traitorous jarls that helped him. Eric had confirmed those rumors.

"Traitors! Tell us who they are!" shouted a few in the crowd.

"The traitors are the men you see before you, Jarl Öster, Jarl Svendsen, Bjorn Jannic, and Jarl Agarson's brother, Gunnar. Notice, all escaped the Thing unscathed, while the others perished. I was to be among the slain, but the killing started before I arrived. In fact, because I knew of the treachery, I was to be the main target."

The clansmen of the named jarls began grumbling about the lies Eric was spreading, but Eric reminded them the battle was turned by Olin's courage and what promised to be a rout became a great victory.

"Many of you who are here were meant to die on the battlefield to enrich our so-called leaders," Eric continued. "You all knew Olin to be the most honorable among us. He would not lie to me."

"Proof! We want proof!" came calls from the crowd.

I was not sure about Eric's claims, but if true, I had no doubt of the complicity of Öster, Svendsen, and Jannic. However, despite my personal animus toward the Agarsons, I knew they would never engage in such dealings. I was anxious to hear what proof Eric had.

"I have the proof right here," Eric said. "Bring them forth!"

Knute and two of his retainers stepped out from behind the livery, each dragging a man, bound and gagged. They lined the men up, holding their bound hands tightly behind their backs and removed their gags.

"You will recognize each of these men," Eric continued. "Trusted clansmen of those I have named. Now each will speak of the treachery of their jarls."

Knute pulled up hard on the first man's arms, and I hear a crack as his shoulders threaten to separate.

"I am Calder of the Jannic clan. I was sent by Bjorn Jannic to parlay with Dragowit for a larger portion of the bounty in violation of our agreement," said the man.

"I am Rangvald Svendsen, cousin to Jarl Svendsen and his femunirgaetir. I was sent to parlay with Dragowit for a larger portion of the bounty in violation of our agreement," said the second man, his arms likewise jerked upward. A silent gasp ran through the crowd. Being Jarl Svendsen's pursekeeper meant Rangvald was highly trusted. A man in that position would not likely turn on his clan leader unless he valued his own honor more than his loyalty to a corrupt jarl.

The third man, reluctant to speak until, with a distinct crack, the pressure exerted by Knute's retainer separated both shoulders, croaked, "I am Hjalmar, brother of Jarl Öster. I was sent to parlay with Dragowit for a larger portion of the bounty in violation of our agreement."

Jarl Öster yelled, "Lies", but was quickly silenced as Eric turned the tip of his knife swiftly upward, driving it through Öster's chin and severing his tongue. Noticeably absent was a representative of the Agarson clan, but Eric covered that by announcing that Agarson's man was killed in the fighting during the pursuit of Dragowit.

I reasoned that none of these men gave their confessions without coercion. One need only look upon each man's battered and bloodied face to know they made their rather repetitive admissions under duress. But what struck me was that none of these men chose death over dishonor, not even Rangvald Svendesn, which led me to believe that perhaps they were telling the truth about the deceit.

Denials rose from the Öster, Svendsen, Jannic, and Agarson clans, even as their leaders remained silent. Eric quickly ended the grumbling, saying, "Before we decide what to do with the traitors, I will give you that which you and your comrades have bled for."

Eric raised his hand and a few more of his men came forward with five satchels of silver, spilling them, one after another, upon the ground. "There are hundreds more satchels, and they belong to you."

I saw the men's eyes widen with greed. Clan loyalty was melting away as each satchel spilled its contents. Sensing what was happening, Bjorn Jannic and Jarl Svendsen began to loudly protest their innocence, but were quickly subdued and gagged by their own clansmen. Gunner Agarson remained silent, electing instead to throw an ax at Eric. Surprisingly accurate, the ax passed Jarl Öster's head and clipped Eric's ear, slicing it off as one would fillet a fish. Eric grabbed the side of his head, and, losing his balance, fell on his side. Öster stumbled forward where he was grabbed by several Norsemen and bound up.

The four, their hands and feet bound together in front of them, were tied face down to posts and the ritual execution performed. The men also wanted the accusers, Calder, Hjalmar, and Rangvald Svendsen executed for disloyalty, but Eric convinced them to set the three men adrift and let Aegir, the God of the Sea, decide their fate, just as he had done with me. Eric had successfully made himself merkis and purchased an army. His grave losses of men in the Szczecin Lagoon pursuing Dragowit would be forgotten.

As Knute and I bandage Eric's head, Knute offers to sew the ear back on. Eric refuses, saying that if an ear is all the vengeance the gods were allowing Gunner, then so be it. It isn't an outright admission of the Agarsons' innocence, but I take it as such. Of course, all may have been innocent, but as they are all dead now, it doesn't really matter. Death comes to everyone, eventually – everyone but me.

I follow Eric as he escorts the three accusers to their boat. It is filled with sixty satchels, a seemingly small price for their disloyalty, but a tidy sum which would afford them an excellent living in their exile. Calder is especially eager to get under way, thinking if he remains any longer, his clan may decide to kill him anyway. He need not have worried, for as his binds are being cut, Knute thrusts his knife into the back of Calder's neck, severing his cervical spine and killing him instantly. The others are quickly dispatched in the same way. The dead men are thrown into the skiff, tied to satchels, and set adrift. The skiff floats out into the bay and, having been scuttled prior to its departure, sinks to the bottom along with the bodies.

"That's a lot of silver to send to the bottom of the sea," I say.

"Rocks, Shadow. I'm not stupid," Eric says, smiling. "Though, I did leave each a penningr for their passage into Helheim."

"Hel doesn't collect tolls. She collects souls," I say.

"Well, you would know Helsvein. Now, let's go and drink ale and bed women. We leave tomorrow with my army."

The evening proves uneventful for me. After a good meal of mutton, brudet, and several cups of ale, I retire to the livery where Fenrir is staying out of sight. The survivors of the Thing are still wondering who may have conjured up the blardraugr, the blue demon, that attacked them. Many believe it was Jarl Svendsen, who was known to employ the services of seers on a regular basis. It is somewhat amusing, given his penchant for seeking foreknowledge, that he didn't know what was going to happen to him. But, then again, seers have a bad habit of speaking in riddles, so a person may not even recognize that a prophecy is coming to pass, especially a prophecy of their own death. I do wonder, though, how Fenrir intends to make the journey with Eric and I considering nearly everyone will try to kill him.

As I pass from drunkenness to sleep, I reflect on the day's events. Somehow, Eric, by manipulating the loyalties and avarices of the men, managed to gain control over all of them. Just as he had made blood eagles of his rivals, so Eric became an eagle himself, soaring higher than I could have imagined. It was, I understand now, pure theater. Eric had honed every detail, from the confessions of the accusers to the spilling of the silver. But how did he engage Fenrir to attack the Thing in the first place?

It was too well organized for him not to have known ahead of time what the Wolf-God would do, but he had absolutely no direct contact with Fenrir. Of that, I am sure. In fact, except for me, no one even knows of Fenrir's existence, let alone his presence in Peenemunde — at least not in this time. It is a mystery I need to solve. I want to think I am in control of my own destiny, but these recent events have me doubting that control, and possibly, my own sanity.

CHAPTER TWENTY-FIVE

KINGS AND KINGDOMS

A barren forest of birch trees gleams in the moonlight. Stripped bare of their branches and leaves, the destitute trunks sway in the gentle breeze while ghostly creatures devour them from the roots. Occasionally, you could see a sapling desperately clinging to its little plot of ground until a creature rips it up and spits it out to fly and tangle with its moribund parents. The sturdier ones are split and shredded and tossed into the black void of the forest floor. The stealth of our advance party is a wonder to behold as they cut the riggings and destroy the oars of forty ships at anchor in the strait and bays between the islands of Björkö and Adelsö.

I'd hoped to be home in Lagarvik, but Eric has other plans. With his army of nearly a thousand men, he sees an opportunity for more than fortune. By attacking the Swedes, and their most precious trading town of Birka on the Isle of Björkö, Eric will increase his reputation beyond anything anyone could have imagined. Östen Beli rules here as king, but is essentially a vassal to Randver, the king of the Danes. From his stronghold

180

in Hovgarden on the Isle of Adelsö, Beli has amassed quite a fortune in the fur trade and has a trading network that extends deep into the Rusland and south to the Byzantine Empire and the riches of the East.

This kingdom, if you could call it that, lies in the northern fringes of the lands claimed by the Yngling kings, the lineage of which is mostly of the Skilfingar clan. It is loosely bordered by the Kvens to the north and east and the Geats to the south. Of course, clan vendetta, tribal fighting, and battles with neighbors make the area practically ungovernable, just as it has been for hundreds of generations. Kings and kingdoms rise and fall like the tides. Not even Randver can exercise complete control here, settling instead for an annual tribute that allows his vassals to rule on his behalf. However, silver is power, and Östen Beli has enough to challenge the Yngling dynasty, something that no one has done with any measurable success in five hundred years.

I question the wisdom of such a venture, but I have come along at Eric's request. I feel I owe him an allegiance for at least one expedition, given that he guided me to Högni's tomb, though his memory of the adventure differs from my own. Had I known how bold an attack he was planning, I may have declined and just gone home as I still so desire to do.

Fenrir, or Blardraugr as he is now known, has come along too, caged as a prize and a symbol of Eric's power. The cage, of course, is useless, but Fenrir is being a sport about it and staying put, at least for now. Eric must figure very heavily into Hel's plans if Fenrir is willing suffer this humiliation. I am still quite surprised that he agreed, thinking he would rather finish what he started at the Thing than be thrown into a cage. He also prefers his new name to Blarulf, which he constantly reminds me was moronic and unimaginative. He may be right; Blue Demon does seem to be more intimidating and aligns better with his true nature.

Having disabled most of the fleet of Beli's ships, and commandeering several others, we make landfall south of Birka and begin our journey toward the town on foot. Eric left a few of our ships, fully manned, just outside the bay to catch any trading knarrs trying to leave and to intercept any armed vessels that may try to cut off our escape.

"Is it wise to leave so many of our men at oars?" I ask, as we claw our way through the dark birch forest toward our objective. "I would think we may need our full complement of men for the raid."

"You needn't worry about that, Shadow. I know exactly what we will be up against," Eric replies. His absolute confidence puts my mind at ease. Not that I am worried for my life, but many of these men are my friends, and though they know me only as Helsvein, the Drengr Røkkr, I would not like to see them slaughtered in another of Eric's glory-seeking follies.

The attack begins at daybreak. We enter the town unopposed and begin ransacking the wharf houses along the docks. Several men break off into the town and begin terrorizing the residents, killing the men, raping and killing the women. There is very little resistance. A small garrison of soldiers is quickly cut down, and the armed townsmen are no match for our seasoned fighters. The amount of pilferage we acquire is beyond comprehension. I haven't seen a pile of treasure this high since the Niflung Hoard. Strangely, there is a distinct absence of silver and gold. Not that there wasn't some, but I expected to see much more.

One boat in the bay that was untouched by the early morning vandalism attempts an escape. One of our ships runs down the knarr, executing the crew and scuttling the ship. From what I could tell, they took no booty before sending the ship to the bottom of the bay.

"You may need a few more ships," I tell Eric. "I think we may have crippled too many."

"I don't need any more ships," Eric says. He is keeping his plans very much to himself. I could ask Knute if he knows fully what Eric is planning, but he has been made captain of the offshore fleet. I suspect, though, were he here, he would tell me he doesn't know either.

Eric gives orders to have several of the derelict ships set ablaze. As well, he orders the town to be fired, the smoke column of which will be visible for miles. I am dumbfounded. Eric has cut off our escape route through the town and made the bay a dangerous inferno to navigate. Whatever he is planning, it will happen right here in the harbor of Birka.

The remainder of the townsfolk is gathered at the docks, bound, and placed into a few of the boats still seaworthy. Barrels of seal oil are loaded into the boat with them, the contents of a few being emptied into the hull, drenching the terrified people. Eric is making fireships, but I don't know why. We have captured and burned the town and there is no opposing fleet to block our escape.

"So, what do we do now?" I ask.

"We wait, Shadow. We wait," answers Eric, a crisp, thin smile crossing his face.

Morning passes into afternoon, the choking smoke of the fires burning my eyes and throat. I walk with Eric to the furthest point of the peninsula that forms a natural jetty for the harbor. From here, the air is clearer, and, at a distance, I can make out the shoreline of Adelsö. Sails, dozens of them, sprout from the horizon like wheat, growing ever larger as they approach Birka.

"It seems I finally got Östen Beli's attention," Eric speaks in almost a whisper.

"So, your plan is to lure Östen Beli into a battle?" I ask, amazed. "But why? We have more than enough riches from Birka, as well as, the recompense from Dragowit. You are, as of this moment, the wealthiest man in the north, if not, the world."

"I told you a long time ago, Shadow – it isn't about wealth. With Andvaranaut, wealth is easy. I have made and lost a dozen fortunes since last we met in the Savonian Forest. This is about power and who is daring enough to seize it."

"You're insane. Regardless of his extraordinary wealth, Beli is still a vassal of Randver, who may see this raid as an attack on him," I say.

"Who do you think sent me?"

"King Randver commissioned you for this?" I am awestruck. Lagarvik is not part of Randver's Danish empire, having fought against the Yngling's for generations, despite some of our jarls having Skilfingar ancestors. Even so, we also pay tribute for passage to the east through the Kattegat Sea and the Danish Straits. That Eric would enter into a pact with Randver, one where Eric accepts all the risk and the Danes profit by avoiding an insurrection in their northern territory makes no sense to me at all.

"Well, not Randver, but Sigurd, his son," Eric replies.

"Sigurd Hringr!? Sigurd the Jarnhringr, the Iron Ring. What do either of you stand to gain by this?"

"Much," says Eric, amused by my astonishment. "We've been planning this for years. We just had to wait for the right time."

"And what makes this the right time, Eric?"

"There are two things, actually. First, I needed an army large enough to pull off this raid, one that Sigurd, for political reasons, could not give me. I had tried several times in the past, but something always happened that wrecked my plans. I had the money to buy men, but Olin had the respect and ability to lead them into battle. In the end, loyalty to Olin always won out over riches. They would rather die for him than fight for me – regardless of the profit. I tried several times, unsuccessfully, to get Olin to help me, to be my merkis, but he refused. Our father thought it was a bad idea, and Olin would never go against our father. Now, with Olin gone and my exposure of the 'traitors', the men trust me to lead them. That, and I handed them, literally, a king's ransom in silver."

The way Eric says 'traitors' makes my blood run cold. Though I had thought about it many times, I'd never confronted him about the veracity of his accusations. "So, the men we executed were not actually traitors?"

"Oh, they were traitors. Every one of them, except Agarson, retreated from the Battle of the Sees when they thought we were losing. They left while many of the clans were still engaged. They left my brother to die. They even left many of their own to die. I wasn't lying about that. Surely, they didn't make separate arrangements with Dragowit, but Dragowit had no intention of paying the silver he owed us. I did what I needed to do to ensure our bounty, for the lives lost, and for the future of our people."

"How do you know this? You were not at the battle."

"No, but Stigr was. He was standing beside my brother when the Franks threatened a rout. Olin sent him from the battlefield to find me, to bring up reinforcements. Of course, I was in pursuit of Dragowit, so there were no reinforcements. But I guess they weren't needed after all. If my brother didn't send him, Stigr probably would have fallen in battle and been received into Valhalla. Instead, he was killed in an unnecessary melee – not the most honorable death. Certainly, not one that would warrant a place at Odin's table."

"I grieve his passing, too, but Stigr was a true warrior, and I'm sure his eternity will not be spent in Helheim."

"Well, I would hope that being Hel's servant, you would be in a position to ensure he doesn't."

"It doesn't work that way, but I'll see what I can do." I peer into Eric's eyes, but I see no true feeling of loss. It is as if Stigr is a necessary casualty for a bigger gain, albeit a regrettable one. "So, you admit the Agarson's stayed on the field. Gunnar was innocent."

"Yes, but I needed the Agarsons gone. I could have no rival for my leadership. Besides, I saw you slit the jarl's throat as he lay wounded. You didn't even give him his sword so that he would die honorably. Perhaps he and Stigr are together in Helheim cursing the both of us."

"Perhaps," I say, pensively. We stand a long moment, watching the approach of Östen Beli's armada. "You said there were two things."

"Hmm?," says Eric.

"Two things that make this the right time. The first is your army. What is the other?"

Eric pauses and turns toward me. "The other? ... You."

Eric locks his eyes on mine, staring into me and through me, as if he is trying to figure out who I am – not the Twilight Warrior, but who I truly am. I can tell there is a glimmer of recognition beyond our shared experience, beyond his believing me to be his shadow of fortune. But that glimmer is shrouded in a fog denser than that upon a fjord on a crisp spring morning. He will never know me. Even if I were to use my bargain with Hel to allow Eric to know me as Asger Agnarson, which of course I wouldn't, he will never truly recognize me because I am no longer Asger Agnarson. I am Helsvein, the Drengr Røkkr. Only now, do I finally accept that I will forever be a mystery to my best friend, nothing more than a forgotten memory, or rather, the shadow of a forgotten memory that never truly existed.

"They're getting close," says Eric. "Come, Shadow. Let's go win me a kingdom."

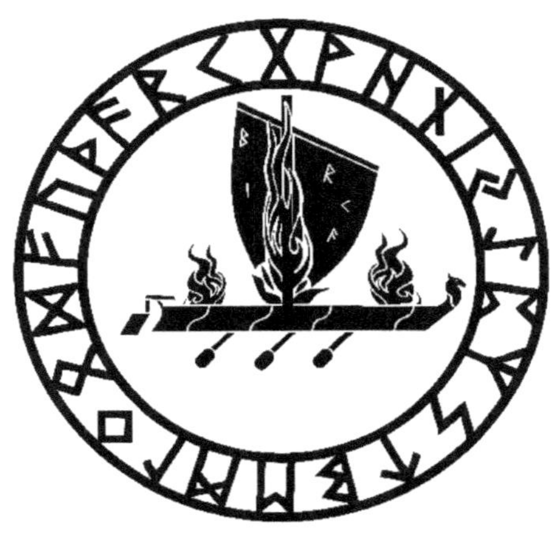

CHAPTER TWENTY-SIX

THE BATTLE OF BIRKA

The choking, swirling darkness of Muspelheim envelops us as we prepare for Surtr's arrival. We light our torches and send them spinning toward the pit, their brilliance dying until all that is left is a sheen of candlelight reflected by the obsidian. From the pitch, flames explode in orange and yellow, illuminating the forms of a dozen dragons pulling a chariot with Surtr standing high in it, hurling fireballs at us. Our fireships are finding some targets but have failed to set ablaze the massive platforms drawn by Östen Beli's drakkar longships and bearing his ballistae and mangonel catapults.

The battle does not seem to be going according to Eric's plan. Our offshore fleet is engaging with Beli's ships, but there are just too many of them. I think Eric has underestimated the size of Beli's forces and just how many he would deploy against us. We hold our lines along the docks, but the fireballs and bolts from the siege platforms are taking a toll on us. Several of Beli's ships split off and make land on the peninsula where Eric

188

and I stood watching only minutes before. Eric has put his army on desperate ground with a large enemy force to our front and the town of Birka, now an impassible inferno, to our rear.

"They're landing on the peninsula. We need to hold them to the narrows where their superior numbers will be negated," I tell Eric. "It's high tide, so the narrowest part of the peninsula is only wide enough for maybe forty men, shoulder to shoulder. We can form a shield wall and hold them there. I'll take the lead. I can wreak havoc in their ranks while they try to break through."

"My men can hold them. I need you here," Eric responds, dispatching a hundred and fifty men to the peninsula.

I do not doubt the steel of these men, but I am not sure a hundred and fifty men will be enough against a host three times that size. The sheer pushing force of that many men will drive back and crush the shield wall as a dominant elk buck would drive off a younger, leaner rival. When the clash comes, I am impressed by how well the wall holds, but it is only a matter of time before the force of the enemy becomes too much to bear.

I think it would be better to have Fenrir here. He would give us quite an edge against the landing of Beli's forces, and he may have been able to silence the ballistae and mangonels, leaping from ship to ship as he had done in the Szczecin Lagoon. Instead, Eric has left him caged on one of the offshore ships. I can't understand the logic of keeping our best weapon out of the fight. Not that I view Fenrir as a weapon, but I am sure that is how Eric sees him. I don't think Eric trusts that Fenrir would attack Beli's forces instead of his own. Of course, Eric may have thought differently about his strategy had he been aware of my bond with the one he calls Blardraugr, but the Wolf-God made me promise to be silent about that.

Östen Beli's flagship, its bowpiece bearing an image of Freyr upon his boar, is the first to make a landing, crashing into the boardwalk between two docks. The force of the collision throws some of his men into the water, but they recover quickly and come ashore, forming a shield wall and awaiting their comrades who are only a minute behind. The sight of that bowpiece emerging from the smoke and flame triggers the memory of my hensbane visions, though it appears that both god and jötunn have allied against us rather than fight each other.

"READY! STAND!" shouts Eric as the rest of the enemy fleet hits the docks and begins to disembark. I draw Dainslief and attack from the flank as the mass of Beli's soldiers crashes into our shield wall. From behind our wall, a hail of flaming clay jars filled with seal oil are thrown, reigning down on the enemy and setting men and ships afire. We are outnumbered ten to one. Even I cannot kill fast enough to stifle the assault. Eric is completely unfazed by the direction the battle is going. He is standing atop a wharf shed, overseeing the battle and directing groups of men to shore up gaps in the line.

I glance out on the peninsula, and our men there have been driven back almost to the docks. That part of the peninsula is much wider, so our wall is now thinly stretched across it. The men are retreating in stages, a few yards at a time. When the wall finally fails, our men break for the docks down a narrow beach and form a semi-circle on our flank, with the water to one side and a large warehouse to the other. We are now hemmed in by Beli's main force to our front and the forces from the peninsula to our left flank. I hack and kill like a madman, suffering grievous injuries that heal instantly, but I can tell something is different this time. Where in past battles my immortality had the effect of destroying the enemy's spirit, the morale of the Swedes is not so easily broken. These men are well-trained and have absolutely no fear. I hope that whatever surprise Eric has in mind, if he has one, he springs it now.

Eric lifts his crutch above his head. Attached to it is a large red flag which he begins waving back and forth, as if signaling someone in the distance. I drive my way onto an enemy drakkar where men are still trying to disembark and cut my way to the stern. From there I see who Eric is waving to. Knute and a handful of men are sailing their longship straight into the rear of the enemy. What's more, Fenrir's cage is resting in the bow. When they are close enough, Knute pulls the pin on the cage door, and he and his crew jump overboard.

Fenrir bursts from his prison with a ferocity I have never seen. He tears into Beli's forces, ravaging dozens of men before they even realize what is happening. At the same time, the wall of the warehouse on our flank is broken down and a river of seal oil pours down on Beli's men from the peninsula. More flaming clay jars are hurled into the river and the entire enemy host is consumed in a conflagration reminiscent of the funeral pyres of Ironwood.

The battle lost, Östen Beli retreats to his flagship with several dozen of his men. Others follow and soon, the remnants of Beli's army are pulling away. A resounding cheer goes up from our men, but Eric is screaming in anger.

"Don't let Beli escape! Go after him!" Eric yells, but his voice is barely heard above the din of the roaring fires and the victory celebration of his troops. Several dozen men climb onto the few seaworthy ships remaining to make pursuit, but it is clear they will not catch Östen Beli. As well, the offshore fleet, having been decimated in their sea battle, are not able to intercept.

It seems, for all the effort and loss of life, Eric did not win this battle decisively. In the end, I think the Swede numbers were just too massive to overcome with such a small force, even one made of men as seasoned and disciplined as ours. Is this raid really all for naught? Our haul of spoils from the town of Birka would certainly indicate success, but that was never the purpose of Eric coming here. He came here to destroy Östen Beli and seize his kingdom. On that account, Eric has failed.

The fires burn into the night as we take an accounting of our losses. From the fierceness of the fighting, I expect casualties to be high. Surprisingly, they are not. Of the six hundred men Eric brought ashore on Björkö, only sixty or so have been killed, with another hundred wounded. Given the forces arrayed against us, I think we are lucky to have not lost a third or even half of our men. I search for Fenrir among the ruins of the docks and town, but he is nowhere to be found.

"Are you looking for your dog, Helsvein?" Eric asks.

"My ... my dog?" I am taken aback by Eric's question. I did not think he knew of my relationship with Fenrir.

"Blardraugr. He is yours, is he not?"

"Uh ... no. He is his own. How did you know about us?"

"Well, I had my suspicions, and you just confirmed them."

"But how did you suspect?"

"Well, it wasn't hard to determine you two were working together, Shadow. You suddenly appear, after years of absence, and at the same time, a great beast also appears and clears my path for this," Eric says, waving his arm in a circle, laying claim to the destruction. Besides, a monster like that would not have remained caged for very long unless someone could coax him to do so."

"That is true, but if you knew, why didn't you just ask me?"

"Well, you are the Drengr Røkkr. I figure if you are keeping secrets from me, you must have a good reason."

"That is true as well," I say. "Blardraugr and I have a complicated relationship. It is not so much that we work together as that we are bound to one another."

"You know, the best working relationships are forged by necessity," says Eric.

"That's a bit too profound coming from you, Eric," I laugh.

"I have my moments," Eric chuckles. Taking a more serious note, he adds, "You did well today, Helsvein. I couldn't have done this without you. The men fought exceptionally well, not because I was leading them, but because they wanted to prove their mettle fighting beside the Twilight Warrior. They may have faltered had you not been here."

"I'm sorry you didn't win your kingdom, today. I guess the gods had other plans," I say, laying my hand on Eric's shoulder.

"Oh, but I did!"

"I don't understand."

"Svitjod was never the kingdom I was after. They already have a king – Randver, or rather, Sigurd, when he takes his father's place. This battle was simply to pave the way for Sigurd's ascendancy. Surely, it would have been better to capture or kill Östen Beli, but it wasn't a necessity. Sigurd can finish the job himself. I just needed to weaken Beli so he wouldn't be a threat. I have done that."

"Why didn't the Jarnhringr just do this himself? Why did he commission you for it?"

"Like I said before – politics."

"And you think you've weakened him enough?"

"Oh, I am sure of it," Eric says, smiling that deviously thin smile again. I look at him inquisitively. I know he wants to tell me; he's just drawing it out for dramatic effect. It is part of Eric's charm, I suppose, but sometimes it can be annoying. "While Östen Beli was engaged with us, Knute sent some of our ships to Adelsö. We raided Beli's stronghold at Hovgarden. It was completely unprotected. We took everything."

"Birka was a diversion?" I am aghast at the sheer audaciousness of the plan. "And you split your forces three times?"

"Yes. Splitting my forces was the risky part. I wasn't totally sure it would work," Eric answers, his eyes staring blankly as he contemplates the outcome had it not worked. "But, you know, I did have some help. There were certain individuals here in Birka that could be persuaded to assist us for a price. Like the warehouse – that trap has been sitting there ready to be sprung for nearly a year. And, of course, there were people in Hovgarden as well."

"Who knew what you were planning?"

"No one knew all of it, not even Knute. Everyone knew their part. That's all they needed to know. Still, you were right, Shadow. I should have had more men. Beli would not have escaped, then. But I figured you and Blardraugr may be worth three hundred men or more. Turns out, you were only worth about two hundred," Eric chuckles.

"Two hundred?" I laugh. "I think more if you would have let me go up the peninsula."

"No. I needed Beli to think he was winning. Otherwise, he might have."

"So how much did we take?"

"Remember the Niflung Hoard? Not quite that much, but we will be able to bring it all home this time."

"And how much does Sigurd the Jarnhringr get?"

"Half. And in return, I get my kingdom – Raumarike – with no annual tribute while I live and no payment for passage through the Danish straits. And since my family controls a substantial part of Vestfold as well, I shall rule over a sizable kingdom."

"That is impressive. You have truly made quite a reputation for yourself. Skalds will tell your stories for centuries. And, you may not know this, Eric, but my wife is from Raumarike," I say.

"I didn't even know you were married, Shadow. But that is something we have in common. My wife also hails from Raumarike. It's why I want it so badly. I want it for her."

So now I understand why Eric is so important to Hel and Fenrir. The separation of Raumarike and Vestfold is something discussed in the ancient stories. According to prophecy, the gods of the Aesir lay claim to Vestfold, while the gods of the Vanir lay claim to Raumarike. That Eric will unify both under a single kingdom can only bring the Aesir into conflict with the Vanir. As long as they are fighting each other, they won't be bothered to interfere in the affairs of the children of Angrboda. I am beginning to understand Hel's plan and what role Eric plays in it. I will also have a role to play, but will it be the role Hel intends for me, or will it be a role I choose for myself.

CHAPTER TWENTY-SEVEN

THE SPECTER

Deep in a forest on the Isle of Eysysla, we encounter Heimdallr, Guardian of the Bifrost, keeping watch with his nine eyes, one for each of the mothers that bore him. To see him in this form is rare indeed, as he usually travels Midgard in the guise of Rig, spreading his seed among humankind. It has long been rumored that the Rainbow Bridge makes its earthy connection here, but few ever venture into this wood and live to tell the tale. We make camp among the nine Lakes of Kaali, each a near perfect circle, awaiting Sigurd Hringr, the Iron Ring.

Why Eric has chosen this spot, I do not know. Perhaps he hopes the stories of this place will cause Jarnhringr to behave himself. Though Eric has made a deal with him he clearly doesn't trust him or else this transaction would be taking place in Kattegat. Perhaps he is right; Sigurd Hringr does have a reputation, and in the presence of this much treasure, may become a bit too greedy. At least here, on neutral ground said to be in the realm of the gods, Sigurd may think before he acts. A betrayal in plain sight of Odin

196

and the Aesir would cost him his place in Valhalla and doom him to the darkest pit of Helheim.

"Where is Blardraugr?" asks Eric. Fenrir had sailed with Knute upon a trading knarr laden with pilfered silver and gold, uncaged this time as a defense against piracy. But since our arrival, he has disappeared. For some reason I cannot fathom, Knute has no fear of Fenrir, and the Wolf-God seems to like him, too.

"Roaming the woods looking for food, I should guess," I answer. "This island is a well-known den of brigands and malcontents. Fen ... ha haak ... Blardraugr has a real appetite for that sort." I almost said Fenrir's name but covered my mistake with a laughing cough.

"Well, better he gets his fill of them than turn on us," Eric laughs. "When Jarnhringr arrives, I want you to be ready. I suspect he may not honor our arrangement."

"Why wouldn't he? You've done your part. Sigurd would not risk a war. His father wouldn't want that."

"His father doesn't know about this. And Randver may be dead soon, anyway, so all the better to keep these proceedings hidden from view, lest one of Sigurd's kin seize an opportunity."

"Sigurd is going to kill his father?" I ask, astounded by the revelation.

"I do not think so, but maybe. Either he or Randver's brother, Harald Wartooth."

"I would not believe than any of Randver's blood would do him harm."

"Nor would I, but a seidr once told me that 'upon the king's death, there will rise two thrones, one of iron, the other of stone; the iron throne, you should mistrust, lest the throne of stone be crushed'," Eric says, his eyes glowing with belief.

"Ahh!" I laugh. "Sigurd the Jarnhringr, the Iron Ring ... the iron throne, and you, Eric Halvorsen, Halvorsen being the Defender of the Stone. That is very lyrical for a seidr. But since when do you put any stock in the musings of a magician? You've never believed in that nonsense, even though you were once accused of being one yourself."

"When was I accused?" Eric asks, angrily.

I keep forgetting Eric does not remember certain things from our past, like our escape from Peenemunde. "I heard some of the Swede captives talking about you. They were sure you must be a seidr. They had no other explanation for your victory in Birka," I lie.

"Well, I can tell you, I was very skeptical of the seidr I spoke with. But, as he sought me out, rather than I go to him, I listened to what he had to say. Many of his tellings have come to pass, like this," Eric says, holding his chain with the cursed ring. "The seidr told me I would acquire Andvaranaut, and with it, my destiny."

"Seidrmen are very good at talking about destiny. I met one once who told me I could make my own destiny. Yet, here I am, somehow tied to yours."

"Our destinies are intertwined, Shadow. Do you not see that? You could no more make your own destiny as I could swallow the sea."

"It is strange you should say that. I remember a time when you tried to swallow the sea. You claimed you were greater than Thor. It happened very near here, across the strait, on Dago."

"I've never been to Dago. You are odd, Helsvein. You seem to live in a dream where things are not as you think them to be. But, as you are my Shadow, I owe you my fortune, and for that I am grateful. Now, you must help me once again to keep that which I have won. When Sigurd comes, you must be ready."

After two days of waiting, Sigurd Hringr finally makes his appearance. He has with him a thousand men, which would be more than enough to subdue Eric's forces were it not for the presence of Fenrir and myself. Thankfully, Sigurd is not inclined to fight for his treasure and has brought a host of Danes to ensure he doesn't have to.

As the two groups of soldiers bond over ale and meat, Eric and Sigurd retire to a tent. I linger outside, at Eric's request, keeping my ears open and my sword at the ready. I admit, I am impressed by Sigurd the Iron Ring. He is, surprisingly, quite young to have earned such a reputation, but given who his father is, I guess it is to be expected. I listen to the negotiations, the tallying and division of the riches, the expectations of peace, prosperity, and mutual trust, and the understanding that Eric will have sole reign over his dominion along with freedom of navigation. Sigurd seems very happy to give Eric all he asks, but something in his tone belies his amenability. Perhaps Eric's suspicions are well founded.

A few hours pass, and the two men conclude their business. Sigurd emerges from the tent, his face stoic as his men inquire about the discussion. I note his fleeting glance to the specter of a man standing at the edge of our encampment, who then disappears into the darkness of the woods. I check inside the tent and see Eric, Knute, and two others of Eric's inner circle, drinking and laughing, as they believe they have accomplished what they set out to do.

I decide to follow the specter into the forest, but I cannot see where he has gone. Every one of my senses is telling me that something is amiss. Perhaps he is an assassin. Should I return to camp and protect Eric? I am not sure. Eric's tent is in the middle of the camp surrounded by his men.

Could an assassin even get close to Eric? I think not, so I continue circling the camp, keeping in the shadows, searching for the unknown man.

Near daybreak, Sigurd's men, some still drunk, begin to filter out of camp. There is some commotion, and a fight breaks out. Axes and swords are drawn, but Knute steps in, and Eric's men return their weapons to their belts. With a stern look from Knute, Sigurd's men do the same, clearly not wanting to test Knute's reputed ability to cut down a dozen men without breaking a sweat. My attention having been drawn away briefly by the excitement, I do not notice the specter enter Eric's tent. I realize my mistake too late. Eric emerges from his tent, a dagger held to his throat.

"Helsvein!" calls the specter. "I have your captain. Surrender to us, and he will not be harmed."

I run toward Eric, Dainslief drawn and ready for blood. The specter stops me in my tracks, slicing a gash into Eric's neck, not a fatal cut, but deliberately and expertly applied to get my attention.

"Sheathe your sword, Helsvein," the specter says calmly.

Eric mouths the words 'Kill him'. I am inclined to do just that. A mere scratch from Dainslief is all it would take, but the specter is clearly capable of killing Eric before dying himself. I return Dainslief to my belt and am immediately apprehended by several men, forced to my knees, and bound in chains. Knute and others rush to assist, but Eric waves them off with a glance.

"We will only take that which has been agreed to," says Sigurd, strolling up to us. "Eric Halvorsen will be free to go and become the King of Raumarike, taking with him his share of the spoils from Birka. All we ask is that you allow us to return to our ships with our share of the bounty ... and the Twilight Warrior. He is not worth your blood, so do not shed it for him."

I can see the men, their hands twitching on the hilts of their weapons, waiting for Eric to give the command. Knute, in particular, has already murdered dozens of Sigurd's soldiers in his mind, but Eric remains steadfast in his unspoken orders to stand down. I look deep into Eric's eyes, searching for a sign of betrayal. He is not the same person I knew as a boy, not the same man I knew before we parted ways after finding the Niflung Hoard. Could he have made me part of his bargain with Sigurd? Would he really put on this show just to make me think he had nothing to do with it? Or is he trying to save face with his men, who would surely rebel if they knew he had sold out the Drengr Røkkr to Sigurd the Jarnhringr? I search, but I cannot see deceit in his face. Then again, Eric is a master when it comes to deception.

As I am dragged away to Sigurd's drakkar longship, I expect Fenrir, at any moment, to jump from the thicket and lay waste to the men holding me prisoner, but he does not. I am secured in the bow, tied hand and foot to the dragon bowpiece. Sigurd takes Dainslief. I am sure he would like to test it on someone, but for the moment, he straps it to his waistband and leaves it sheathed.

The specter brings Eric to the shore and holds him there until all but one of the ships, overflowing with treasure, disembarks. He releases Eric and jumps onto the final ship, which follows the others. Eric raises his hand to staunch the bleeding from his neck and stares at me from the shore, a thin devious smile crossing his lips.

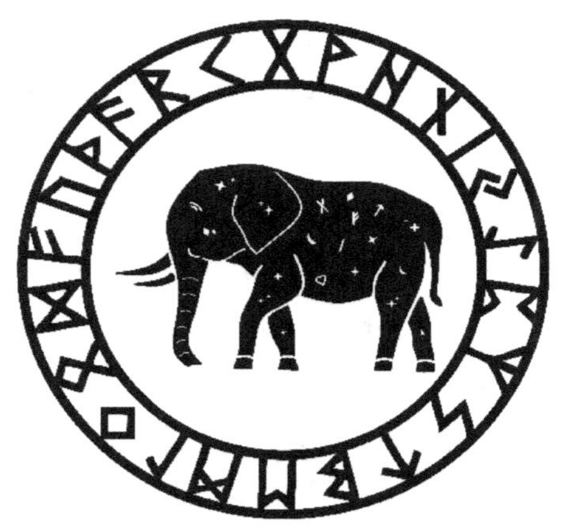

CHAPTER TWENTY-EIGHT

GIFTS OF GLASS

A solitary dragon mystically appears on the horizon, soaring low over the sea, driven by vengeance. It is no ordinary dragon, for it carries a rider, a jötunn impatiently pacing the creature's back, spurring it onward. The dragon closes on our flotilla at great speed, its rider now abreast the beast's shoulders, his hedinn cloak of shocking blue brushed back by the wind. The Danes ready themselves for battle as the drakkar longship approaches, bearing the Wolf-God, Fenrir.

Just before impact, I note that there is no sail set, nor oarsmen driving the ship. It is as if Fenrir, by power of will, is propelling the drakkar on its deadly course. Fenrir's ship strikes mine amidships, savagely breaking its spine and cleaving it in two. Danes are thrown into the air by the collision and fall like stones into the sea, their armor and heavy clothing dragging them to the bottom. Still chained to the bowpiece, I am drawn over as the broken ship capsizes and see a river of bright rainbow colors pass beneath me just below the surface. The children of Angrboda have come, Fenrir

202

and Jörmungandr honoring their commitment to me.

Unable to break my chains, I languish in the bobbing bow watching Fenrir ravage one Danish drakkar after another. Jörmungandr, as well, is heaving his mighty body upward, breaking the backs of several ships and drowning their crews. Somehow, Sigurd Hringr has survived and is pulled aboard an undamaged longship. Fenrir jumps aboard the same, tearing through Danes like a scythe until he comes face to face with the Jarnhringr. Sigurd draws Dainslief and slashes down on the Wolf-God's head. Strangely, the blade impacts heavily on Fenrir's nose before melting away and leaving no mark. The blow is sufficient to stun Fenrir, who steps backward shaking his great head to regain his faculties. Rather than risk another strike, the blue wolf leaps to another ship and clears it of Danes.

Jörmungandr comes up beneath me, lifting my wreck out of the water on his back. The top of his great head emerges from the waves, his pearly eye flashing a few meters from me.

"I am chained, Great One," I say. Jörmungandr's head retreats gently beneath the sea. A moment later, his tail breaks the surface and smashes down on the wreck resting on his back like a blacksmith's hammer striking an anvil. The longship is reduced to splinters in an instant, and I find myself sitting on Jörmungandr, unscathed by the precision of the World-Serpent's strike.

Jörmungandr swims alongside the drakkar where Fenrir sits, exhausted from the combat. I jump aboard and the serpent begins pushing us away from what is left of Sigurd's fleet.

"My sword! Dainslief! The Iron Ring still has it. We must go back," I say. The longship whips around so quickly that it almost capsizes. Fenrir and I barely manage to remain in the boat. Our ship pulls gently alongside Sigurd's, where he is the only one still alive. I step over the gunwale and board his ship.

"I believe you have something that belongs to me," I say softly. Sigurd, his face etched with rage, strikes at me. Dainslief melts away, refusing to penetrate my body. He thrusts again and again, but he cannot touch me.

I hold out my hand. "My sword?"

Sigurd, beaten and confused, relinquishes my weapon. I have a mind to strike him dead for what he has tried to do, but Hel suddenly appears behind him, her beauty radiating and staying my hand.

"Sigurd must live. He is important to us," she says, her words becoming gulls that flit about the ship.

"I don't care," I say in defiance.

"You mustn't, for all our sakes, including yours and your family's," says Hel. I see a pleading glint in her eye, but I am not sure if it is real. She could be using my wife and children against me to force me to comply.

"I am at your mercy, Helsvein," says Sigurd, the anger melting from his face. "I should never have tried to capture the Drengr Røkkr. I should have known that a warrior of your renown would have the gods at your side. My father has often told me that my brashness will be my undoing, and now it has come to pass."

His words ring of truth and honor, which is surprising, given his reputation. I lower my sword and look him in the eye. "Did Eric Halvorsen have anything to do with this?"

Sigurd's eyes tell me his answer before he speaks. "Why would he?"

"You do not know him as I do. He is ambitious and not very trusting."

"Then, why do you help him? You could do anything. You could defeat the gods themselves if you dared. Why would you waste your time with the likes of Eric Halvorsen?"

I resist the urge to brag that I have already defeated Thor and Aegir in battle and taken Tyr's hand as well. "I cannot say. He is important to my destiny, so I help him with his. And you, Sigurd the Jarnhringr are also important to my destiny, so I will let you live. But you must honor your commitment to Eric." Hel gives me a slight, thanking smile and disappears.

"I will, Helsvein." Sigurd Hringr looks at the dead men lying in his boat and wrecked vessels around him. Then he looks back at me, his eyes asking a silent question.

"No. They will not go to Valhalla," I say. "Hel has already collected them."

Sigurd sits down in his ship, putting his hands to his head. He has lost almost a third of his men, ships, and treasure. It is the price he paid for his treachery. I daresay he will be more prudent in the future. He is an impressive young man, and once he learns to temper his arrogance, as this escapade seems to have, he is destined to do great things

I return to my ship and am whisked away by a fast-moving wave rolling off the back of Jörmungandr.

"How did you end up in a drakkar by yourself," I ask Fenrir.

"Knute. Soon after we arrived, he and a few others took out two ships. They left me on one and rowed back in the other. Eric's mistrust of Sigurd Hringr seems to have been well founded."

"And you went along with it? I know how much you hate the sea. You could have stopped him on the island, you know."

"True, but Eric did not know exactly what Sigurd had planned. Besides, out here in the middle of the sea, Eric's hands are clean."

"But what if Sigurd had tried something on Eysysla. Suppose he decided to fight Eric for the booty."

"Then you would have stopped him. There was no need for both of us to be there. And, judging from the way it turned out, Eric was smart to deploy us this way. I never would have imagined it would be you who was captured," Fenrir chuckles.

"Well, you would know all about being captured," I retort.

"BY A KRAKEN!" Fenrir declares in mock offense.

One final push from the World-Serpent and Fenrir and I are hurled onto the beach, our drakkar running nearly halfway aground. The men assembled on the shore loading supplies and treasure into Eric's ships scatter as Fenrir jumps from our boat. Knute strides up to Fenrir, scruffs him on the head, and shouts "Well done, Blardraugr!"

I nearly fall out of the boat at the spectacle. I would never deign to pat the Wolf-God on the head, lest he try to take my hand off. I give a sideways glance at Fenrir who returns a look saying, "Are you jealous?"

I approach Eric, who is speaking with a few men next to a large pile of supplies. "I bet you didn't expect to see me back so soon," I say, clapping him on the back.

"On the contrary, Shadow. I was wondering what took you so long," he says, not even looking up from an ornately etched, cobalt blue water basin of glass he is inspecting. "Look at this. It comes from Constantinople or maybe somewhere farther east." He hands me the platter. "Feel the weight of that."

I can feel the weight, and I appreciate the beauty, but I am no expert on glass. Only a few Norse craftsmen work in glass, and I have never met one. I peer into the crate Eric is standing over, and it is full of such pieces, all brilliantly forged and blown into platters, glasses, goblets, and animal shapes. One of the pieces catches my eye, cobalt blue, like the water basin, but in the shape of an animal I do not recognize with legs like tree trunks and a long snout that curls up over its head between large leaf-shaped ears. I find another in yellow-orange, sleek, with a neck longer than its legs.

"My children would love these," I say, lifting the blue one from the crate.

"Then take them. They are yours," says Eric. "You may have all of these treasures if you wish, except for this basin. This is for my wife."

"I have no need of your treasure, Eric. But thank you for these pieces. Will you see they get home, intact?"

"Of course. I am sending Knute ahead to Lagarvik with the bulk of my wealth. You and I have one more thing to do – Raumarike. If I am to rule there, I must first take the city."

"Raumarike is a fortress. It will not be as easy as Birka. Besides, I thought Sigurd the Jarnhringr gave you the throne."

"Oh, he did. Unfortunately, someone is currently sitting on it who I will have to remove – Eystein Halfdansson."

"Do you ever think, Eric, that one day your luck will run out on you?"

"Never ... not while you are with me, Shadow. You are still with me, are you not?" Eric turns a suspicious eye toward me.

"You know, I thought you had betrayed me to Sigurd," I answer.

"I thought you might," Eric says earnestly. "I didn't know what Jarnhringr was planning, but I knew it had to be something. He is not one to simply leave things alone, even when they favor him. It was Knute who suggested using Blardraugr. He seems to have established some kind of rapport with the beast. Knute says he 'understands' it."

"Well, he would be the first," I say amusedly under my breath.

"Their relationship certainly came in handy in Peenemunde," Eric adds.

Peenemunde! So that's how he did it. It was Knute who convinced Fenrir to attack the Thing. He must have found Fenrir hiding in the livery. And now that I think about it, it was Knute who first called him Blardraugr.

"But, if it will put your mind at ease, my friend, I will say it," continues Eric, oblivious to my shock at the revelation. "I did not betray you." He pauses and turns his eyes to mine. "So, Shadow, I'll ask again. Are you still with me?"

"To the end," I say.

Eric places the basin gently back into the crate, and his men load it onto a ship. By nightfall, fourteen of our ships, eleven knarrs with three drakkars as escort, have set sail for Lagarvik, laden with the fruits of our exploits – a king's ransom in silver and the spoils of the raids on Birka and Hovgarden. Eric is not the least bit worried that every penningr will make it to Lagarvik safely or that the ships' crews, which are much fewer in number than usual to make room for the treasure, will resist the urge to take what is not theirs.

The next day, the rest of us set sail for Raumarike. Fenrir rides, uncaged, in the bow. The men still fear him but trust my word that he will not eat them. I am amazed at the fighting spirit of these men. They endured a brutal battle against the Franks and another against Östen Beli at Birka. Most men would be spent, sick of fighting, and lusting for home by now, but not these men. They are loyal to Eric and trust him completely, ignoring all of his flaws and failures. I, myself, still have my doubts; yet I continue to follow him. Hel may have made me her spear, but it is Eric who is wielding me.

As Eysysla passes from our view, storm clouds begin building on the horizon. I have a queasy feeling in the pit of my stomach that this storm is one of the gods' making. Eric doesn't remember our last storm at sea when we escaped Peenemunde and were shipwrecked on Dago, but I do. That was a storm created by the gods to capture Fenrir, and somehow, Eric and I survived it. But this time, Eric is the target. With the potential unification of Vestfold and Raumarike, the Vanir will do anything to ward off a war with the Aesir; they must keep Eric from taking the throne. Eric and the crew seem unperturbed by the threat of a little rain, but I know this storm will be much, much worse. Fenrir knows it, too, his eyes telling me, "I really do hate the sea."

CHAPTER TWENTY-NINE

HINRIC

The sea goddess, Ran, sings her siren's song for the dead, the melody both enticing and frightening. The chorus is taken up by her nine daughters, as the souls of our crew are taken, one by one, to Aegirheim for Ran's amusement until Hel finally comes to claim them. I know the song well. I have heard it many times. But for me, the strains have lost their beauty, my immortality making me tone deaf, my soul unmoved by the melancholia of the music. I walk the shore among a half-dozen whooper swans, singing their swan songs as they die beside my brethren.

Like us, the swans were caught in the storm and separated from their flock. And like us, they were driven down into the rocks, battered, and drowned. Of the forty-two men on our drakkar, twenty-five of us have survived including Eric and me. Fenrir has fared better in this storm, having to swim only the last fifty yards or so from the rocks where our ship foundered, to the shore where I am pulling the survivors to higher ground.

210

Eric is in a bad way. His splint has been shattered and his ankle along with it. He is not quite conscious, so I take advantage of his state to reset his ankle as best I can. I fashion a new splint from the remnants of an oar and tie it on with strips of hide I cut from the coat of one of my dead comrades. I feel guilty for desecrating the honored dead in any way, but given the circumstances, I think it best to make use of whatever I can to save as many of these men as possible.

Besides Eric, seven men are seriously injured, and two of them I do not expect to survive. Regardless, I tend to their wounds assisted by the other able-bodied of my party. I should like to gather what supplies I can from the wreck, so I enlist Fenrir to act as a ferry. He, of course, balks at first, not wanting to set one paw in the water, but I persist, and he relents. It is good to know he must still follow as I direct, but I rarely resort to ordering him. I think we both prefer a relationship as equals, but in the backs of our minds, we know we are not. I suppose that is why he has a fondness for Knute. They share a kinship of status. Knute is to Eric as Fenrir is to me – a loyal friend to be sure, but ultimately, a warrior under the command of his captain.

"Do you know where we are, Shadow?" asks Eric, groggily.

"Well, the evening sun is over the sea, so I know we are not in Karelia," I joke, but the humor is not well received. "We didn't sail far enough west to make Öland or the Kalmar Strait, so my guess is, we are on Gotland."

"Ergh, Gotland," croaks Eric. "I hate this place. I hate these people."

"But they do make great ale!" I say. I don't remember ever accompanying Eric to Gotland, but, then again, our memories and histories have changed.

"True. That is the only thing great about Gotland, and I could certainly do with a cup or two right now." Eric tries to get up, before he realizes his special splint-and-crutch contraption is gone. "What happened to my splint!?"

"What do you think happened?" I say sarcastically.

"And this thing here? This is your work, Shadow?" says Eric holding up his splinted leg.

"Yes."

"It's a good thing you are a fighter and not a healer." Eric begins untying the leather bands.

"You weren't so particular the last time I splinted your leg after a shipwreck."

"I have never been shipwrecked, Shadow," Eric rebuts. A second later, he looks up at me in mock realization. "Ooohh, you mean when we were shipwrecked on Dago!"

"Yes, of course," I say, knowing he has no memory of the event.

"And I drank in the sea, and I nearly drown, and I broke my leg – all when we were shipwrecked on Dago."

"Yes. I am glad you finally remember," I quip. Eric breaks into a laugh, and I join him. At least if he's able to laugh, he's not in much pain.

He asks one of the men, Geir, to help him refashion his special splint-and-crutch, making a show of it, saying, "See, Shadow, this is how it's done."

Able to walk again, Eric, I, and ten others set out to look for a town, while the rest, including Geir, stay back to tend to the wounded. After an hour's walk, we come upon a large fishing village with a good harbor. In the harbor, to our surprise and relief, is another of our longships, giving us hope that others may have made landfall and not foundered at sea. We stride into the village and find the olstafa, betting that we will find more of our comrades there.

'Heill ok saells', claps on the back, and cups of good ale greet us as we enter the olstafa. There are about twenty men from the other ship here, the rest having been dispersed throughout the town, foraging for supplies to fix the ship, which according to the men, is severely damaged and barely afloat. We are all relieved to hear that not a single man on that ship perished, and another round of ale toasts their good fortune. Eric directs several of the men to return to our wrecked ship and bring back the injured and the supplies.

Others, he sends out in small groups of three or four men to scour the shoreline looking for other ships and survivors. It is a monumental task. Gotland has about one hundred forty miles of coast, although we will only be looking on the eastern edge. Given that we only got separated from the rest of the ships a few hours before making landfall, we are hoping that any survivors will be within a twenty-mile stretch of the coast. Some of the men commandeer horses from the local farmers to expedite the search. Eric makes each man promise to return the horses when they are done. Perhaps he is trying to reform his reputation here.

"Eric Halvorsen!" yells the proprietor of the olstafa. "I hoped to never see your face again!"

"Sven!" Eric replies, giving the burly, gray-bearded man a hearty clap on the shoulder.

Though Eric acts like he is greeting an old friend, Sven is not so amiable.

"I mean it, boy. You are not welcome here," Sven says, his stone face stiffening.

"Sven," Eric pleads. "That was years ago. Can't we leave the past in the past. Besides, Sara must be happily settled by now."

"Happily settled? Not after what you did!"

"We were both young, Sven. I'm sure you had your share of trifles when you were that age."

"I take it you two know each other," I intercede. Sven is getting hotter with anger by the second, and I don't want to see him killed. He seems like a nice old man, and his ale is the best I've ever had. It would be a true crime if he couldn't make any more.

"Yes, I know him. The last time he came here, he made me a grandfather," Sven says, glaring at Eric with murderous eyes.

Eric is dumbfounded, his eyes widening and his mouth dropping open. He had no idea. I step in and pull Eric down into a chair. This may be the first time I have ever seen him at a loss for words.

"A grandfather," I say, using my body to gently corral Sven to another chair. "You must be so proud. Boy or girl? How old?"

"Err, boy. Seven ... seven years old ... Hinric." Sven is answering my questions, but he hasn't taken his eyes off Eric.

"And is Hinric about?" I ask. "Perhaps he would like to meet his father." I am hoping that creating a familial bond between Eric and Sven will cool the anger and settle the tension.

"He is outside, churning butter."

"Okay, let us go fetch him," I say, guiding Sven back to his feet. His anger has cooled, but his mind seems in a daze as I lead him outside.

We return a few moments later with a fair-haired little boy, skinny but firm, his eyes unmistakably his father's. Sven sits down and urges Hinric toward Eric.

"Hello, father. I am Hinric. I am glad to meet you," he says.

Eric does not respond at first, fixating on the boy's face. Slowly he puts his hands on his son's shoulders, and then, finally pulls the boy into his embrace.

"Where is Sara?" Eric finally speaks, still holding Hinric.

"Dead," says Sven. "She died giving birth to Hinric." Tears well up in Sven's eyes with the memory of his daughter's death, but not a single one falls, and his voice is strong and unwavering. I have never experienced grief like Sven has, but I can only hope that, was I in a similar circumstance, I could keep my composure as well as he does.

The good cheer and whispered hilarity of Eric's sudden fatherhood melts into a solemn silence. Every man suddenly thinks of his own children and are grateful to not be sitting in Sven's chair. A runner breaks the silence, entering the olstafa with news that three more ships and nearly one hundred thirty men have been found alive an hour north of us.

Eric declares the olstafa to be his base of command and continues sending out small groups of men to search for the others. By sundown the next day, a total of nine ships have been found, seven of them sea-worthy, along with six hundred fifty-four men. That leaves six ships unaccounted for and a loss of nearly three hundred. By mid-morning the day after, nearly everyone has arrived in the village. Eric sends out several more parties on long range sweeps. They all return within two days having found only one more sea-worthy ship and twenty-nine more men.

The influx of men has strained the resources of the village, so Eric sends men to neighboring villages and towns for food and supplies. He insists that they pay for all they take. Beside the fact that most of the treasure is on its way to Lagarvik, Eric has wisely held some back which he uses to do good commerce on Gotland.

"I thought you hated this place," I say.

"I do. But if I am to be King of Raumarike, I must start acting like one," Eric responds.

"Well, it sounds like there was a time you liked this place," I say, nodding at Hinric who is helping to repair one of the ships.

"Maybe. I suppose it wasn't all bad, but then again, we raided a lot of villages here on our way to the Savonian Forest all those years ago, remember?"

"I do," I lie. There is no point in responding otherwise.

"Who would have thought that a bunch of farmers and fishermen could put up such a fight. I lost a quarter of my men for nothing – my first defeat. I have learned a lot since then."

"Well, you seem to be redeeming yourself, now," I say. "Hinric is learning what a true leader looks like. He is very proud to have you as his father."

"When we leave, Shadow, I'm taking him with me," Eric announces.

"Do you think that is wise? He's just a boy and we have some serious fighting ahead of us."

"He'll have to learn sometime if he is going to rule Raumarike."

I never thought I'd live to see the day when Eric Halvorsen would put the future of someone else ahead of his own ... and I am going to live forever. Yet, here he is, thinking about his legacy with young Hinric, a child he did not even know existed until a week ago. It is a good thing, but I wonder what his wife will think when, finally, he returns to Lagarvik with a son by another woman.

CHAPTER THIRTY

OF BARGAINS AND PROPHECIES

The eyes of Baldr shine brightly at the news, providing light and affirmation, born of the love he shared with humanity. But soon his brother, Hödr, bedims the room, sowing darkness and doubt. That the two can coexist amiably in the same place, playfully jostling with one another, testifies to their brotherly bond. I watch the twin gods wrestle across young Hinric's face as he wavers between his excitement of accompanying his father to Raumarike, and his fear of leaving his home and his grandfather.

A month has passed, and finally, the ships are ready to sail. Eric busies himself with the minutia of preparation, a quality of care and attention to detail he has rarely, if ever, exhibited. In the past, he would be more extemporaneous, going off on an adventure without a second thought and just as likely to encounter trouble and failure as a result. Now, however, he seems overly cautious, almost to the point of stagnation. I do not know if it is because he will soon be a king, or if it is because now, he is a father. In either case, the men are grumbling. They are ready to sail to their destinies and are waiting for Eric to give the command.

To pass the time, as I am not skilled, nor inclined, to the task of repairing ships, I have taken to exploring Gotland. Fenrir accompanies me, creating fear and havoc among the islanders to be sure, something he seems to revel in, but behaving himself for the most part. After a while, they become accustomed to seeing him and are not so anxious. We travel far, sometimes twenty miles in a day. Everywhere, I am recognized as the famous Helsvein, but am kept at arms-length because of my relationship with Eric. News of his presence on the island quickly spreads, and despite his attempts to make amends with the people, they still despise him.

Not knowing exactly what happened, I make inquiries, but only one man chances a conversation with me. His name is Tholf, a man who has seen many years and hardships, years and hardships that had taken his eleven older brothers and sisters, he comments before relaying his story. Tholf says that Eric Halvorsen spent several months on the island. He remembers the young man boasting about his adventures, enticing the young men of Gotland to follow him. Several did, willingly, but others were less interested. To encourage their cooperation, Eric would threaten the lads' families and villages, and when they did not comply, he would have his men kill their fathers and burn their houses. Eric, Tholf said, wreaked havoc across Gotland, swelling his numbers by way of fear and intimidation. Finally, the Gotlanders had had enough and fought back. Eric was defeated and sailed away to the east, supposedly to find some ancient treasure. The cream of the young men of Gotland either perished or sailed with him, never to be seen again.

The story Tholf tells makes my heart sink. I have known Eric a long time, and this did not sound like the Eric I knew. Surely, Eric was not a man to shy from killing when it was warranted, but he was never cruel, and

I witnessed many times when Eric would drink ale with an enemy, having made him a friend. But the Eric Tholf describes does seem to fit better with the man I know now. Eric has always been ambitious and determined, but now he has a new quality – ruthlessness.

I am beginning, again, to doubt my decision to stay with Eric and help him with his destiny. Fenrir, on the other hand, has no qualms at all, saying "He is a better man for his ruthlessness. He would not have come this far without it." Fenrir is probably right, but I wonder from all he has gained, what has been lost from the man I once knew.

We set camp near the remnants of a fishing village. There is a high point, not quite a cliff, overlooking the beach, covered in pink dogrose. The sweet smell triggers a memory of an old fort and an old man. The memory overtakes me to the point where I swear, I smell the aroma of smoked seal meat wafting down from the heights. I blink my eyes to recover my senses, but the smell of roasting flesh does not disappear. As well, Fenrir's nose is high in the air, taking in the glorious aroma, his mouth opening slightly, drool dripping from his fangs. We follow the smell to its source, a decrepit long house with its far wall fallen and part of its roof collapsed. In the void, we find an old man tending a røykhus, smoking meat.

"I was wondering when you would show up," the old man says without giving me a glance. "And you've brought Fenrir. I am at your service, brother of Jörmungandr." He turns to Fenrir and gives a slight bow from his bent, stringy shoulders.

"You're the seidr!" I say in surprise.

"Well, of course, boy. Whom did you expect?"

"I would expect you to be on Dago," I say.

"I go where the Great One needs me," says the seer, cutting off a large slab of freshly smoked seal which he tosses to Fenrir. The Wolf-God voraciously devours the meat, staring at the old man until another slab is flung his way. "So, it sounds like you were successful in your mission. Here stands Fenrir, and the Kraken is slain. Well done, Asger."

I hadn't heard my real name in so long, I'd almost forgotten it myself. "You called me Asger?"

"That is your name, isn't it. Or do you prefer Helsvein, now?"

"But the curse?"

"I told you before, curses have conditions, and one of those conditions is that I can see past it, though it took quite some time and effort to finally know you. I nearly lost my sight in the attempt.

"But, how do you know of my mission to save Fenrir?" I ask. Even as I am famous for defeating the Kraken, not a living soul knows it was to free the Wolf-God.

"Know of your mission? Was it not I who summoned the Great One for you? Just because you crossed the plane into other realms and have returned to Midgard a bit out of your time doesn't mean the things in your past never happened. As I recall, it has only been a few months since our encounter on Dago."

"I ... I ..."

"Don't think about it too much, boy. Your head'll fall off."

"I suppose you're right. Until now, I was doing well to ignore the differences, the memories of others." I say, coming back to myself.

"Well, if it will help, my memory is aligned with yours. So, tell me. I'm curious. How did you kill the Kraken?"

"From the inside."

"Well, I guess you had some practice with that," laughs the seer, holding up a dried finger of Vörnir he has tied to his belt.

Fenrir chuckles. I don't think he knows the story, exactly, but as he can read my thoughts, I'm sure he is quite amused. The seer points to a stack of meat he wants me to carry. As I throw the slabs over my shoulder, one of them drops. Fenrir rushes to seize it, but I quickly stab it with Dainslief, denying him the tasty morsel. "That will teach you to laugh at me", I think, and the Wolf-God glares at me.

"So, you knew I was coming. Did you see that in one of your visions, or did you just hear it from the locals?" I ask as we make our way to a deep inlet.

"Ah, boy, you see through me. I heard it from a farmer. Shipwrecked by that storm, I hear. You know that was no ordinary storm."

"Yes, we know. We've been through enough of them to know when the gods are involved."

"The Vanir are very upset. They do not want Eric Halvorsen on the throne of Raumarike. They do not want the unification with Vestfold."

"You know about that, too? Well, it's done, except for deposing the man currently sitting on it," I say as if there is nothing the gods can do about it.

"I would not be so sure. If Eric tries to leave Gotland, he will be killed," says the seer, very assuredly. "I've have seen his demise and that of his fleet in the entrails."

"I would not be so sure of your visions, old man. I've seen Eric rise stronger every time he is knocked down. He learns from his defeats. The gods themselves have already made two runs at him, and he is still alive."

"He's not immortal like you are, boy, and my visions are never wrong. If Eric leaves with his fleet, they will all perish."

"So, what do you want of me? Do you want me to keep him here? I think you overestimate my influence with him, and I know you underestimate his pigheadedness."

"I am just providing you with the information. What you choose to do with it is your own business."

"You know, Eric claims a seidr told him many things, things that have come to pass, including his becoming a king. Of course, to hear Eric, his prophecies were much more poetic."

"I know what I told him. And he expected mystery and poetry, so that is what he got. They always want mystery and poetry and smoke and mist," the seer chortled.

"Oh! It was you who told him those things? Why does he get poetry, where I get the unsung truth?"

"Do you really want me to sing your prophecies, boy?"

"I suppose not. But why would you drive his ambitions with your visions, and then tell me if he tries to achieve them, he'll die?

"I don't know. It's a mystery," says the seer as he begins throwing meat into the water. Within minutes, the World-Serpent surfaces.

"Hello, brother," says Fenrir.

"Fenrir," Jörmungandr responds. "You s-s-seem no worse for the s-s-storm."

"You could have helped us," the Wolf-God barks, seeming a bit perturbed.

"You're alive, brother. You're here. Who's-s to s-s-say I did not help you."

"Great One," I interject. "I should like to ask a favor of you."

"As you wish-sh. What would the Drengr Røkkr have with me?" Jörmungandr asks.

"Could you see Eric's fleet safely to Raumarike?"

"I could, but I won't," the World-Serpent responds with a certain finality in his booming voice.

"But it shall benefit you as well. The Vanir and Aesir will fight one another, and you will be left in peace," I say, my argument strong and unassailable.

"That is-s-s true, and it is precis-sely why I cannot. It must be mankind that sets-s-s the gods-s-s on each other. I can have no part in it."

"But you already have, Great One. You and Fenrir rescued me from Sigurd the Jarnhringr."

"That was-s-s for your benefit, as we are bound, you and I, but not for the benefit of your friend. He mus-st do this on his-s-s own. Fenrir and I cannot help."

Fenrir looks at me like he has betrayed me, remorse falling over his face like a veil.

"Are you not coming with us?" I ask Fenrir.

"I will come, but I will not take part in the battle," says Fenrir. He knew this but kept it from me. I should be angry with him, but I'm not. It's the first time he has cared how I regard him.

"Well, then, Children of Angrboda, I respect your decision and withdraw my request. You have honored me greatly with your companionship and the deeds we have done together. If Eric is to fulfill his destiny, and I to fulfill mine, we shall do so of our own accord," I say courteously. Jörmungandr's eyes flash waves of translucent colors in acknowledgment, and then he sinks beneath the water.

Fenrir and I return to the fishing village where I must try to convince Eric to remain. I find him in the olstafa finalizing his attack plans for Raumarike. It seems he is finally satisfied with the preparations and is planning to set sail in the morning. I'd hoped he would still be entrenched in the details and reluctant to leave, but this is not the case. And having made up his mind, it will be useless for me to try and change it. I can only hope that we survive another assault by the Vanir.

Eric calls me over to go over what he plans for Fenrir and me. In past engagements, he was always a bit cagey with the details, but this time he is making sure I know exactly what he wants me to do. I tell him that Blardraugr will not be participating, but he ignores me.

I retire to a table with a cup of ale and try to figure out what I can do. I notice a grizzled sea trader sitting across from me. His face is familiar, but it is his hobbled leg and missing ear that truly catch my attention. I know this man from Dago. I have a bargain with him to take two people to Lagarvik for fifty pieces of silver. The seer's words return to me – 'If Eric leaves with his fleet, they will all perish.' But what if Eric doesn't leave with his fleet? What if he leaves on a trading knarr? I quickly fish through the pouch under my tunic and find half of a silver coin. I approach the old man and drop it on the table in front of him. Slowly, he raises his head, and his wondering eyes meet mine. Many things have changed since I returned to Midgard, and it is possible that this man has no knowledge of our agreement. My eyes remain fixed on his, as he absently fiddles with a money pouch, finally producing a half coin, the mate of my own.

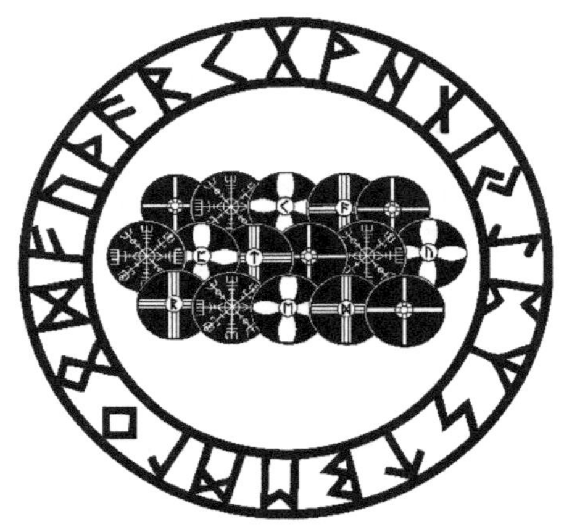

CHAPTER THIRTY-ONE

A GRAVE ERROR

The road of black moonstone leads the way home, the hue of the larvikite pavement beckoning me. It is said that larvikite has healing powers, increasing one's strength and security, and enhancing the ability to achieve one's desires. Most importantly, it is said to repel curses. And here before me is a pathway tiled with it, one that promises to end my curse and take me where I desire most to be. It has been months since I've been home, years since I've seen Gyda and Brant, and an eternity since I've lain with Inger. Alas, I am only passing by the deep, dark blue of the Larvik Fjord on my way to Raumarike and my destiny. To be so close to home, and yet so far away is the greatest pain I have ever suffered.

Our escape from Gotland has been, thankfully, uneventful. The seer's prophesy having been defeated by the bargain I struck with a hobbled, old sea captain, Eric has sent his army ahead to Raumarike with me as his merkis, while he and Hinric sail on a trading knarr, unseen and unmolested by the gods. I paid the captain double the agreed price, one hundred pieces

226

of silver, to ensure they sailed to Lagarvik first. I hope Eric takes my advice and leaves the boy there, safe in the care of his wife. But, then again, I know Eric. He may double the payment again and sail straight to Raumarike.

As general, I have nearly six hundred men under my command, and they, having the Drengr Røkkr leading them, feel invincible. As I have never led men in battle before, I protested strongly against the position, but Eric would hear nothing of it. He trusts only Knute and me, and since Knute is in Lagarvik protecting the spoils of Eric's adventures, it is left to me to lead these men, at least until Eric arrives.

Our mission is clear. We make camp on Haøya and the group of islands surrounding it, just south of Raumarike, where the fjord pinches down into a narrow channel on its way to the sea. Our position affords us a great advantage, the islands being separated by narrow straits and thus forcing any attacks by sea to be easily seen and the maneuvering of a large fleet to be difficult. Our escape route, should we need one, would be south through the channel, thus reducing any advantage the enemy would have in men and ships.

We set our main camp on an island to the southeast of Haøya, while we deploy some of our men to the heights at the southern end of Haøya to serve as lookouts. As well, we occupy the island to the southwest, thus allowing each encampment to support the other. In the event of an attack on one camp, the other would take to oars and come to their aid. I don't necessarily like splitting my forces like this, but Eric thinks it best that the entire army is not put at risk in one place. To that end, of my own accord, I keep a fleet of ships south in the southern channel, rotating the ships and men once a day to keep them fresh. From this position, we make raids to the north in an effort to draw out Eystein Halfdansson, the man currently sitting on Eric's throne.

The first few raids go according to plan and soon Halfdansson sends warriors down the fjord to engage us. In their first attack, they sail for the island of our main camp, and as we had planned, they are trapped in the narrows. Our ships in the channel now close from the south, while troops from our supporting camp sail around the northern end of Haøya and attacks from the north. Eystein's forces are caught in our vice and unable to maneuver. We board their ships, and the battle ensues. Though I am leading the army, I do not take part in the battle. Eric explicitly forbade me from fighting. I believe he wants my identity to remain unknown to Eystein Halfdansson. He needn't have worried. Eric's warriors are well seasoned and make quick work of our foes. We destroy eight ships and kill more than four hundred with a loss to our own forces of less than twenty.

The men are pleased with the victory, but I know this was just a test. Our enemy was clearly untrained and made up mostly of conscripts and slaves. Halfdansson is no fool. He is probing us to see both our numbers and our weaknesses. It would make no sense to waste his best warriors on such a suicide mission. His tactic works to near perfection. He now has a very good idea of what he is up against with one direful yet unforeseen exception – me.

I anticipate the next attack will come in a day or two, and it will be massive. Eystein will most likely try to land troops on the north end of both islands, thus making it impossible for either of our camps to support the other. He will then send the bulk of his forces around the islands and attack us from the south as well. All he needs to do is hold off our southern fleet long enough to get his men ashore. Then it will be us who are caught in a vice. And if we set sail, as we did today, his best ships and warriors will be there to stop us from escaping. Then he'll bring the weight of his remaining forces down on us. It is a gamble for sure, but Halfdansson has the men and ships to do it. If the battle drags on long enough, we will be crushed.

I decide to break with Eric's plan. If I am not to fight, then I must move this army. We board our longships at night and sail south through the channel, uniting with our southern fleet where the channel widens again. I decide to remain on the water which has the men grumbling. They prefer a battle on open ground to one fought on ships, but I know we would lose a land battle. At sea, I can array my fleet in such a way that we can isolate and swarm a few enemy ships at a time as they come through the channel.

For two days, we wait, but Eystein Halfdansson does not attack. It is as if Halfdansson has given up pursuing us. I am flummoxed by his lack of response. I was so sure he would attack; I was so sure he would have numbers five times our own; I was so sure of his battle plan that I moved my entire army to lay in wait. It is exactly what I would do in his situation, but he is not doing as I would. Eystein remains in his fortress and refuses to engage.

I realize I am not the tactician that Eric is. Perhaps he knows Eystein would not risk a full-scale attack. The third day I reverse my decision and sail north to our original position. I realize quickly I have made a grave error. As we disembark, we are attacked by land and sea, Halfdansson's army emerging like a swarm of hornets from the tree line above us while three dozen longships round the flanking islands and cut off our escape. We are now caught in the exact trap we had set for Eystein. I get as many men ashore as I can, and we quickly form a shield wall. The few ships still at oars form a semi-circle around our beachhead and prepare to be rammed. They must hold off Eystein's fleet to our rear or we will be slaughtered.

Fenrir would be a great asset in this fight, but as he had informed me, he cannot help. I put him ashore on the peninsula that forms the eastern shore of the fjord when we first arrived many days ago. The men were glad to be rid of him. They had witnessed first-hand what he can do to an enemy, but they are still deathly afraid of him. Without Knute, they believe Blardraugr cannot be controlled, despite me being the one who kept company with him. However, I am sure, given the graveness of our circumstances, they wish as I do that he were here.

We repel the first assault but are split into small pockets of thirty to sixty men each. If we could consolidate our forces, we may have a chance. I call on the two groups closest to me to fall in on my position, but as they do, a second wave of Eystein's men come crashing in. As the men in those groups are engaged in fierce hand-to-hand combat, I direct my group to advance in formation to cover the pocket of men to my left, while leaving the men to my right to be cut down. A river of regret flows over me, but I could not save both groups. I know I must do something to protect the soldiers I have left. I cannot sustain losses like this. We are fighting a much larger force, and they have the high ground. We are in a desperate situation. I think to myself, "What would Eric do?"

I see now that I will not be able to bring all my forces together in a cohesive defense, so I make the decision to withdraw to our ships. On the water, we may be able to break out, whereas on this island we have nowhere to go but Valhalla. I know the only way to affect such a retreat is for me to engage directly, even though it is against Eric's instructions. But, as I am responsible for this debacle, it is incumbent upon me to try to reverse it. I yell for the men to retreat to their ships, while I break from my shield wall and rush into the enemy steel.

More than a hundred of Eystein Halfdansson's men fall to Dainslief before I am subdued. The grievous injuries I suffer heal instantly, leaving the enemy with no other conclusion than I am Helsveir, the Drengr Røkkr. As I am bound and dragged away, I see that nearly all my remaining men have taken to oars and are engaged with Halfdansson's overwhelming fleet. It appears that our semi-circle of defending ships has collapsed and the enemy drakkars are driving hard into my retreating men. I search for a weakness in Halfdansson's formation, but he has left some ships to form a perimeter leaving no avenue for escape. I have led these men to their doom. I alone am responsible. Eric left his destiny in my hands, and I have failed him, utterly.

The sea battle drags on. Each of my ships has at least two enemy ships alongside, making it impossible to row or maneuver. The clanging of steel on shield and the cries of the dying pierce my ears like arrows. The men fight valiantly, in some cases even gaining an advantage, if only until more enemy reinforcements arrive. Odin's Great Hall will certainly be full tonight. I think, where mere days ago these men were praising the name of Helsvein, in Valhalla they will surely be cursing it. I want to close my eyes to the slaughter, but I cannot. Instead, I turn them briefly southward to the long, narrow channel of the fjord and see the masts of two dozen ships.

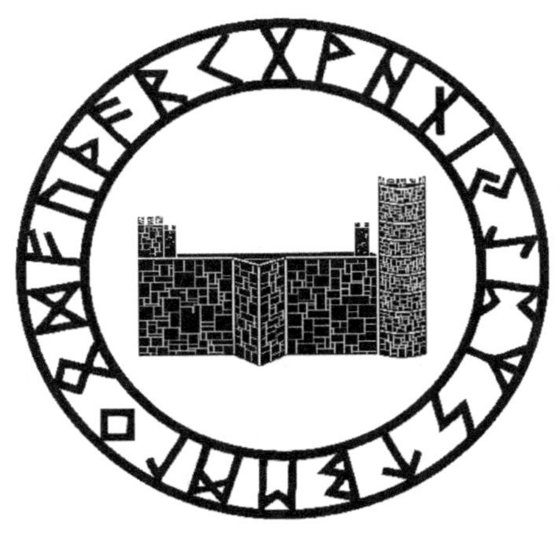

CHAPTER THIRTY-TWO

LOYALTY AND BETRAYAL

Unsure of its own beauty, the budding flower shyly takes its time opening in the brilliance of the midday sun. Gaining confidence, its petals begin to emerge in hues of deep burgundy, azure-blue, and yellow-white. A gentle southern breeze ripples each petal driving it outward until the flower, finally, spreads wide into a full lustrous display intended to capture the eyes of men and gods alike. The bloom of Eric's sails is a beautiful sight as his drakkars fan out and engage the forces of Eystein Halfdansson's.

Eric's arrival could not have been more fortunate. Our army was barely hanging on, fighting desperately in close ship-to-ship and hand-to-hand combat, boardings and violent engagements happening on nearly every ship, both ours and Eystein's. Scores of men had died on both sides, either by sword, ax, and hammer blows, or by falling into the frigid waters of the fjord and drowning. Into this melee, Eric sails, smashing through the perimeter ships, some of which are torn straight in half. Eystein still has the numbers, but his fleet is now in disarray as Eric's ships engage in small

232

groups, like packs of wild dogs taking down a herd of deer. As they are forced to the defensive, several enemy ships disengage and break for home.

Bound, I am thrown into an enemy drakkar, the oarsmen of which pull so hard we are soon at ramming speed. A dozen other ships surround us, rowing hard toward the mass of ships engaged in battle. It is clear we will not be joining the fray when the men not rowing cast up a cover of shields. The men on this ship mean to drive through the battling drakkars and escape with me as their prisoner. I can see nothing, but I can hear the crash of ship on ship and the thumping of arrow, ax, and sword onto our covering of shields. A small gap in the cover allows an expertly thrown ax to penetrate, cleaving into a man's chest. He falls on me, dead, the shield he was holding almost crushing my skull.

More thumps and more men fall, opening more gaps in our cover. Several oarsmen on our port side are killed, their heads scythed from them as if they were stalks of wheat. As a result, our longship takes a hard turn to port causing a few of the standing shield bearers to topple into the water. We are buffeted from all sides by friend and foe alike, but the oarsmen keep pulling. A sudden crash throttles our momentum, throwing oarsmen onto their backs and their protectors onto their backsides. We have struck another longship. Perhaps we have been stopped, and I will be rescued.

I manage to right myself enough to see that we have indeed rammed one of Eric's drakkars amidships and broken its back. Some of the men from the doomed ship jump onto this ship and begin fighting for control. One of them is Eric.

"What have you done, Helsvein?" asks Eric while he dodges a blow from an ax and dispatches the man wielding it. "You were ordered to take up positions on these islands and remain there until I arrived."

"I know, but it seemed our position was not as defensible as you thought," I protest.

"It seems to have worked well enough for Eystein Halfdansson. He would have destroyed my army had I not arrived to save it."

"Was that not your plan all along, Eric ... to arrive just in time to keep us all from being slaughtered?"

"Of course, but you were supposed to hold the islands, not give them away to the enemy."

"I did protest your making me merkis," I say, trying to get to my feet. If nothing else, I could act as a human shield for Eric, absorbing the blows meant for him.

"Well, I may have made a mistake in that, Shadow." I took Eric's referring to me as 'Shadow' as a sign of forgiveness, or at least, a sign that his anger with me was waning. "I take it that they know who you are since they have you bound and are trying to escape with you."

"I had no choice. I had to do something to get the men off the beach."

"Well, it is certainly not how I wanted them to find out about you, Helsvein, but we may be able to make it work. I am going to let them take you."

"WHAT?" I cry out.

"I said, 'I am going to let them take you.' Halfdansson will feel he has won this battle, having captured the Twilight Warrior. He may even want you to fight for him. You must let him think that you would be willing ... no, eager ... to do just that, for I have been a tyrant to you, Shadow, ransoming the lives of your family for your continued support of my quest." That familiar thin smile crosses Eric's lips. "And when the time comes, you will kill Eystein Halfdannson!"

"So, I am to be your assassin?" I ask, somewhat angry at Eric's request. I have no time for assassins, believing them to be cowards who would not face a man in combat.

"You were always going to be my assassin, Shadow. I could never hope to take the fortress at Raumarike with five thousand men, let alone the five hundred you've left me with."

Eric's words are a backhand to my skills as a general, intending not only to show his displeasure, but to infuse me with guilt. It works, as he knows it would.

"So, I am to kill Halfdannson at the first opportunity, then?"

"No! You must wait for the right time," Eric shouts, killing another man who dared to cross swords with him.

"How will I know the right time?"

"Don't worry about that, Shadow. You'll know."

With those last words, Eric lifts me up and kicks me into the water before ordering a retreat and jumping onto another of his ships that has come alongside. Eystein's men pull me back aboard, reclaim their oars, and begin rowing in earnest, pulling us north away from the battle. I look down the length of the longship strewn with dead and injured. Of the eighty men I estimate were on this ship, some at oars, the rest at shields, there are barely twenty able-bodied left. And every one of them believes himself a hero for the ages, for they have successfully captured and escaped certain death with the Drengr Røkkr.

We arrive in Raumarike after sunset, the full moon hanging low over the shimmering harbor. Even in the darkness, Raumarike is magnificent, its battlements of limestone gleaming in the moonlight. The Norse rarely build fortresses of stone, but this is a grand exception. It has two outer walls, also of stone with four smaller palisades of birch, fully manned, guarding the harbor entrance and flanks of the city. I estimate Eystein Halfdansson has nearly three thousand men in defense of this place. Taken together with the forces we just fought with at Haøya, he must have close to six thousand men in all, a staggering number for one man to have at his command.

As I am brought up from the harbor, I can see the lower town within the first wall. It is mostly stick and brick dwellings, with a few larger buildings of birch and oak, arrayed in a chaotic mix of narrow roads and alleys. An army seeking to attack the citadel at the center of this maze would have an extremely difficult time getting there, which I suppose is the point. The whole place reminds me of stories I've heard about the walled cities of Francia, and it is clear Eystein Halfdansson has purposely modeled his fortress to replicate one.

Inside the second wall, the buildings are very ordered and ornate. The homes and buildings here have the purpose of keeping the wealthy and well-connected close to the king so they know exactly what his patronage can bring them. I have never seen a place like this anywhere I have traveled, not even in Birka, which was a very wealthy town, and though it is true I did not see the stronghold at Hovgarden, I cannot imagine it looking anything like this.

Like the outer walls, the citadel is limestone with a curtain wall nearly twenty feet high. Within them is a stone tower twice as high as the curtain wall, with timber towers in the corners and along the sides enclosing a courtyard that is nothing more than a killing zone. Given what I have seen already, however, it would be nearly impossible for any army to come even this far. And if an enemy were to lay siege, there are dozens of storehouses in the lower levels of the city filled with food and supplies. Halfdansson could easily hold out for more than a year, but of course, he need only wait until winter when his enemy would either have to withdraw or freeze to death.

I am brought through a door into a large open room with a vaulted timber roof and stairs leading to an upper loft at the far end. Additional stairs branch from the loft and disappear above the ceiling to the levels above. I expect there to be a throne on the raised deck below the loft, but there is none. There are several long tables, and near the head of one of them, sits Eystein Halfdansson on a common bench, surrounded by soldiers with whom he is sharing his strategy for the city's defense. For all the splendor of his fortress, his inner sanctuary is quite simple, devoid of any of the trappings of wealth and power, and much less grand than many great halls I have been in.

"Konungr Eystein, we have a prisoner," says one of the men dragging me.

"I said you were to give no quarter!" Halfdansson barks, obviously annoyed by the intrusion.

"We had no choice. This particular prisoner refused those terms," the man says, beaming at his own cleverness. "He is Helsvein, the Drengr Røkkr."

"What?" Eystein says, his attention instantly drawn to me.

"It's true," says the other man holding me.

Eystein Halfdansson rises from his seat and approaches me slowly, eying me from head to foot as if I were a prized horse.

"I always imagined him taller," Eystein says, drawing his dagger from his belt.

"You would think me a jötunn?" I ask in preparation for Eystein's blade.

"No. Just taller," he says, driving the dagger into my belly and pulling it upward like he was gutting a fish. I just stand there, completely unfazed by the cut. He withdraws the blade with a few drops of blood and runs his hand up my midsection seeking a wound that has already healed. Unbelieving, he stabs me in the neck, a spray of my blood striking him in the eye. As he blinks away the blood, he sees I am still standing, uninjured.

"You really are the Twilight Warrior," he concedes but his eyes tell me he still cannot believe it.

"I have been called such, yes," I admit. He is so close right now I could kill him easily if I weren't bound. I struggle against the ropes and am instantly kicked in the back of my leg and brought to my knees.

"Why were you attacking me? What have I got that you would want?"

"The throne of Raumarike," I say.

"Well, if you can find a throne, you can have it!" Eystein says waving his hand around the room and drawing a raucous laugh from everyone. "So, what am I going to do with you?" he asks, grabbing my hair and shaking my head.

"Well, we can't kill him," says the clever man, drawing even more laughter.

"We could throw him in a well and bury him," says the other.

"Or maybe ..." starts the clever man, but before he can finish, another of Halfdansson's soldiers bursts into the hall. "Konungr Eystein, the enemy is in pursuit. They have made camp west of Raumarike."

"How many?" Eystein asks, throwing my head down so hard it smacks the floor.

"A thousand, maybe more?"

"A thousand? Valhalla can't hold that many. When they attack, we'll send them to Hel," Eystein laughs then looks at me. "It's a pity so many good men should die trying to save one who can't. But I'll tell you what, Helsvein. I will spare your men if you agree to join me. There is no reason to kill good soldiers in a pointless battle. I could certainly put their talents to better use. And yours as well."

"I will be happy to join with you, but I cannot speak for the men," I answer.

"Why is that?"

"They are not my men."

"Then whose men are they?"

It appears Eystein does not know it is Eric Halvorsen who desires his throne, but he will find out soon enough even if I remain silent. "Eric Halvorsen of Vestfold."

"The seventh brat of that ill-famed Jarl?" Eystein says with obvious disdain. "Who does he think he is?"

"The King of Raumarike," I answer. I am rewarded with laughter and a brisk slap to the face. Then I burst into laughter. "You know, Eystein, you've slapped me, pulled my hair, even gutted me like a fish, but you have still treated me better than Eric Halvorsen."

"Then why would you serve him?"

"He threatens my family. I have no choice. But, if you were to promise to see to my family's welfare, I would be more than happy to help you defeat Eric."

"I need no help for that, Helsvein. Besides, I don't trust you."

"I can be a great asset. I am worth a hundred of your soldiers. You can trust me."

"Two hundred, if the legends are true, but I still have no reason to trust you, even if Eric is threatening your family, as you say."

"Eric betrayed and abandoned me in battle, today. He blamed me for losing half of his army. He boarded the ship carrying me and could have freed me, but instead, he threw me overboard. His last words to me were that I had failed him, and my family would pay the price."

"That is true, Konungr Eystein," says the man holding me. "Eric Halvorsen boarded our ship after we rammed his and nearly took it before we beat him back. He could easily have taken Helsvein, but instead, he kicked him into the water. He seemed quite angry."

"There, you see? Eric Halvorsen's rage has delivered me to you. If you know anything of him, then you know how brash he can be."

"He does have that reputation. All right. I will give you a chance to prove your loyalty to me. Cut his bindings and give him his sword," Eystein says to the shock of everyone. Reluctantly, the man holding me does as he asks. "Now Helsvein, you may strike me down, and I will not stop you. Either that, or strike down Garmr, here, the man who has vouched for you. You must do one or the other, else I WILL do as Garmr suggests and throw you down a well and bury you for all eternity."

My sword is placed in my hand. I can claim Eric's throne for him with a single stroke. I raise Dainslief and let it fly.

CHAPTER THIRTY-THREE

THE NECKLACE AND THE SPEAR

A few drops of misty rain kiss my cheek, trickling downward, tickling my bearded jaw and neck, almost imperceptibly. Heavier drops follow soon afterward, splashing on my forehead, nose, and eyes before the deluge truly begins. My head still turning with my body, I am, in a few brief moments that seem to drag on for hours, drenched in the torrent of blood spewing from Garmr's neck as my backhand stroke slices clean through it.

Garmr's body drops to the floor, his head rolling away like a knattleikr ball.

"So, you have chosen to serve me, then – a wise choice," says Eystein Halfdansson.

"To serve you, no, not without your promise to protect my family. But I have chosen not to kill you, at least not yet."

"Kill me? You could not have killed me. I am like you – immortal. The goddess, Freyja, has made me so."

241

"Freyja? The Goddess of Magic has made you immortal?" I question the veracity of his claim, and my tone reveals my doubt.

Eystein plunges his dagger into his own chest and leaves it there, spreading his arms open as he nods at me, his eyes bidding me remove it. As I step forward, I notice something glowing beneath his shirt just above the knife haft, its faint bluish hue fading as I draw out the dagger. The wound closes quickly, a slight blood stain on his tunic the only evidence of the miraculous event.

"So, this was a test." Eystein knew I could not kill him which is why he felt safe to cut my binds and return my sword.

"Exactly that, a test, a test of loyalty. After you told me about Eric Halvorsen, I had to be sure you were not still doing his bidding. But the goddess would not let any harm come to me."

"Well, as I have proven I have no loyalty to Halvorsen, and you have shown me we have nothing to fear from one another, I will take my leave."

"I think not, Helsvein. I think you need to remain here with me, at least until Eric Halvorsen and his army are defeated. That is, unless you would like to kill Eric yourself."

"I will leave that to you, Eystein. But I will remain as you ask, if for no other reason than to see Eric's face when you give him the same challenge you just gave me."

Eystein laughs hardily. "I had not thought to do that, but it is an excellent idea." He orders his men to take Eric alive.

I accompany him to the battlements where we can oversee the carnage. "Your family, Helsvein? I will see to their safety," Eystein says as we gaze out at the city and the smoke from the fires of Eric's camp beyond. "Where are they?"

"I am not sure. I left them in Lagarvik, but knowing Eric, he may have brought them along to keep me in line. They may already be dead." Eystein has bought my lie completely. He will be sure to keep me close now, thinking we are bound by his offer. Unfortunately for Eric, when the time comes, I will not be able to kill Eystein Halfdansson.

"Well, if they are not, then I give you my solemn promise that they will be brought back to you. I will not ransom them to keep your loyalty." I can tell by his voice that Eystein is serious about his promise. I know little about this man, but he has already shown me who he is – a man who would sacrifice one loyal man to gain the loyalty of another, especially one with better skills and talents, but also someone who will extend a hand of friendship to someone who has shown him loyalty. I realize, now, he never expected me to kill Garmr. He expected me to try to kill him, in which case, he would have, no doubt, thrown me in a well and buried me alive. He is, however, perfectly fine with either outcome. In many ways, he is exactly like Eric, intelligent, ambitious, and ruthless, but, perhaps, a little more mature and less likely to take any real risks.

Our conversation drags into the night as he waits for Eric's attack. He asks me if I know Eric's battle plan, which I honestly say, I do not. Knowing he has superior forces and a superior stronghold that can sustain any attack or siege, Eystein expects something dramatic, something he has not thought of. As confident as he is in his victory, he still has a nagging fear that there is something he is not prepared for, some weakness that Eric knows and will exploit.

"You shouldn't worry," I say, noting his apprehension. "I have seen your defenses, and I know Eric's strength. He cannot win."

"I am not worried. He cannot kill me. Freyja has seen to that. I would just like to know what he has planned," Eystein responds pensively.

"How did you come under Freyja's protection. Did you call on her?" I ask, curiously. I expected the gods' involvement in the war, but the goddess making Eystein Halfdansson immortal did not cross my mind.

"She came to me. We of Raumarike have always revered the Vanir, Freyr and Freyja, but I would not have expected she would grant me such power in the face of my enemies."

"Yes. That does seem a bit out of character for Freyja. She never uses her magic to impact the lives of mortals or change their fate."

"That is not true, Asger Agnarson. When my realm is under assault, I will intervene." a soft voice calls from behind me. I turn to find a woman of eclipsing beauty, dressed in an exquisite silver-laced gown, appearing almost like mail armor but flowing like satin. Upon her shoulders were plates of golden armor from which a magnificent cloak of falcon feathers was draped, and around her neck hung Brisingamen, a necklace of gold inlaid with rubies, sunstone, and other precious gems. A deep blue sapphire at its center is incredibly large and appears to be glowing. The necklace is so splendid in its beauty that I am spellbound, scarcely able to take my eyes off it.

"Freyja," I gasp.

"Yes," she says, circling me as if inspecting a piece of livestock. I follow her with my eyes and notice everyone on the battlements, including Halfdansson, is frozen like a standing runestone. "So, you are Hel's creation? Hmm. I would have thought you taller, given your reputation."

"I've heard that before, quite recently in fact. What would you want with me, Goddess?" I ask, her presence wrapping my body in both the warmth of love and the coldness of death.

"I would know your intentions. You have brought war to our doorstep, and I want to know why."

"I have brought nothing, Goddess. Only myself."

"That is not true, Helsvein," says Freyja, purposefully calling me by my alias. "You brought a great army – Eric Halvorsen's army. A man of your ... abilities ... could do anything he chooses, yet you choose to help him. Why? And why do you now betray him? You had the opportunity to kill his enemy, yet you did not."

"He threatens my family."

"That lie may work for Eystein Halfdansson, but not for me. The Drengr Røkkr has no family."

"But I do, Goddess. I have a wife and children."

"Helsvein, you may have been a man once. You may have had a wife and children, but I can assure you, you are no longer a man, and you no longer possess those things. So, I will ask again, why do you help him? You must know we will never let him lay claim to Raumarike. He will be destroyed."

"My destiny is tied to his."

"His destiny is to die this very day. It seems rather odd that you should entwine your destiny with that of a dead man."

"All men die, Goddess. It is the one destiny we all share."

"But you do not share that destiny, Helsvein."

"And that, Goddess, is your answer. It is true, I was to help Eric become king, but in the end, it does not matter. Whether he sits on the throne of the unified kingdom for years until his death or is struck down today, it will not change my fate. But, that he has used me, betrayed me, and given me over to his enemy, I would see the latter. If I am destined to live forever, then that shall be my only destiny, and I will be beholding to no one, man or god. My life will be mine to control."

"You would defy Hel and deny her this victory?" Freyja asks doubtingly.

"I defy no one. Given the opportunity to kill Halfdansson and deliver the throne to a man who has become tyrannical in his ambition, I simply chose not to. And if that means Eric dies and Hel is defeated, so be it. I have accepted what I am, but I have chosen to follow my own path," I say. "You know, it is strange. To finally accept that I am no longer Asger Agnarson, I think I should feel a great weight has been lifted from me, that I am somehow newly empowered, free from the bondage of false destiny, but instead, I feel no different than the moment before I swung my sword. In fact, I had not even decided my target until that very moment."

As I say these words, Brisingamen begins glowing orange, and Freyja's hand instinctively goes to it. "Your words ring true," she says. "Even so, had you decided differently, you could not have struck down Eystein Halfdansson. My magic protects him, and even Dainslief, the weapon that fell the Kraken, could not have hurt him."

"Yes, I know. He showed me, rather dramatically, the gift you bestowed on him," I say, amazed at how well my words can deceive the Goddess of Magic.

Freyja smiles like she has won at knucklebones, besting everyone, mortal and god. I stare at her lovely face, trying to detect any hint of doubt, but I find none. I know that Freyja has great magic, and all the magic of the gods, Aesir and Vanir alike, flow from her teachings. And if her magic has truly made Halfdansson immortal, as it seems to have, then this battle was over before it started; Eric was never really destined to become king of Raumarike and Vestfold. It all seems entirely pointless. Eric has been chasing this his entire life, and I have chosen to help him because I believed his success would get me what I want – to end this curse and return to my family. But that is the paradox of destiny I suppose. Are the choices you make preordained, or do you have control of your path? Is your destiny determined by your choices or are your choices governed by your destiny? I do not know the answers, but I do know if the Vanir will go to these lengths to stop Eric, it is because they fear the outcome. And, if they fear the outcome, it can only mean one thing – they cannot control it. Freyja cannot control it.

"What does it mean when Brisingamen glows like that?" I ask.

"Brisingamen has an enchantment that helps to focus my magic in this realm. Each stone glows with the magic empowering it. When the sunstone glows orange, it tells me that a man is speaking the truth."

A shudder runs through me. I had thought my admissions about Eric and Hel to be a successful deceit, only to find that there was truth in them. Have I been deceiving Freyja or myself? Are my words merely lies to placate a suspicious goddess, or are they the true expressions of my soul? I briefly turn my face downward so Freyja cannot see my disquiet.

"And what of the blue sapphire?" I ask, noting its similarity to the azure glow beneath Eystein's tunic.

"That is my protection for Raumarike and its king." Freyja looks reverently at her necklace. For all the power she wields as a goddess and magician, it is but a trifle to the power Brisingamen has over her. She is both obsessed and possessed by it.

While she regards her treasure, the battlements erupt in a flash of lightning followed by a crash of thunder. Something whistles past my ear. Freyja makes a quick gesture with her hand while she shouts "BREGDA!", sharply altering the path of Odin's spear, Gungnir, which drives into the stone wall with a sharp crack and a spiderweb of lightning.

"I'll have you, witch!" cries Odin as Gungnir mystically reappears in his hand. "You will surrender or die." The spear flies again, this time passing through my body. Burning pain erupts from my chest, radiating into my head and extremities, shafts of brilliant white light shooting from my fingers and toes. A mortal man would have been struck down, instantly reduced to dust, yet I have survived. I gape in awe at my fortune as the battle between Odin and Freyja ensues, their celestial bodies swirling into the sky as tornadoes of blinding light.

The battle of Raumarike has begun. The Aesir and Vanir are fully engaged, and soon, the mortals will be as well. The children of Angrboda are getting exactly what they want. Eystein's immortality makes Eric's victory all but impossible. Regardless of the outcome of this battle, destiny will ultimately win out, but I must be the one to control that destiny. I have only a moment before the spellbound statue of Eystein Halfdansson reanimates. I snatch from around his neck a silver chain holding a sapphire shard, and with it, his immortality.

CHAPTER THIRTY-FOUR

SLAUGHTERBOX

Stars glint and flicker in the murky blackness like fireflies on a summer evening. They grow in number and brightness, revealing the heavens as if a veil of clouds is being rolled back from the horizon. Atop the ramparts, I watch as fires light the lower town until it is indistinguishable from the bay beyond where pinpoints of reflected starlight dance in the gentle ripples. Within minutes, much of the town is engulfed in flame, the shrieks of the terrified townsfolk a dreadful accent to the low roar of the fire.

"So, this is how he does it," I think to myself. Eric must have sent some of his warriors into the city in disguise to await his arrival. But we were delayed by the storm, so how could Eric have sent anyone ahead of us. "Knute!" The realization struck me. I thought he'd be in Lagarvik with Eric's treasure, but he is here, inside the city. I know it. He is the only one Eric would trust with a mission so critical and dangerous. It would be extremely difficult to remain hidden for so long among the enemy without sound leadership.

The fires do their hellish work, sowing chaos in the soldiers and citizenry of Raumarike. Eric's plan is obviously to force the gates to be opened to allow the people to escape. He and his army are, even now, waiting in the shadows somewhere beyond the wall for their chance to enter the city amid the pandemonium. Having met Eystein and witnessing him allow a trusted friend to be killed just to make a point, I believe Eric may have miscalculated. Eystein Halfdansson would see his city and people burn before he would open those gates to an enemy.

Recovered from their trances, many of the men begin funneling down the battlements toward the street below. Eystein, likewise awakened from his unnatural sleep, takes in the horror happening below him, and understanding instantly his enemy's intention, orders his men back to their posts. Most freeze, caught between their duty to their commander and their desire to save their families from the growing conflagration. Irate, Eystein brushes past me, quickly overtaking a soldier who had ignored the order. Screaming "COWARD!", he bashes in the man's skull with a hammer. The rest of the men immediately return to their stations on the battlements. Eystein Halfdansson is in complete control of his troops, but it is clear they obey him more out of fear than respect or duty.

I could end this now. Eric said I would know the time to assassinate Halfdansson. This is clearly it. As I have taken Eystein's immortality, I can sever the head of the snake, and with it, the iron grip he has on his men. They will break ranks and rush into the unfolding chaos, the advantage of their superior numbers effectively nullified by their loss of discipline. No sooner do I have the thought, than Dainslief flies. Eystein's neck offers no resistance as his head spins around, fixing his shocked eyes on mine. I wait a few brief seconds for the head to drop off, but instead, it grows a smile.

"Did you think it would be that easy?" smirks Halfdansson. "Look in your hand, Helsvein. Look!"

I glance at my left hand. Dangling from it is a length of silver chain but no stone. When I return my gaze to Eystein, I find him staring at me with wild eyes, his face lit by a shimmering chain laced in his fingers with a gleaming sapphire dangling from it partially obscuring an impish grin.

"You cannot take it by force, Helsvein. Only the King of Raumarike or Freyja herself may remove it." The glimmer of fear I had seen in him earlier has been extinguished. Halfdansson was never anxious about a weakness that Eric might exploit. No, his anxiety concerned his immortality. He'd not tested it against another immortal, and I have just provided the proof of it. I was wrong about him not taking any real risks. Eystein Halfdansson had just bargained everything and won.

"You may have made a mistake," I say, trying to pull his attention away from his victorious revelation. "You called back your men, and they obeyed you out of fear, but what of the ones on the outer wall? You may have left them with orders to keep the gates closed, but as I have witnessed, only the power of your presence can ensure that order is followed. Yet, you are stuck here with no way of reaching them through the fires and chaos. If they do falter and open the gates, you cannot stop them."

"Who says I would want to stop them?" Eystein's smile widens until the corners of his lips almost reach his ears.

"A trap," I utter sheepishly.

"Yes! A trap!" Eystein confirms smugly. "But there is no reason you should be caught in it, Helsvein. I knew about the infiltration almost from the beginning — all those trading knarrs suddenly appearing in our bay, a few laden with goods and silver, but most completely empty. All those crews clumsily running about the city, overpaying merchants, trying to gain intelligence, buying access and bribing soldiers. For a day or so, it seemed like a boon to our city. Commerce is not usually that good this time of year, but as word of the Drengr Røkkr's sacking of Birka reached Raumarike, it was not hard to see that my city was next. I admit, it took some time to prepare a proper defense, but then again, I thought I was preparing for you. Had Eric attacked sooner, he might have had an easier time of it."

It is clear our foundering on Gotland has utterly disrupted the timing of Eric's attack, fatally so, in fact. Eystein Halfdannson has the total advantage: a nearly impregnable fortress, foreknowledge of Eric's attack, and of course, his immortality. Eric's destiny to unite Vestfold and Raumarike is a fool's errand.

"So why the theater? Why let me kill Garmr?" As soon as I ask, I answer my own question. "You needed me to kill you, or at least try to kill you."

"I had to know, and now I do," replies Eystein, seriously. His tone becoming more animated, he continues, "Helsvein, you are the Drengr Røkkr. You are above the people that inhabit Midgard. And so am I! Think about it. We are immortals living in a mortal realm. As the gods have their realms to rule, so you and I have this one! Why be subservient to Eric or any man when you can rule over them?"

"My experience with rulers is that there can really be only one."

"Fine. You don't have a desire to rule? You can be my merkis."

"I may not be the right man for that job. After all, I am Eric's merkis and look where I am now."

Halfdansson breaks into a hearty laugh and claps me on the back. "You and I will do great things, Helsvein."

I thought I had the destiny of Raumarike and Vestfold in my hands. Now I see the entirety of Midgard is at stake. I could take Eystein up on his offer, but I know what has started here is nothing less than the end of all things – Ragnarök. If I let this play out, my curse would end along with my life, and my tenure as Eystein's merkis may be shorter than my tenure as Eric's. But, if the prophecies hold true, Freyja will survive the great battle, and Eystein Halfdansson will be ruler over all of Midgard. "NO!" I think to myself. Midgard is the realm of mortals, and if any immortal is destined to spend eternity here, it cannot be Eystein Halfdansson. If the Twilight of the Gods is indeed upon us, then it is up to the Twilight Warrior to bring a stop to it. It is up to me, and I know the first thing I must do is keep Eric from breaching the gate. I leap from the ramparts and head into the flames.

The calamity is more than I expected. The narrow streets are clogged with people moving in every direction, trampling over each other in a vain effort to flee the fires. There are some who have formed a bucket brigade, carrying water from a handful of wells in a valiant effort to quench the flames. But the fire fighters, jostled by the surging crowds, slosh much of the water onto the ground before their buckets ever reach a burning house or store.

Try as I might, I cannot make my way through the streets to the gate. I do not wish to add to the bloodshed, but I am left with no choice. I draw my sword and begin slashing and bashing my way through the mob toward the outer wall, hoping to find a less crowded way to the gate. Their deaths, though regrettable, are for a greater purpose, and so I keep my conscience at bay, praying the gods will accept their sacrifice and give them standing in the afterlife.

Reaching the wall, I find dozens of ladders have been assembled and laid against it. Hundreds are crowding around them, scaling the wall to make their escape. I had considered climbing to the top of the wall too, but the mass of people crawling along the narrow planking would make it impossible for me to reach the gate from there. Fortune favors me, though, and I find an easier path along the wall underneath the ladders where there are fewer people blocking my way. I must get to the gate quickly before it is opened.

I arrive too late. The gate is already raised, and a mass of humanity is pouring out. I am almost caught in the wave but manage to flatten myself to the wall just below the winching room where the ropes and counterweights for the portcullis are housed. Though much of the outer wall is augmented with wooden logs and scaffolding, here it is only roughhewn stone with few handholds and footholds I can use to climb. I must use my ax to chip additional niches, but having to do so slows my progress. I finally reach the top and am greeted by a half dozen soldiers. To my surprise, they are not Eystein's, but Eric's men who have captured the gate and are keeping it open. They are elated to see me until I remove the head from one of them. The shock of the blow allows me to dispatch the rest in short order, tossing their lifeless bodies from the wall onto the crowds below. From here I can see outside the wall all the way down to the wharf where people are clamoring onto boats, attempting to flee the blazing city.

With the first traces of morning sun, the scene unfolds before me like a play being performed for an audience of one. I see Eric's men, spurred on by the open gate moving up from their encampment, slaughtering everyone in their path, but their progress is slowed by the sheer press of people. I do not see Eric, but I notice a few dozen of his men have managed somehow to enter the city and are moving toward a large section of the upper town, which flanks the Keep's largest tower and where, surprisingly, the fire has been kept at bay. Despite his maniacal lust for power, Eystein is a brilliant tactician. He knew Knute was in the city with Eric's acvance guard and that they would set the town ablaze, so he took steps to secure a path for Eric's troops to follow – one that led them into a slaughterbox.

Volleys of arrows rain down on Eric's men from the tower and from the surrounding buildings, laying the lot of them low in a few brief minutes. If I am to save Eric and his army, I must shut this gate now. I slip through a doorway into the winching room and, with a single stroke from Dainslief, sever the rope.

The portcullis, a massive oaken gate five feet thick and banded with iron, slams down, crushing a dozen or more people, their blood spraying out like a swatted mosquito. The panicked screams of the people, as their only escape route is shut off, fills the air around me. I know I must find Eric, but I have no idea if he was held up outside the gate, or if he is already in the city. I must decide quickly which way to go, but I am frozen by an unimaginable sight on the horizon.

CHAPTER THIRTY-FIVE

BROTHERS IN ARMS

Claps of thunder rumble down from the northeastern mountains, growing louder as they roll across the hills and plains toward Raumarike. From the west, more thunderous crashes can be heard, the noise pounding its way toward the besieged city, reaching my ears in a deafening cacophony of stereo sound. From my position on the wall, I bear witness as the two storms rapidly approach one another, threatening to create a tempest, the fury of which has not been seen in a thousand years. The billowing clouds are not of water vapor descending from the sky, but rather are of dust emanating from the ground, stirred up by enormous legs sporadically visible through the pother, gruesome heads bobbing above them in the stygian heavens. The Jötunn have joined the battle.

This is an unexpected turn of events. Having armies of humans engaged in combat can be devastating enough and having the Aesir and Vanir warring overhead only adds to the potential destruction. But to have great bands of giants doing battle would bring absolute ruination.

256

Clumsiness alone could level an entire town, but when suffused with blood-rage, even a single jötunn can bring utter desolation. And here are dozens, perhaps hundreds, of murderous colossi rushing into the conflict, bringing immeasurable chaos and annihilation with them. At the finish, I will surely be the only one left alive.

Unable to escape through the gate, the survivors are left with no alternative but to try fighting back the fires. They have some success as many of the fires have already burnt themselves out, but the choking smoke of the smoldering remains hangs low and forces many to cower on the ground gasping for breath. The approaching storm they hear and its promise of cleansing rain, no doubt, has many beginning to hope they will survive this day, if they can just hold on for a few more minutes.

That hope is short lived. Though unaware of the jötunns' approach, they can feel the thudding of the giants' feet and realize that it is not a storm of divine rain destined to save them. Apprehension gives way to unbridled panic as soldiers begin fleeing the battlements and flooding into the streets spreading the alarming news. The fear and chaos of the previous night is no comparison to what I am witnessing now. The hundreds of people who had managed to escape the city are now running in all directions, desperate for shelter, some even trying to claw their way back over the wall.

The clash of titans is imminent, as the first of the jötunn enter the arena, crushing people underfoot and clearing swaths of shattered bodies with clubs hewn from trunks of spruce trees. Suddenly, a dark mass plunges from the sky like a meteor, tearing through the giants approaching from the east. The speed and ferocity of the attack astounds me, the heads and limbs of jötunn after jötunn being flung in every direction, tracing bloody arcs through the air like the fiery tails of blazing trebuchet stones. The shimmer of blue fur in the rising sun leaves no doubt that Fenrir has chosen to fight, and at his true size – twice that of his prey.

Though valiant, Fenrir's efforts fail to stop several giants from breaching the walls of the city. Two of them attempt to smash down the large tower of the Keep with their clubs but are met with a volley of arbalest from the surrounding parapet, the enormous steel bolts tearing through the giants and dropping them dead. One, a bolt through his eye, spins and slumps against the tower, his tree-trunk club still in his hand propping him up like the cane of an old man leaning against the wall of an olstofa, passed out from too much drink. Two more giants break through and attack the Keep, using their tree-clubs as shields to fend off bolts from the arbalests. Sustained battering from their clubs and hammers finally topples the tower, killing many defenders, destroying many arbalests, and exposing the inner courtyard and long houses within. As one of them enters, he is cut down by a volley of arbalests from the opposing wall. The other, unable to evade the falling tower, is crushed beneath the stone, swarmed by Eystein's soldiers, and killed.

Near to where I stand, a jötunn cracks his club against the gate, beating on it until the oak begins to splinter. Another joins in, and it seems the gate is about to buckle when a massive wave crashes against the wall, driving a drakkar longship through the torso of the first jötunn, while the other's body explodes against the stone superstructure of the portcullis, shaking it violently until it shatters and crumbles, the naked gate left standing for a brief moment before being swept inward.

I am knocked back by the force of the water, driven into the winching room, which quickly fills in a spinning whirlpool, threatening to drown me. The wave washes over the wall with ease and rolls up into the city, extinguishing the remaining fires before washing humans, animals, and the ashen debris of the lower city back through the now gaping hole left by the pulverized portcullis.

As the winching room drains, I crawl out, spewing water and gasping for air. I see a massive rainbow of shimmering color erupt from the harbor as Jörmungandr enters the fray, swinging his coils like a scythe, cutting down the jötunn approaching from the west. In an instant, a quarter of their number are erased, their crushed bodies floating into the air like dandelion pappi. Transfixed by what I am witnessing, I feel as though I have left my body, my gaze slowly taking in the destruction and mayhem around me before falling back on Jörmungandr and Fenrir and their ferocious assault on the jötunn. I am returned to myself by a familiar voice.

"This is not their fight. It is between men and between gods." Hel says, appearing before me. "The Jötunn must learn to stay out of matters that do not concern them."

Startled, yet unsurprised to see my tormentor come to watch her brothers lay waste, I ask, "So why have they come?"

"To take advantage of the situation, of course. With the attentions of the gods on other matters, the giants of Jötunheimr and their outcast cousins of the western mountains see an opportunity to increase their realms."

"And your brothers? They made it quite clear to me that they would not take part in this battle, and yet, here they are."

"Because, Midgard is their home, and they must protect it," Hel responds, pointedly. "There is no other place where they can be free, so they must live here in the realm of men. They cannot allow the giants to destroy it. Utangard must remain utangard. The chaos which lies beyond the fence must not enter here, especially between such mortal enemies as this lot. Their squabbling could bring about Ragnarök."

"Ragnarök? Is that not what this is? Is this not what you have been striving for all this time – this war of realms, the end of all things, the great rebirth." I say, waving my hand at the carnage around me.

"No, Asger. Contrary to what you may think, the stories you've heard, the children of Angrboda have no desire to bring about Ragnarök. Quite the contrary, we are trying to prevent it, and that is why you must help us."

"How can setting the gods against each other prevent Ragnarök? It seems it would have the opposite effect. You know what I think? I think you brought about this war hoping to gain some advantage over the gods, but now you have discovered that you can't control the outcome."

"We do control the outcome – through you."

"But why should I help you. If I do nothing, I can end the curse you laid on me."

"And you would never see your family again!"

"AND THEY WOULD NOT KNOW ME!" I yell. I glare hard at Hel until my rage subsides, and I soften my tone. "You can't use my family as leverage anymore, Hel. I know what I am. I am the Drengr Røkkr. And if I choose to stop this war which you have brought about, it will be for my own purposes, not yours!" Even though our interests are aligned, I do not want Hel to think I am doing her bidding.

A dozen or so jötunn from the opposing sides evade Fenrir and Jörmungandr and commence fighting each other in an open field just west of the wall. In a death struggle, two of them crash through the western wall, crushing several soldiers and townspeople under their massive bodies. Dozens of people descend on the fallen giants with axes and swords and hack them both to death. The other jötunn continue their fighting until a brilliant kaleidoscope of colors streaks from the sky like lightning and consumes the combatants in a single mouthful.

"There is more at stake here than you know, Asger," Hel responds. "There is a deadlier enemy we are fighting – Surtr. As the two pantheons of the Aesir and Vanir have become complacent, willing to share their power and influence in Midgard, Surtr has become aroused by fear. If he rises, his army will rain fire and destruction across all the realms, starting with Midgard."

"And you think pitting the Aesir and Vanir against each other will prevent that?" I ask cynically. "It makes no sense. The gods will only be weakened and more susceptible to invasion by Surtr and the Sons of Muspel."

"I do not believe so," Hel says, but there is a hint of hesitation in her voice. I give her a questioning look, and she responds, "As the Vanir have grown in favor in Raumarike, Odin has become inclined to ally with them. It is an alliance between the Aesir and Vanir that Surtr fears the most, especially since both Thor and Freyr have sworn to kill him. Neither can do so alone, but together, they may succeed. That is what spurs his paranoia. Hence, this battle – with the Aesir and Vanir fighting one another, Surtr will not feel threatened. As long as the Jötunn are kept out of this war, my great uncle will remain in Muspelheim. He will not risk an invasion unless the giants are able to establish a foothold in Midgard. Of course, it also benefits the Children of Angrboda to have our enemies fighting each other."

I shake my head at Hel's naiveté. "You know, the Aesir and Vanir will eventually tire of fighting and come to a truce, and you will be right back where you started."

"Perhaps."

"And, I have met Surtr. He is quite insane. You cannot count on him remaining in Muspelheim, regardless of how the Aesir and Vanir view one another."

"He came to you?!" Hel, asks, anxiously.

"In a vision, yes – or perhaps it was a prophecy. I'm not sure there is a difference. But, in my vision, he used me to defeat Freyr."

"If that is true, it is even more imperative that you complete your task. This affair must end quickly. Eric must be made king."

"I'm afraid that is impossible," I say with all seriousness, but without defiance. Hel looks at me with confusion and a spark of rage.

"Did you not know?" I continue. "Freyja has used her magic to make Eystein Halfdansson immortal. He cannot be killed."

Hel mouths the word, "What?", but no sound escapes her lips. Instantly, she disappears, leaving me alone amid the chaos. I laugh to myself, "if this is Hel's grand plan, she is a worse tactician than I am." The gods are truly not as smart or all-knowing as we give them credit for.

Fenrir and Jörmungandr continue battling the jötunn as more and more of the city and citadel are destroyed, but it seems they are gaining the upper hand, as many of the giants start to flee back from whence they came. From the remains of the warehouses on the wharf, nearly wiped away by the World-Serpent's wave, I see Eric and several hundred of his men move up to the city and pour through the gate and gaps left in the outer wall from the jötunn attacks. They engage Eystein's soldiers and jötunn alike, taking numerous casualties as they cut their way toward the Keep. I estimate less than half of his men are left, certainly not enough to successfully assault the Keep even though it has sustained much damage and many of its defenders killed.

I am about to jump down from the wall and try and stop Eric from his foolish attack, when I am caught by the sight of a blazing sun rising in the west. But just as I know the sun does not rise in the west, so I know that I am right, and Hel is wrong. It is the Sons of Muspel; Surtr has arisen.

CHAPTER THIRTY-SIX

THE SONS OF MUSPEL

Twisted trunks of a once great forest litter the ground, their stumps hunched over like old men, their branches sheared away like sickled wheat. Some are burnt into ash, standing in curled misery awaiting a gentle breeze to whisk them away and give them solace. Others are merely toppled, cut with a hundred ax strokes, their sap running into the dirt as slow flowing streams. Still others remain upright, shaken of their leaves, dazed and frozen, as their grime-covered bark tells the story of their tragedy. I stumble among the dead and dying people of Raumarike, some caught in the blazes of the previous night, others butchered in the battle or trampled by jötunn as I try to catch Eric and stop him from making his gravest mistake.

I make my way to the upper town beyond the interior wall to a place just below an angular battlement of the Keep which juts outward into the middle of the city, the place where Eystein and I stood the night before. The upper town has fared surprisingly well, considering the jötunn attacks

264

and the fires that had all but destroyed the lower town. Though the top of the battlement would be a better spot to observe the city, there is no way to scale it, and I would have to fight whatever remains of Eystein's forces. Climbing a tall skurdgod totem carved in the image of Freyja for better visibility, I can hopefully see well enough to locate Eric and his men.

Beyond the outer wall, I see Fenrir and Jörmungandr have won their battles with the giants, dispatching the few who remain with brutal efficiency. I hope that the rout of the jötunn would give Surtr pause, but as I see the brilliant light of Surtr's fiery sword continuing to climb above the western horizon, that hope is quickly dashed. Perhaps, with the jötunn defeated, the Children of Angrboda can combine forces against Surtr and the Sons of Muspel. I know they don't usually get along, but they fight together very well, as I have witnessed. We may yet escape this day without the whole world burning. We may yet avoid Ragnarök. No sooner do I have this thought, than lightning cracks the sky and the ground shakes violently. Thor has descended on Jörmungandr and dealt him a devastating blow from Mjölnir, one the World-Serpent did not see coming. An agonized howl tells me that Fenrir has also been attacked, most likely dealt in vengeance by the one-handed Tyr. Now, Tyr knows very well it was I who took his hand, and yet he continues the charade that it was Fenrir, lest he be ridiculed for being bested by a mortal. "God of Justice, indeed!" I quip to myself.

I don't want to involve myself in the battle of the gods, but it seems I have no choice. I am beginning to formulate a plan to prevent the Sons of Muspel from achieving their victory, but I will need Eric and his remaining men to do it. I know his power-lust is driving him to defeat Eystein Halfdansson, but I also know it will not be possible. However, there is more at stake now than the unification of Vestfold and Raumarike. I only hope I can find him and convince him to fight with me in my battle before the Lord of Muspelheim sets fire to the world.

Hamingja favors me as, from my vantage point, I locate Eric making his approach to my left, taking care to avoid the slaugherbox that took so many of his men earlier in the battle. I can see what he is planning. He intends to make it to the wall of the Keep and move along it to the destroyed tower where he can enter the inner courtyard. His men are holding their shields above their heads to deflect the arrows that are already raining down on them. I descend from the totem pole and slide along the wall to intercept Eric, taking care not to be seen by the Keep's defenders.

"Eric!" I call out as he gets close enough to hear me. Eric, of course, is at the front of his column, leading his men.

"Helsvein!?" Eric runs to me, laying his back tightly against the wall to avoid a hail of missiles. "Is Halfdansson dead?"

"No, the goddess Frey..."

"NOT DEAD? Did you not understand your instructions? You were to kill him when the battle started!" Eric fumes.

"I CAN'T", I yell back. "And neither can you. Freyja has used her magic to make him immortal. He cannot be killed, not even by me."

"What?" Eric grimaces in confusion.

"I tried. Dainslief passed right through him like he was water. He is immortal. You cannot win this battle."

"Impossible! It is my destiny to sit on the throne of Raumarike. It is my DESTINY!"

"I know something of destiny, Eric. It is not always what we think. But that is irrelevant now. I have a more pressing matter, and I need your help."

Eric's face is a tangle of anger and confusion, but he waves his men up to the wall, nonetheless.

"Eric, you must listen to me," I continue. Surtr has risen from Muspelheim. He is approaching Raumarike as we speak. If we don't stop him, Midgard will burn – all of it. It will be Ragnarök."

"I don't believe in fairytales, Helsvein."

"Fairytale? Am I a fairytale, Eric?"

Eric does not speak, but his eyes say 'no'.

"No. I am the Drengr Røkkr, the Twilight Warrior, the Immortal Soldier. Are you saying you will believe in me, but not in the end of the world?"

Eric pushes past me. He is so set on fulfilling his destiny, he does not want to hear what I have to say. I draw Dainslief and lay it across his neck, blocking him. I lock my eyes on his so he will know my heart. I will kill him, here and now, and take his men into battle against the Sons of Muspel. Eric pushes against my sword, daring me to cut his throat, but I do not yield, even as his blood begins trickling down his neck.

"Alright. What do you want, Helsvein?"

"I need you to take up positions on the forested hill west of the outer wall."

"You're thinking the high ground will give us an advantage? I am sorry my friend, but you do not have a head for tactics. The high ground will not be enough. We will be fighting giants. What you need is a force to engage them on the flat ground from the front, drawing them in so that the men on the hill can launch a surprise attack into their flank. I do not have enough men for that."

"I know. I am going to get the rest from Halfdansson."

"WHAT?"

"He has no choice. He wants to rule all of Midgard. That will be very hard to do if there is no Midgard to rule."

"Rule ALL of ..." Eric trails off shaking his head.

"There is a large gap in the western wall. Go through and take your men into the woods. I will do the rest."

"Even if we can defeat the Sons of Muspel, what about Surtr? I hear he has a flaming sword with which he will burn everything in his wake. How do you plan to defeat him?"

"Leave that to me. Go now. There isn't much time," I say, leaving Eric to his task as I slide along the wall to the destroyed tower.

I am met by a hail of arrows as I climb over the rubble, yanking them out as quickly as they hit me. I enter the courtyard, cutting through a half dozen of Eystein's men, crying out, "I AM HELSVEIN, THE DRENGR RØKKR. WHERE IS EYSTEIN HALFDANSSON?" The soldiers melt away in fear, one even pointing to the western tower. I climb the scaffold and find Eystein. He is not pleased to see me.

"You were supposed to serve me, Helsvein ... ME! Yet you chose to abandon me in a vain effort to help that would-be usurper, Eric Halvorsen", says Eystein. "I see you've convinced him to tuck and run. It won't matter. Don't think I won't hunt him down and kill him, and don't think I'll forget this disloyalty."

"You have bigger problems than Eric Halvorsen," I say, crossing the floor to look out over the western part of the city, not bothering to give

Halfdansson a passing glance.

"Oh?"

"See that light in the west?" Though it is late morning now, the sun rising in the west is still very noticeable.

"A fire. Set by Eric no doubt," Halfdansson says dismissively.

"No. It is Surtr," I respond.

"Hmmph."

"I tell you, Surtr has risen from Muspelheim and his Sons are coming. He will burn all of Midgard, starting with Raumarike. You and I will be the only ones left in this realm. No, that is not correct. It will be Ragnarök. My curse of immortality will end. You will be left here, alone, to rule over the ashes."

Eystein looks at me in disbelief.

"Do you doubt me?" I ask.

Eystein's disbelief turns to rage. "You did this! You brought this on to end your curse!" An ax cleaves into my head, staggering me. As Eystein struggles to remove the weapon, I slap his hand aside and pull it out myself.

"The Children of Angrboda brought this on, but things have gotten out of hand. Now it is up to me to stop it."

"Why would you?" asks Eystein, still fuming.

"Because I would not see you rule Midgard, even if you are, quite literally, the last man on earth."

Screaming incoherently, Halfdansson buries another ax in my chest and a knife in my belly. I fling him aside and punch him hard in the face.

"If you want to stop this, you need to listen to me. You need to position every able man you have in the field beyond the western wall, and when the Sons of Muspel arrive, you need to fight."

"This is just a ploy to get me to abandon my Keep so you can deliver Raumarike to Eric."

"Eric is not even here. You saw him leave the city. You said so yourself."

"Then where is he?"

"On the forested hill above the western field, waiting for you to engage the Sons before attacking their flank."

"He agreed to this!?"

"Like you, he has no choice."

I see Eystein Halfdansson's mind working over the battle plan. I know he is a brilliant tactician, much like Eric, and he can see this is his only chance to save his city and this realm.

"Okay. But Eric better not be late in his attack. And if, somehow, we emerge victorious, do not think that I will not immediately dispatch Eric and all of his men."

Eystein Halfdansson orders his men to the field beyond the wall. There is much talk among them as to why they are abandoning the advantage and safety of the Keep, but they follow their orders and take up their new position. Halfdansson wisely does not tell his men what they will be facing.

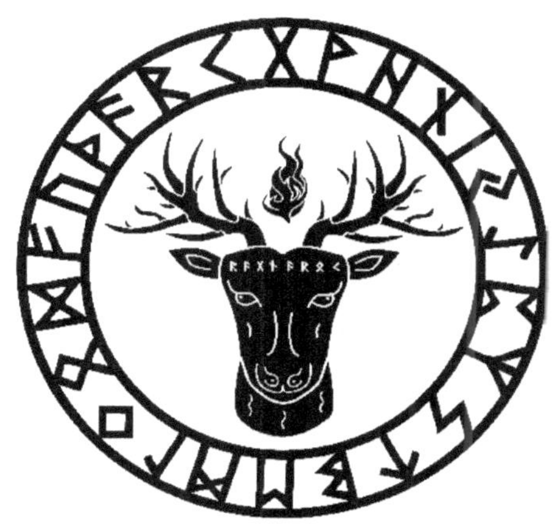

CHAPTER THIRTY-SEVEN

RAGNARÖK

The musky aroma of kvann fills my nose as I sip mead on a spring evening while Inger prepares a stew of venison, leeks, and pigweed. When spiced with kvann, known to the Franks as angelica, the sweet drink of fermented honey is even more intoxicating. I find myself drifting in and out of a dream, where I am at one moment preparing to do battle with a host of Charlemagne's foot soldiers on a plain between two inland seas, and the next, nuzzling Inger's neck as she giggles and curls away, almost spilling a ladle of stew she is pouring into Gyda's bowl. The dream brings me no terror as I know I am, at last, home with my family, enjoying the simple pleasures of a rustic life. Though the war is a fading memory, a horrible remnant brought to the surface in a moment of inebriation, my drunken mind slips once again into the battle. As I steel myself for the Frankish onslaught, I look around, seeing thousands of my comrades staring into space, sharing the same memory of home and hearth. I snap to my senses, the battlefield in my mind transforming before my eyes into a field of burning angelica choking the air with fragrant but intoxicating smoke, and the imagined Frankish army dissolving into an all too real horde of flaming giants.

I rally the few of Eystein's men around me, waking them from their collective dream, encouraging them to do the same for their allies. Before our army is fully revived, the Sons of Muspel are upon us, their enormous, swollen, deformed bodies with emberlike skin radiating a searing heat as they charge in. "SHIELDS!" someone yells, and as if by magic, a wall appears, a mass of men and wood stretching more than two hundred yards wide and twenty yards deep. If nothing else, Eystein Halfdansson knows how to train an army. The defensive shield wall is impressive, and no doubt would be sufficient to fend off an army ten times its size, but I fear it will be nothing more than a pebble in the path of the oncoming host, easily kicked to the side.

"WEDGE!"

A moment before the Sons crash into the shield wall, a gap opens in the center and the flanks extend out in a V-shaped formation. The maneuver has the desired effect. The giants take the path of least resistance and are soon tripping over one another as they are funneled like livestock into a smaller and smaller space.

"NOW!"

With a ferocity I have scarcely witnessed, the defenders of Raumarike cut, slash, and pound into the mass of smoldering giants, wreaking havoc, chaos, and confusion. For a moment, it looks like we may be winning, but that hope is short lived, as the advantages of size and fire begin to swing the battle in favor of the Sons. Some break through or circumvent our right flank while our center is barely holding on despite our numerical advantage. Every giant who falls to a sword or ax crashes to the ground in an eruption of flame, burning to ashes the men who cut him down.

With Dainslief drawn, I cut through the jötunn, hacking off blazing limbs, impervious to the flames that are incinerating my comrades. "WHERE IS ERIC?" I scream aloud, my words dissipating unheard into the din of the battle. Surely, he must see what is happening. Surely, he knows Eystein's forces are on the verge of collapse. Perhaps that is what he wants – to win his throne without having to shed more of his blood for it. But to allow the Sons of Muspel to dispatch his enemy for him would be foolish and short-sighted. Surtr's forces would surely destroy Raumarike – all of Midgard for that matter – and Eric, should he survive, would be king of nothing. I know Eric is no such fool, but I wonder why he is holding off his attack.

As I successfully hack my way through dozens upon dozens of giants and emerge at their rear, my question is answered. My destiny, a destiny I fought so hard to change rises like a summer sun before me. Cresting the low hill to the west are thousands upon thousands of red, glowing jötunn, the rest of Surtr's Sons of Muspel, and leading them, mounted on his reindeer with flaming antlers and wielding his blazing sword is Surtr himself. There is no escaping the truth of my hensbane induced vision. Even knowing the outcome, I cannot help myself. I am compelled forward to meet Surtr. A last grasp at hope, I pray for assistance from the Wolf-God and the World-Serpent, my lamentable brothers-in-arms. Unfortunately, Jörmungandr is still engaged with his arch-foe, Thor, while Fenrir battles the one-handed Tyr. Neither will be able to help me stop what is surely going to be the Twilight of the Gods – and my twilight as well.

I meet my adversary in the scorched vestiges of the angelica fields. Surtr takes no notice of me until I cleave the hoof from his reindeer and topple him. Enraged, he climbs to his feet, screaming a shaft of fire that splits the sky above us. The reindeer, undeterred by his amputation, charges me, tilting its fiery rack. I step aside, easily avoiding the goring, and as the wounded animal passes, I thrust Dainslief downward into its belly, attempting to disembowel it. Unfortunately, my blade misses its mark, and as I turn to ready myself for another pass, I am cleaved in half, head to groin, by Surtr's blazing sword. For a moment I lie on the ground fearing I may be dead, but the searing pain coursing through my entire body tells me otherwise. Even Odin's spear did not inflict this much pain, and I am slow to recover. By the time I regain my feet, both Surtr and the reindeer are gone.

I quickly look around, but Surtr is nowhere to be found. I can feel the heat radiating from the Sons of Muspel closing behind me as I look east toward Raumarike. The smoke makes it impossible to see the battle, but I do see a silhouette illuminated by the risen sun emerging from the haze, taking the shape of a man riding a boar. It is Freyr upon Gullinbursti, the boars bristling mane gleaming of gold, charging me at great speed.   In his hand, Freyr wields not a sword, but the antler of a hart, the very one he famously used to kill the jötunn, Beli. According to the stories, Freyr had given away his sword, Sumarbrander, to procure his wife Gerdr's hand in marriage. I wonder if he regrets that decision now. Freyr must know Surtr is significantly more powerful than Beli, and he has little chance of defeating the great fire giant with an antler. It is a suicide mission. Ragnarök is playing out just as the legends predicted.

Suddenly, a fire explodes inside me, as I am run through from behind by Surtr's flaming sword and hoisted high into the air. In the next moment, I am hurled helter-skelter at Freyr and impaled on the antler. The impact spins Freyr around, and he is unboared, crashing to the ground with an earth-shaking thud as Surtr's flaming sword passes harmlessly over him.

I free myself from the antler just in time for Freyr to pick it up and fend off another attack. The sword of Surtr shatters the antler, leaving Freyr totally defenseless. As Surtr wheel's his reindeer around for a killing pass, I see Dainslief lying on the ground just a few yards away. I roll quickly towards it, and in a single motion, retrieve the sword and throw it into the outstretched hand of Freyr, who, while ducking a slash from the flaming sword, opens a gash in Surtr's side. Molten lava pours from the wound, opening a fissure in the earth that consumes Surtr and his reindeer, sending them both back to Muspelheim. Freyr barely avoids falling into the hole as well, pulling me to safety as he makes his escape. The Sons of Muspel have no such luck, as wave after wave of them topple into the chasm, likewise returning them to their fiery realm.

I have no time to reflect on the events of the moment and how the few details that diverged from my dream left Freyr alive and triumphant. With Surtr defeated, my focus turns again to the battle for Raumarike and defeating the advance guard of the Sons of Muspel still engaged with Eystein's army. I rejoin the fight just as Eric and his men emerge from the tree line and descend the slope, slamming into the flank of the fire giants who are on the verge of completely destroying Eystein's forces. Eric had learned something watching the battle from the safety of the forest. His men strike their enormous foes quickly but do not linger to finish them off once they are brought down. The swift hit-and-run attacks by small bands of men against a few jötunn at a time keeps them from being consumed in the flames of the enemy fallen. The battle rages for a few more hours, but in the end, we are victorious, dispatching the last of the Sons of Muspel in a crescendo of steel and fire.

Devastation surrounds me. The dead of Raumarike are piled three deep while the fallen Sons of Muspel turn to ash upon the field. The survivors make their way back to their ruined city, heads hanging low despite their victory. I find Eric who is gathering his men into a fighting formation.

"What are you doing?" I ask, astonished.

"I have come to take this city and take it I will!" he responds.

"But you have just fought alongside Eystein Halfdansson and his men, claiming a victory that neither of you could have achieved on your own. How can you continue to press your attack against those who were your allies just a moment ago?"

"We were allies by necessity, but we are enemies by nature. I must defeat Halfdansson and claim my throne. I must fulfill my destiny." With that, he gives the order and his men attack.

The battle rages between Eystein's depleted army and Eric's exhausted one, the former falling back into the city where the fighting continues through the rubble-strewn streets. Many men on both sides are slaughtered, shield and steel shattered, as Halfdansson's forces retreat into their fortress. But the Keep, its towers and walls partially destroyed, offers no protection from Eric's onslaught. As the sun sets, Eric Halvorsen, the would-be king of Raumarike, meets face-to-face with its current king, Eystein Halfdansson, on the very battlements where the latter and I stood the evening before.

"You have lost, Halfdansson. Surrender to me now, and I shall let you live," says Eric, a surety in his voice that commands the attention of everyone present, be they of Raumarike or Vestfold.

"You cannot kill me. I am under the protection of the goddess, Freyja. She has made me immortal. And it is you, Eric Halvorsen, who will surrender to me," Eystein retorts with as much surety in his voice as was heard in Eric's.

"Your army is demolished. You have no one left to fight for you. Immortal or not, you cannot keep me from my destiny. I will unify Vestfold and Raumarike. I will rule ..."

"You'll rule nothing, skraeling. I am Eystein Halfdansson, and it is my destiny to rule all of Midgard. Surrender to me now, or I shall not only kill you, but destroy your legacy as well."

I find myself holding back a chuckle as these two men trade in bravado, acting more like young boys arguing about who is better at fighting or fishing or whatever boys of a certain age argue about. That is, until Eystein waves his hand and one of his men steps forth holding a young boy by the scruff of the neck. It is Hinric. Despite my warning, Eric has foolishly brought his son to this battle.

"Lay down your sword and submit, or I shall kill your son," Eystein says coldly as he grabs the boy and holds him at the edge of the wall.

I look at Eric's face. His rage is immeasurable. Were it fire, it would consume all the nine realms just as surely as Surtr would. Eric stands frozen, locked in a death stare with his enemy. I see his resolve begin to waver as he starts lowering his sword. But just at that moment, he leaps forward, hacking into Eystein's chest, the sword passing through his enemy to the hilt as if cutting through air. Eystein is completely unfazed by the assault. Eric's eyes grow wide with disbelief. Even though I told him so, he never believed Eystein Halfdansson was truly immortal. With a faint smile, Eystein calmly draws a dagger and drives it into Eric's belly. Wincing in pain, Eric watches helplessly as Eystein gives his beloved son a hard shove. I rush to catch Hinric as he topples over the parapet, but his grasping hand is just beyond my reach.

CHAPTER THIRTY-EIGHT

THE DEATH OF THE KING

The cold gray of winter gives way to spring, marked by the wildflowers that seem to bloom overnight, covering the valleys, low hills, and mountain slopes in blankets of white, pink, and red. My favorite has always been the red poppies that fill the fields and gently sloping sides of the fjords of Lagarvik. Inger and Gyda adorn their hair with the blossoms, interlaced with delicate white and pink bergfrue. But here in Raumarike, the winter seems to cling like a babe to its mother, refusing to yield to its inevitable passing. In anticipation, I watch the small poppy bud struggle against the winter, awaiting the moment when it will burst open, its red petals flaring out in glorious triumph. Alas, winter wins out. The crimson flower of Hinric's blood spraying out from his broken body as he strikes the stone below never blooms.

I am oddly amazed that such a fall did not produce the gruesome result I had expected. To my further amazement, a moment after an impact that should have killed him outright, the young boy groggily climbs to his feet

278

and stares back at me, equally amazed, his eyes searching mine for an answer I cannot give. I can make no sense of Hinric's good fortune until I see an azure glow illuminating the ground around him and the glint of a silver chain clutched in the boy's hand, at the end of which is dangling the source of the mysterious aura – a blue sapphire. He must have grabbed Halfdansson's necklace in a desperate attempt to keep from falling as the tyrant pushed him to his death.

While wondering how Hinric may have been able to remove the stone whereas I was not, I realize that Eystein has been stripped of his immortality. Not knowing when or if the sapphire will magically return to its master, I waste no time drawing Dainslief and spinning quickly to decapitate him. My stroke misses its mark, however, as Eystein, at that very same moment, slumps forward with Eric's blade still embedded in his chest. He turns his head to look at me, the garish smile of his immortality dissolving into disbelief, his mouth dropping open slightly as he collapses, dead.

Everyone stands frozen in silence, as if in the presence of a goddess, though neither Hel nor Freyja have appeared. The silence is broken by Eric's moaning as he doubles over, stumbles, and falls to the ground next to his enemy. Knute, who had witnessed the events from a dozen yards away, rushes to help his cousin.

"Eric. Eric!" Knute cries out, turning Eric's body over, revealing the mortal belly wound.

"Knu ... Knute," coughs Eric as Knute lifts his shoulders, cradling his head.

"Fetch a healer!" yells Knute as he places his hand on Eric's bloody stomach, attempting to staunch the flow of blood.

"Thro ... Throne," croaks Eric. "Take me to my throne."

Knute looks up at me as if asking my permission to move the dying Eric.

"Take him," I say, "I will see to things here."

Knute and another man lift Eric and carry him out draped across their shoulders. Some of Eystein's soldiers, recovering from the shock of their dead commander, begin to advance bent on revenge. To them I shout, "I AM HELSVEIN, THE DRENGR RØKKR. EYSTEIN HALFDANSSON IS DEAD. IF YOU DO NOT WISH TO JOIN HIM, LAY DOWN YOUR WEAPONS! MEN OF VESTFOLD, DO THE SAME!" I am well aware that the tales of my exploits, real or embellished, have become mythic, and I am viewed now more as a god than a man. The threat has the desired effect, and the men stand down.

Word of Eystein's demise spreads quickly to his remaining soldiers, many of whom are still fighting with Eric's men. But, when they hear the Drengr Røkkr threatens to kill any man still engaged in combat, regardless of their allegiance, most stop fighting, and the ones who would continue are pulled back by their comrades. It seems my very presence helps to quell the bloodshed as the name of Helsvein strikes fear into even the stoutest of hearts. Soon the din of war dies out as the victors and the vanquished cease their hostilities.

I make my way to Eystein's hall where Knute has taken Eric. I find my friend slumping on a bench, leaning against the table, a cup of ale in his hand. I am reminded of when I found him drinking in an olstafa after the Battle of the Sees, the beginning of our great adventure together. I sit on the bench across from him.

"I killed my son. I killed Hinric," Eric chokes.

"No. He lives. I saw him rise after his fall," I reassure Eric.

Eric's weakening eyes luster briefly at the good news. "And Eystein?"

"Dead – by your hand."

"But I thought he was …" Eric's voice trails off.

"Immortal? Yes, he was."

"How, then?"

"Hinric," I say without explanation, as I have none.

Eric nods, his familiar thin smile straining to crease his face.

"No throne. He doesn't have a throne. He doesn't even have a chair," Eric laughs weakly, coughing the last word.

"Yes, I know," I say. "Despite his affinity for Frankish architecture," waving my hand at the stone rubble of his once grand tower visible through the archway, "he was still a Norseman at heart. Just like us, all he needed was a long table, a cup of ale, and the company of good comrades."

"Comrades. Yes. Good comrades," Eric slurs, his eyes turning glassy. "To good comrades," he says, raising his cup a few inches off the table, an effort that sapped whatever strength he still had.

I grab a cup and raise it, saying, "To the Clan of the Crescent Moon!"

Eric looks up at me, familiarity filling his eyes. "Long days, my friend."

"Do you know me, Eric?" I ask, hopeful for the recognition I have craved for so long, even from a dying man.

"Yes, I know you. Of us all, you were always the most cunning," Eric answers.

I do not see nor hear the Valkyries as they collect Eric's soul and take him to Valhalla, though given my interactions with the gods since Hel cursed me, I thought I might. But I am not disappointed. I am sure that Eric will be sitting at the Allfather's right hand, the place of highest honor at Odin's table. Though his reign over the unified kingdoms was brief, Eric fulfilled his destiny. Despite the odds and despite the gods, he accomplished magnificent things, from his dubious victories in the Battle of the Sees and the Szczecin Lagoon, to the finding of the Niflung Hoard, to his sacking of Birka, and culminating in this impossible feat – the taking of Raumarike. Any one of those would be enough to make a man legendary, but I think when the skalds tell the stories, Eric Halvorsen, the seventh son of Jarl Halvorsen, will be known as the greatest hero of our age.

I sit alone with Eric's corpse for a while, thinking back on the times when we were boys and all of the adventures we've had since then. Outside I hear the storytelling and laughter of drunken comradeship as the men of Lagarvik and Raumarike come together, talking about their great feats of bravery against the Sons of Muspel. I know it will be short-lived. Soon the animosities of the locals will rise against their invaders and fighting will break out. And of course, there will be the sam-eign, the bloody one-on-one combat to determine the succession now that both Eric and Eystein are dead. I expect Knute will feel the kingdom should be his, not out of ambition, but out of loyalty to Eric. I also expect there to be a number of Eystein's elite to take issue with Knute becoming king. "Where is Knute?" I ask myself silently.

As I rise to go look for him, the laughter outside is broken by fearful shouts of "Kill it!" while others are merrily chanting "Blardraugr!". There is a clanging of weapons that quickly abates as Fenrir enters the hall, returned to his normal size, though still twice that of an ordinary wolf. Upon his back sits Hinric, looking quite majestic for a seven-year-old.

"Father!" cries Hinric, dismounting and running to Eric's side.

Tenderly, he lifts Eric's head and gently kisses his forehead. "Rest, Father. You may rest now," he says, his voice wavering slightly, but shedding no tears.

"Hinric, I am glad to see you. Are you injured?" I ask, believing I already know the answer.

"No, Helsvein, I am ...". His words are cut short, his tiny mouth frozen in time as a flash of light fills the room.

"Hel, I am not in the mood," I say, my slightly raised voice reflecting my annoyance. Hel is the last person or goddess I wish to see at this moment.

"No, Asger, it is Freyja," the goddess corrects me as she circles the table to face me. Fenrir growls, but a sharp look from Freyja silences him.

"I thought you were battling Odin," I say dryly. At this moment, I am disinterested in having a conversation with any gods or goddesses. I am weary, and I only wish to mourn my friend with his son.

"We have worked out our differences. Or, should I say, you have worked them out for us. That was quite a victory you orchestrated over the Sons of Muspel. And my brother thanks you for your assistance in defeating Surtr."

"Well, I found it was in my interest to stop Ragnarök."

"And stop it you did. You saved Midgard from Surtr."

"And from Eystein Halfdansson," I add, drawing a stern glance from the goddess.

"Yes," she acknowledges tersely. "About that, do you not wonder how this young boy was able to snatch the shard of Brisingamen from Eystein's neck?"

"Not really. I had other things on my mind. But as you mention it, I thought only you or Eystein could remove the necklace. I certainly tried ... unsuccessfully."

"Well, it is quite simple. It was never only Eystein or I who could remove the necklace. It was I or the king of Raumarike who could remove the necklace. That Hinric was able to means only one thing. He is the king of Raumarike."

"The seven-year-old bastard child of an hour's long king?" I say, pointing to Eric. "I don't think the people of Vestfold or Raumarike will accept that, and I don't think Hinric is quite ready for the sam-eign."

"If you are referring to Eric, he was never king. True, he won the battle, but his victory only paved the way for Hinric, the true king. You see, Eric felt his destiny was to unify the kingdoms, but I tell you now, that Hinric already had."

My puzzled look encourages Freyja to continue.

"Eystein had an older sister, Astrid, who fell in love with a foreigner, a Gotlander. She refused to marry the jarl Eystein had promised her to, and instead, married her lover. Eystein banished her and she lived out her days on Gotland with her husband, Sven. I believe you have met him."

The realization passes over me like a wave.

"Yes, Asger. Not only is Hinric the son of Eric Halvorsen, but he is also the grandson of the banished Astrid and grandnephew of Eystein Halfdansson. In his veins flows the blood of both Vestfold and Raumarike. He is the true king."

"So, you orchestrated this whole affair to put a boy on your throne?"

"Oh, no. It was Hel who orchestrated this for her own reasons. Oh no, this was pure fate. Perhaps Urdr, the Norn of Fate had a hand in this, but I certainly didn't."

"Hmm," I grunt, the orange glow of Brisingamen telling me she speaks the truth. "Still, I think he will have a difficult time maintaining his crown."

"And that is where you come in, Asger Agnarson. I want you to help Hinric, train him, and be at his side until he is of age and able to lead on his own. The people fear and respect you. With you at Hinric's side, he can rule."

"With respect, Goddess, I do not wish to do the bidding of the Aesir, or the Vanir, or the Children of Angrboda, or anyone else. I wish to make my own way, my own destiny."

"Our destiny is never our own, Asger. I thought you would understand that by now. Even so, this is not a command. It is merely a request. You can make your own decision."

"I'll consider it, but on these conditions. You take back the sapphire shard. Immortality is a curse, not a gift. Leave him to his true fate."

"Done," she says, and the necklace disappears from Hinric's neck. "And the other?"

"Take this and bury it where it will never be found," I say, taking the cursed ring, Andvaranaut, from Eric's finger. "Wealth is also a curse, not a gift."

"No," she replies. "Let the boy have it. It is his birthright from his father. With proper guidance, the boy will not succumb to the avariciousness of the ring."

I nod my head in agreement, and Freyja departs.

"... fine, thank you." Hinric continues where he was cut off.

He is such a soft and well-mannered boy. I hate to think how he will get along in such a cruel and unforgiving world, let alone rule it.

"With my father dead, does that mean I am king now?" he asks.

"Yes."

"But I am just a boy. I do not think I can be king."

"Then I will help you, Hinric. I will remain here alongside you until you are ready to rule. I am the Drengr Røkkr, the Twilight Warrior, and I promise, no one will oppose you as long as I am here."

"Thank you, Helsvein. Will you help me bury my father now?"

CHAPTER THIRTY-NINE

UNFORESEEN AGONY

Their mound destroyed by an errant foot, the ants immediately get to work rebuilding it. Their movements seem random, but somehow, in short order, as if each individual ant knows exactly what needs to be done and their part in doing it, the dirt and debris is removed, and the hole is prepared for the next step. They draw up wood to lay in the hole to make their home stronger against the next catastrophe, taking such good care that everything they do is done perfectly. After a few hours, the men of Raumarike and Vestfold have completed the burial mound for their departed kings, two graves waiting to be filled and a drakkar longship placed between them, ready to be sailed into the afterlife.

The days pass uneventfully. Surprisingly, Hinric is accepted by all his people as he plans for the funerals of both his father and his great uncle. He proves himself to be wise well beyond his years as he enlists the advice and assistance of Eystein's and Eric's soldiers in preparing the rites that the Norse afford their greatest warriors and kings. I am still dumbfounded by

287

Knute's absence. I haven't seen him since the night Eric died, and he wasn't in the hall when I arrived to have one last drink with my friend.

On the day of the funerals my question about Knute is answered as he sails into the harbor with a half dozen longships and knarrs. Aboard them are many people from Lagarvik, including members of Eric's family: Jarl Halvorsen, his mother, Brechtje, his brothers and sisters, less Olin who died in the Battle of the Sees, and several uncles, aunts, and cousins. Eric must have sent Knute home to fetch his family. But why? Did Eric think he was going to live? Did he want his father to see him ascend to the throne of Raumarike, despite the fact the old jarl thought his seventh son worthless? Was it so Eric could sit high while his own father bent his knee to him?

In truth, it doesn't matter what Eric thought. The reality is that they would be attending his funeral, not his coronation. Hinric and I meet them on the docks, surrounded by a dozen of Hinric's elite, unified warriors. Hinric is known to Eric's family as his firstborn, having spent a few days in Lagarvik prior to Eric's assault on Raumarike. Still, it is young Hinric who offers solace to his grieving grandparents and other family members.

The last to leave the boat are Eric's wife and other children, a boy and a girl. "Systir, Brodir!" exclaims Hinric as he rushes to embrace his siblings. I recognize the girl instantly. It is Gyda, but she is years younger than when I last saw her, not more than four. And the boy is my son, Brant, a boy of six, though he should be nearly eleven. I stumble at the sight, my knees buckling, my legs barely able to hold me up.

I drop my eyes and stare at my feet because I cannot bear to see Inger as she steps off the boat. My heart is pounding, and my head is swimming. My wife is Eric's wife? My children are Eric's children? How can this be? My stomach turns, and I feel faint, stumbling once more before catching my balance.

"I welcome my family on this sad occasion," says Hinric. "I am glad you have come to honor my father, and I invite you to honor my great uncle as well. I apologize for the condition of my city; we have had some turmoil here. Still, I have prepared accommodations for you in my Keep. I hope they will be comfortable for you.

"And I would like to introduce my personal guard, some of them you already know, I'm sure. And I invite my cousin Knute to join them as their captain."

Knute dutifully takes his position alongside his new command. Knute was the most loyal of men to Eric, and I have no doubt that he will be even more loyal to Hinric.

"And this is my counselor and merkis, Helsveir, the Drengr Røkkr."

There is a collective gasp from the assemblage. They have obviously heard of me but may not have known that I serve their new king. I reluctantly raise my head to meet Jarl Halvorsen's strange, cold stare. He turns his attention back to Hinric with a grunt and a nod.

"Helsvein, this is my family. Will you protect them as you would me?"

I am unable to answer as my eyes have fallen on my beautiful wife, her long blond hair adorned with red poppies blowing gently in the breeze. She is breathtaking, and I drink her in, my prayers of seeing her again finally answered. But even as I unflinchingly stare at her, she takes no notice of me.

"Come, please, and rest a bit. The ceremony will begin at sunset," says Hinric.

Hinric leads the procession of Eric's family, holding the hands of his siblings. I lag near the rear of the procession, my eyes still fixed on Inger, but I stay behind her, so she does not notice. I remember when she would braid her hair and wrap it on top of her head, but today, she is letting it flow freely. I self-consciously look around me to see if anyone is watching me watching her, but they are all either talking quietly among themselves or staring solemnly at the ground before them.

We are led into the great hall where a feast has been prepared. Sadly, much of the food for the city was destroyed during the siege, but there is still enough smoked meat and fish, rosolje, pirukas, bread, ale, and wine to satisfy the funeral party, which by my estimate, numbers close to two hundred, mostly family members of either Eric or Eystein, along with a few favored friends and soldiers. I sit at Hinric's right hand, but unable to eat with my wife and children sitting across from me, I make some excuse and leave the table.

I linger outside the hall, wondering how I am going to cope with seeing my family and them not knowing me and trying to resolve that they are not really mine, but Eric's wife and children. I have endured terrible pain and hardship as result of my curse, things no man should ever have to endure. But being in the presence of Inger and Brant and Gyda and for them to not recognize me, to not even be mine, is the most agonizing of all. "I curse you, Hel. I curse you for cursing me," I say under my breath.

"Helsvein?" a soft voice calls from behind me. My heart melts at the sound of it. "Helsvein?" A gentle hand on my shoulder, and I am nearly undone. Steeling myself and wiping a tear from my cheek, I turn.

"I am sorry to have disturbed you," Inger says. "Eric must have meant a great deal to you. I had no idea you two were so close. Eric mentioned you when he was home. He gave me the feeling that you were helping him with his quest, but not that there was a brotherhood between you. How long have you known my husband?"

"It seems I have known him my entire life," I answer, and after a long pause, I add, "but perhaps I didn't really know him at all."

"Eric is like that ... I mean, he was. I've known him most of my life and been married to him for almost nine years, but sometimes I feel I didn't really know him either. He wasn't always so driven, but I think he just wanted so much for my father-in-law to acknowledge him. Ours was an arranged marriage, but I did love him. I still do."

Inger's words cut deeper than Dainslief. To hear her express such love for another man, even Eric, is almost more than I can bear. I fight back my rage; it isn't her fault she doesn't know who I am or who we are. That fault is entirely mine.

"I want to see where he died," she says.

"Well, he died within, sitting on the bench where you were sitting. I was with him when he died."

"I'm glad he had a friend such as you by his side. But I want to see where he was killed – where Eystein killed him."

I nod and lead her to the wall, to the very bloodstained spot where both Eric and Eystein fell. She stands quietly for a moment, then asks, "Is it true he died protecting Hinric?"

I nod yes.

"And you have taken it as your duty to protect Hinric until he may rule on his own, both Raumarike and Vestfold?"

"Yes."

She looks at the blood pensively for a while. "I should like to ask a great favor of you, Helsvein," she says quietly, her eyes still fixed on the dried blood of her husband.

"Anything," I say. "Ask, and it is yours."

"I should like you to look after Brant and Gyda as you would look after Hinric."

"Uhh," I stammer, confused and not knowing how to answer.

"I am quite sick, Helsvein. Dying, in fact. I have brjost-sott, an illness in my breast. I haven't much longer to live."

I feel my knees buckle under me and grab Inger tightly in an embrace, as much to keep from falling as to give her comfort. She feels so good in my arms, I am overcome. Choked by my emotion, I whisper, "It shall be done, Inger." I resist the urge to call her my love, though I don't know how I manage it.

CHAPTER FORTY

DESTINY

THUMP! Mjölnir's thunder rips the world as Thor battles his enemies. Each strike fills the ears of the men and women of Midgard, pulsing through their bodies, rumbling in their bellies, and amplifying their beating hearts. THUMP! Another strike splits the skies above, bringing forth a soft rain to drown out the sobbing of the defeated. THUMP! The victorious celebration rings across the land, proving once again that even the strongest may be laid low by the righteous. THUMP! The funeral drums beat as the procession of mourners makes its way from the Keep to the western plain, where a field of freshly planted angelica, red poppies, and bergfrue are like a Bifrost, bridging the gap between the city and the burial mound, between the living and the eternal.

The funeral ceremony is perfect. Both men are laid in their graves with silver and gold coins and their most prized possessions, though neither man seemed to have many possessions of note. A single longship rests between them, the sails bearing the crests of both Vestfold and Raumarike. Homage

293

is paid by those who knew them best, evoking both laughter and tears, particularly Knute's tribute to Eric. The community of the unified kingdoms is forged this night, two tribes coming together as one. In his first test of leadership, Hinric has done well.

In the days that follow, I spend every hour I can at Inger's side as she has taken to her deathbed. Brant and Gyda visit with their mother often as well, but I can tell it is difficult for them, being so young. In a very short time, they will be orphaned, at least, from their perspective. And, of course, there is Hinric, already an orphan, but one to whom I am bound; he tries to be strong and independent, yet he requires so much of my attention. I always thought I was a good father, but I feel I am failing all of them because I cannot give any of them what they truly need – a real father, not an immortal warrior. And my heart is breaking every moment as I watch my beloved slip away.

In her final hours, I am at her side with the children. Hinric has his arms around his brother and sister as the three of them sniffle and try to be strong.

"Why does she have to die?" Gyda cries.

"I don't know, svass. I wish it weren't so. I would do anything if she would not die," I answer.

"Anything, Asger?"

It is Hel, come to torment me in my hour of grief.

"What do you want, Hel? Can't you see what is happening here?" I ask, making no attempt to hide my contempt for her presence.

"Yes, I see. But it doesn't have to happen, Asger. As I once saved your life, I can save hers."

"You didn't save my life, you cursed it!" I snap.

"We've been through this, Asger. It was you who laid the curse."

"Yes, it was me," I relent, burying my shamed face in my hands. "So why would you save her?"

"I would say in appreciation for your efforts in warding off Ragnarök."

"You left me little choice, Goddess."

"That is true, but you did avoid the catastrophe, and for that I am willing to reward you."

It is more than I dreamed of and though I know Hel is capable of doing it, I have reservations. With Hel, things are never as they seem. "You've made me promises before but have failed to fulfill them. You promised I could have one person know who I really am if I saved Fenrir. I chose Inger, but, still, she knows me only as Helsvein."

"But Asger, wouldn't this be so much better? Not only would she know you, but you could spend a lifetime together.

"Would she be immortal like me?"

"No, Asger. You were made immortal by your dead-man's curse. Inger has cursed no one. But I can take away her illness, and she will live a normal life."

"And you would do this for me?" I ask desperately, my fear and grief overcoming my suspicions.

"Of course, Asger. But there is a favor you could do for me in return."

I knew she would want something. How could I let her give me hope? "What's the price?"

"Well, you said it yourself, you would do anything if she would not die.

I only ask that you commit yourself to me."

"Commit myself to you? I will never do that!" I fume.

"Not even for your beloved wife? I can make her remember you, love you. You can have a happy life together."

I feel myself wavering. Everything she is offering is everything I desire. But the price she asks is high. I have no idea what she may have planned for me. Would those plans jeopardize Inger? Would they put Brant or Gyda or Hinric at risk? Knowing her, she would prolong Inger's life only to have her snatched away again within a fortnight.

"And if I do commit myself to you, what would you have me do?" I ask, hoping to gain some insight into her intentions for me.

"Well, first, I think you should just return to Lagarvik with your family. I can call on you there when I need you."

"But I am bound to Hinric. I am his merkis and protector. I cannot leave."

I sense a fiery rage building in Hel. The Hag flashes across her face saying, "You were to be my spear. You were to do my bidding. That was the bargain. But instead, you let that witch talk you into raising a boy that is not even yours." Quickly, she regains her composure and her beauty, "But that doesn't matter. All that matters is that I can save Inger. I can make her remember you, remember that she is your wife, remember how much she loves you. You can be a family again. It is what you want most of all, and it is what I want most for you. Hinric will be fine with Knute to watch out for him. Please consider it."

Hel is right. What she is offering is what I want most of all, and the price is no more than what I have already been paying. The only difference is that her intentions for me wouldn't be hidden. And it is true, Knute would be a formidable protector. Hinric will do well in his care. Still, I don't trust Hel. Unlike her brothers, she is not bound to me by debt or deed. And why did she get so angry when I said I couldn't leave?

The answer hits me like a jötunn's tree-club. She is trying to restart the war. The Aesir and Vanir have already settled their differences and that is not what Hel wanted. It is all clear to me now. With Eric on the throne of the unified kingdoms, the war between the gods would have continued. Eric would never have been accepted as ruler by the people of Raumarike, and certainly not by the Vanir, particularly Freyja. I was the insurance that Eric would not only win Raumarike, but also control it, and as long as he could, the Aesir and Vanir would continue their squabbles giving Hel the opportunity to do whatever she wanted. This was never about Ragnarök or securing Midgard so Fenrir and Jörmungandr would be able to live in peace. This all was done so Hel could bring to fruition some master plan of which the conquering of Raumarike by Eric was just the first step.

The gods normally have no interest in the petty political aspirations of the men of Midgard, but a war that threatened to start Ragnarök would definitely invite the god's participation, each side blaming the other. That is what Hel was counting on. She never imagined that Surtr would actually rise from Muspel nor that Freyr and I would defeat him. Saving the gods from their prophesied doom surely gave them pause to think about why they were fighting to begin with.

Still, any peace between the Aesir and Vanir would be tenuous at best. Hinric is the key. Not only is he the bridge between Vestfold and Raumarike, but he is also the bridge between the Aesir and Vanir. With him on the throne, both sides can claim power in the unified realm, shared in the blood of its new king. The peace would hold as long as Hinric and his descendants reign. But Hel never anticipated Hinric in her plans either.

That is why she intends to have him killed, and the only thing standing in the way of that is me.

"No," I say softly, but defiantly.

"No?" she asks, not sure that she heard me correctly.

"No," I say again, "I won't consider it. I am bound to Hinric, and I will see him become a man – a great man – a great king. The price you ask for my beloved Inger is too high. I will have an eternity to mourn her passing, be it now or a few years from now."

"What about your children? Brant and Gyda will be left without a father or a mother. They will be orphaned."

"But they won't be orphaned. As you have just said, they are my children. They will never be orphaned, and that includes Hinric. I reject your offer as I reject you. From this moment on, my destiny will truly be my own. I will not be beholding to you nor a party to any of your devious plans, whatever they may be."

The shock on Hel's face is without equal. "I will have you DEAD," she screams, the Hag taking her over, her face becoming hideously grizzled, her hair a tangle of thorns, her rag-covered body grotesquely emaciated, her fingers reduced to bone.

"You have your answer, sister," Fenrir says entering the room. "Now, you can be on your way. It is always a pleasure to see you," Fenrir adds, without a hint of the sarcasm he was obviously conveying. "But before you leave, you must honor the promise you made Asger on my behalf. You know what will happen if you don't."

Hel, fuming with rage, looks at Fenrir, then at me, and then again at Fenrir. Fenrir gives her a flippant smile. Exasperated, she waves her arm and disappears.

"I thought you were in on Hel's plans," I say.

"Well, never all of them. She's too much like our father. But as long as I have my place in Midgard, unmolested by Odin and Tyr, I am satisfied with the result. My brother must still contend with Thor, but it is no more than I must contend with fleas."

I stifle a laugh, given the solemnity of the moment, but I am thankful for Fenrir's presence. We may not like each other very much, but we are best friends. I turn my attention back to Inger, as she and the children regain their awareness after Hel's visit.

Holding out her hand, she beckons, "Children, come to me. You too, Hinric." The children obey, grasping her hand, tears now flowing freely. "When I am gone, you must take care of each other. You must rely on each other. And you, Hinric, being the oldest, must set a good example for your brother and sister. Always remember, I love you, and will be watching over you in the next life." Turning to me, she whispers, "Take care of them, Helsvein. Please."

"I will," I say, my voice quivering as I hold back my tears.

A flash of recognition crosses Inger's face, and her eyes suddenly widen. "Asger! My love!" she sighs as her last breath runs out.

I said I had an eternity to mourn her, and so it begins. That will be my destiny, the one I chose for myself. There will be another grand funeral, fitting for the wife of a king, but the planning for that will begin another day. Today, I will hold my children close to me and weep with them.

James W. Truax is a writer of science fiction/fantasy, historical fiction, modern American gothic, and children's mystery stories. His debut novella, "The Wooden Man" received critical acclaim as a "thought-provoking, clever, educational and visionary piece of work (Matt McAvoy)." A former Coast Guardsman, he holds a B.S. and M.S. in mathematics and currently resides in Texas with his wife and children.

Authors always appreciate feedback from their readers. If you enjoyed this novel and would like to recommend it to others, please leave a review at the following URL:

https://www.amazon.com/review/create-review/?ie=UTF8&channel=glance-detail&asin=B0CD4QJG5W

If you are interested in finding more books by James W. Truax, visit his website at:

https://jameswtruax.com

Don't forget to subscribe to get advanced notice of future books and free advance chapters. James W. Truax will never spam you or sell your email address. It is strictly a way for him to communicate with his readers.